My Side of Her Story

2 My Side of Her Story

©

Nichole Jaimes

2020

A special thanks to:

April, the editor. I could have never done this without her. She formed my words into a book.

Beth, my bestie for pushing me along the way. I'm not sure I would have ever finished without her.

My sisters that believed in me before I even started. My mama, meme, Aunt Dee Dee and Uncle Brett for supporting me in everything I have ever done. My husband and best friend, Pedro, and our children: Kaelynna, Amiyah, Araya, Nolan, Avelen, and Espe

Dedicated to:

My ray of sunshine for inspiring this story

TABLE OF CONTENTS

1. The Secret.

2. The Fall

3. Never Alone

4. My Secret No More

5. The Unexpected

6. The Forbidden Questions

7. The Christmas Party

8. What's Mine Is Yours

9. The Fiesta

10. The Vision

11. New Year's

12. The Gift That Keeps On Giving

13. Ice-Cream, Stars, and Annika too

14. Mallory's Side

15. Where There's A Will There's A Way

16. Falling

17. The Appointment

18. My Mama

19. Mama Knows Best

20. Within A Contradiction

21. Afton

22. Thorns Come From Roses

23. Another Chance

24. You're So Close

25. **After the Storm**

26. **And Just Like That She's Three**

27. **Mary Anne**

28. **Dear Diary**

29. **Listen**

30. **Mama's Here**

31. **My Choice**

32. **Thank You**

33. **There's Nothing In The World Like It**

34. **An Angel On Earth**

35. **We Do**

36. **Home**

My Side of Her Story

Chapter 1: The Secret

Rosy, round cheeks framing the sides of her sweet, tiny face. Closed eyelids hiding the deep blue from underneath. Wispy, blonde curls falling around her just so. While I am watching my daughter sleep, soaking up her implied innocence, a deep hurt causes a blow to my stomach and moves up my spine. I shake the shivers off and start a prayer for my sweet baby girl. She takes in a deep breath and lets it out. Her stomach rises and falls. Tiny, precious whimpers escape her mouth, not distressed, but the sweet sound of content sleep. Tears burn my eyes. I go to kiss her, but do not want to wake her. Maybe while she sleeps, she is as innocent as her appearance reflects. My mind races and takes me back to one of the darkest days I've seen.

Annika was clinging so tightly and seemed to be peculiarly distraught, very opposite of her normal, bouncy self. Her father and I, young lovers blessed with the gift of life early on, passed her between us, questioning what could be wrong.

"Maybe she has a diaper rash?"

"Maybe it's her stomach?"

"Maybe she has an earache?"

Her father lifted her above his head, and she let out a faint laugh followed by a breathtaking shriek. She grabbed her father as if to never let him go. He fell onto the couch, tired; we had both lost any hope for sleep. Annika clenched so tightly around his neck the color of the flesh on her fingertips faded, and tiny bones protruded from under her skin. As he hit the couch, his body lost life. My attention immediately went from my eight-month-old to my best friend. His eyes rolled back, and the tight grip on our daughter was lost. She rolled to the side of him. Annika was screaming and turning red, the lullaby CD was still playing in the background, but I went deaf. I heard nothing but a loud buzzing. Goosebumps were tingling down my legs, and heat took over my body. I buckled to my knees, grabbing his head into my hands. "Afton!" I shouted his name as if to call him back, but just as I couldn't hear my daughter's screams, he didn't hear me. Tears streamed down my face, and I confessed my love for him, begging for his response. For a moment his eyes met mine and replied, "I love you too, always and forever." Then, in a moment's time, he was gone.

Annika's body twitches suddenly, and my attention is focused to the present. Though the memory has faded, the stinging pain lingers. The hopelessness that always stays tucked in my heart overshadows the light in this moment. I pull her close and tickle her nose with mine. As her eyes open, a smile appears across her face. She pushes the hair away from her eyes and hugs my neck. I hold her closer, and warmth fills us both. I carry her with me to grab her sippy cup from the kitchen counter.

"Mama, we go mall," she says, very sure of herself.

"No, not today, baby. We are going to stay in and play." The thought of getting out and into the world seems nice, but a single young mother with a single-young-mother budget does not see the mall often. After analyzing my wallet only to find two wrinkled dollars along with some old receipts, the idea did not seem very appealing anyway. Leaving my small, cozy house was also harder than my initial feelings about the idea let on. Anxiety settled in quickly anytime I tried to get out into the busy world, although I would never admit it. I turned to walk back to the living room. "Nana!" The door bursts open, and there stands my mother.

"Natalie, just look at you! You look terrible and so fragile. Give me that baby." She holds her arms, filled with costume jewelry from every other finger up to her wrists, out for Annika. Annika willingly goes to her. As my baby is plopped on her hip, my mother uses her free hand to fuss with my hair. "Your hair is dreadful. When is the last time you ate? Are those your pajamas?" She sighs for a moment as if she expects me to spit out all the answers just as quickly as she poured out the questions.

"This shirt is not a pajama shirt. I got it from the Hidden Closet, and I like it just fine."

"Hmmm," she lets out behind pursed lips, and a disapproving gaze meets my eyes. We stare in silence for a moment. She prisses over to the pantry and pulls out the tea kettle. As she starts the tea on the stove, I can almost hear her thinking. She can be overpowering, but she has good intentions. Her love for me runs deep. I know the sadness that seems to follow me like a shadow worries her. "So your sister is at it again. You won't believe this guy. Well, yes you will. His name is Jace. The tattoo that takes the length of his arm is absolutely dreadful, crossbones overlapping a naked woman." She lets out a disgusted sigh. "He plays the drums for some band called something like Hit This." She rolls her eyes and rattles on. Eventually, my thoughts are heard louder than her words. I am brought back when she says, "Now go!"

"Go where?"

"Were you even listening? Go take a shower and do something with that hair. It'll make you feel better. Annika and I will play right here and have some tea. Isn't that right, baby? Tell Mama to go shower."

"Take shower, Mama."

"I feel fine, Mom, I really do." She just waves her hands as if to dismiss me.

As the water falls down my back, the heat rises up, relaxing my tense muscles. My mind begins to wander. A week ago today, Annika had said she would pet a baby cow. A baby cow, how random the thought seemed at the time. Surely she had seen barn animals on her favorite show earlier that day or maybe on the string cheese package, something to spark the idea. Then later that day, as we walked up to the annual family fish fry, there in a small fenced area, were goats, pigs, and to my dismay a calf. Annika waited patiently in line behind her cousins and other relatives. When it was her turn, the calf found its way to her. She ever so gently and lovingly pressed her little hand down the calf's head and across his back. The thought, so precious, and the look of Annika, so pure, almost brings a smile across my face. But before the smile ever exists, my eyebrows turn down, and the worry takes over yet again.

I clumsily fumble through my drawers for something to put on that won't provoke a negative response from my mother. I walk out into the living room, and she looks satisfied. She hands me some sweet tea with a lot of ice and a slice of lemon (she knows just the way I like it). "I've started some soup but cannot stay; I have a lunch date with Caroline. Just stir it every once in a while, and let it simmer for about an hour."

"Call from Tori-Call from Tori," my mom's cell phone alerts her.

"Hello. Oh hey! Yes, I'm here now. Uh-huh." My mom grabs my phone. "Yeah, her ringer was off."

I lip talk to explain why I had it off. *Annika was napping.*

"She says Annika was napping. Oh, that's right. That is today. I will let her know because she obviously has no idea. Uh-huh. I'll let her know to call you back." I watch as my mother squints and holds her phone away from her, trying to find the end call button. She turns her gaze back to me. "Did you forget something, darling?"

I pretend to think for a moment, but know I don't have any idea, so I have to give in. "I guess so."

"Pictures with Santa at 1:30 today." She looks at me half disappointed and half pleased with herself, as though she has saved me yet again. I try not to look as alarmed as I feel. Annika reaches her arms out for me, and I grab her up. "Well, I'll turn this soup off. I have to go, Natalie. I can't be late; we are trying to make happy hour. Annika's Christmas dress is in the front row of her closet to the left. I saw it the other day when I pulled out her play clothes. Call me when you get back home. If you don't, I'll worry. Maybe y'all can make it to my house tomorrow for dinner? That would be nice. I will cook a roast. Be there at 6." After a kiss for me and a kiss for Annika, she prances out the door. I watch from the window as what looks to be a very wealthy, secure woman walks to a car with a bad paint job and a bent bumper. She proceeds to put her hand through the window in order to open the door from the inside. Then she buzzes down the driveway and is gone as quickly as she arrived.

As soon as her car disappears down the road, I sit Annika down and run into her room. I fling open the closet doors and rip the dress off the hanger. Next, I run to her dresser and pull out the tights. Annika has followed me into the room and laughs at the sight of me running around like a chicken with its head cut off. I drop to the floor and try looking for her dress shoes under the crib. With no success, I rise up to see Annika digging in her closet. She does not have any success either. Then I remember they were in her crib. Stand up, arms up, dress on, sit down, tights on, shoes on, hair half up, oversized bow clipped securely in, and we are good. I give her a small tub of soup crackers and her cuppy. I run a brush through my hair, apply a small amount of mascara, some lip gloss, decide to just pull my hair back, put on my tennis shoes, look at my clock knowing it was probably already five minutes past time to go. *Sure enough,* I verify. As I secure Annika's car seat, my phone goes off. It's Tori. "Hello. Hey, sorry I forgot to call. I was in a hurry to get going. Yes, we are leaving now. Yes, she is in the dress. Yes, she has the matching tights on. Yes, the cute bow is in her hair. We will be there in about fifteen minutes."

I think of my poor niece and nephew that have probably been dressed in their matching attire since that morning, not allowed to move or barely breathe in fear of messing up their outfits and hair. I look in the rearview mirror at my baby, the youngest of the three. The bow is tilted to one side because of the weight. I smile at her, and she smiles back.

"Bwaiden and Bwi?"

"Yes, baby, we are going to see Aunt Tori, Bri, Braiden, and **SANTA CLAUS**!" She couldn't have cared less about Santa, but she loved her cousins and aunt.

My sister was an early childhood teacher and though homeschooling tugged at her heart, she wasn't ready to give up her career. She could easily stay at home without a financial burden. She had married into money; her father-in-law owned more than half of the town. They live in a gorgeous house with a huge yard and pool. They are the perfect all-American family. When she found out I was pregnant before marriage, she claimed disappointment, but I think it was embarrassment. But as soon as I went into labor, any ill feeling had left her, and her heart was filled with love for the precious niece I would give her. She never left my side.

My love for my mom and sisters runs deep. We were all we had, and we know we will always have us no matter what.

I pulled up to the mall, relieved it was only 1:27. I parked and rushed into the building, not even worrying with the stroller. My sister had probably been there waiting since 12:30. As soon as the doors parted and the smell of pretzel teased my senses, I felt something like deja vu. In a hurry to find my frantic sister, I dismissed the feeling. Annika's voice grew louder, trying to get my attention. I somehow managed to pick my sister out of the crowd. Glancing at her watch, tapping her foot, with my four-year-old nephew on her hip, napkin tucked into his shirt, looking around and then glancing at her watch again.

"Mama!? Mama!!"

"Yes, baby?"

"Mama, we go mall."

"Yes, baby, we go mall. We go mall. We?"

I stop dead in my tracks and feel the blood start to drain from my extremities. We are at the mall. She had told me that morning, "We go mall." There was no way we were going to go to the mall, and now we are here. We are at the mall.

"Mama, we go mall!"

I fake a smile and kiss her forehead. I push my way through the crowd, and my sister finally meets my gaze. "Oh, thank God! Two more minutes, and we would have lost our session. Look at how packed it is."

"Yes, it is packed." I grab onto my niece and nephew and kiss them hello. My sister kisses my cheek then puts Braiden down to grab Annika.

"Oh well, at least you made it. After pictures we will get some cookies and hot chocolate." She smiles a true smile. and my nerves are calmed, at least for now.

The older Annika gets the more intense the coincidences seem. I did not tell a soul; it never seemed to mean much of anything after the moments passed anyway. Only in the moment did it feel so real and heavy. When I was alone and the thoughts spun, I felt so hopeless and scared. Thinking of telling anyone just seemed silly. Petting a calf, predicting a mall trip, they were just small, insignificant things that seemed unimportant and explainable. But I knew something was coming; I could feel it the same way my heart would tug when I tried to soak in my daughter. I know the day we lost Afton was the day we found something else. We found what others would call "a gift."

Chapter 2: The Fall

After what turned out to be a long, but nice day at the mall with my sister, niece, and nephew, it was nice to pull down my long, winding driveway. The house was left in Afton's name after his parents died. After his absence, the house went to Annika. It was a small three bedroom house with chipped paint, but it was cute and cozy. It was all we needed. I was in my first semester of college when he left. His sudden absence abruptly ended my school career.

I walk into the house, and the smell of home welcomes us. I flick on the lights and drop my heavy bag off my arm. I hold my breath as it hits the floor, hoping not to wake Annika. I make my way to her room to get her pajamas. I look at the perfect crib with the perfect blankets, a gift from my sister and brother-in-law. Annika has never been in it longer than a diaper change. I turn her lights off and walk into my room.

I hold her close as I drift off into my dreams. Just as I fall asleep I kiss her lips and whimper out, "I love you, always and forever." She replies with a nuzzle. Then just like that, the same way every night, we sleep until morning's light.

I awake with Annika patting my face. "Good morning, sunshine," I whisper. She smiles and sits up. Her ringlets fall around her, and as always, she pushes them out of her face. My mom insists we cut bangs, but I protest. My feet hit the cold floor, and I crawl back under the covers with Annika. Under the blanket, it looks like we are in a dark cave. She laughs as I begin to crawl after her, a mama bear and a baby bear chasing each other. We both jump, startled as we hear the alarm go off. I have to be at work at 9:30. That means playtime is over, and it is time to get ready. I swipe my phone to dismiss the alarm, and Annika covers her ears. For now, she is a typical two-year-old, and so, for now, I feel happy.

I step in front of the mirror and take a long look at myself. I am young, but my big, deep blue eyes seem tired. I am pale and thin. My wavy, dirty blonde hair turns into a poof with every stroke of the brush. My lips, larger than average but not massive, sit just so. My mother always announces my beauty, but beauty is not something I see in myself often. After second guessing, I decide to apply some mascara, but instead of gloss, I grab my chapstick.

"Where's that pretty baby of yours, Nat?" Robby asks with a side smile.

"She is with Mama today, Rob."

"Aw, well it is more fun when she's here," he says as he slips out the door. Robby was one of my dad's distant cousins and offered me this job when I was sixteen. He is a good man with a good heart. His wife sits at the desk across from me and smiles from beneath her glasses. She is a plump woman with short, blackish grey hair.

"He is right. It is more fun when she is here." Caroline smiles. She has as good a heart as her husband, except for the fact she keeps up with the town's gossip. She doesn't let on to many though that she does this. A lot of people confide in her because she is a listener, but what most don't know is she is also a teller. But then again, she just tells me, and I would never tell a soul. I am a genuine listener. I keep my lips closed. Maybe it's in hopes that if my secret was to ever slip, the listener would display the same confidentiality that I have displayed for more than half of this town.

"Missy is having the annual Christmas party at her house this year, and I heard that she has still not invited Macy. You know those two were the closest twins you would have ever seen. All up to when Macy did not go to the hospital when Missy's daughter…What is her name? Never mind, Mallory, that's it. Mallory was having her baby." And so it begins. I get all the latest updates starting at 10 o'clock sharp. Even though I am not big on gossip, my ears still perk every time she switches to the next victim.

"Mr. Collins, poor thing, he just had to put his dog down. He had her for thirteen years, you know? Thirteen years. Just a shame, such a sweet man." The phone rings, and Caroline gets sidetracked. "Robby's Construction…"

Mr. Collins fills my thoughts. He was one of my neighbors growing up, and he still lives pretty close to my mom's new place. When we walk to the park, we usually see him messing with his flower garden when weather permits. I feel so bad for him because he loved that dog, and I begin to think how lonely he must feel after losing his only companion. My thoughts come to a halt when my cell phone goes off. I see my mom's name come across and answer in an instant.

15 My Side of Her Story

My mom's voice, frantic on the other end spins off, "Annika fell and bumped her head, Natalie. She bumped it on the corner of the fireplace, and there's blood. Natalie, I am so sorry. I was right here. I just, I just don't know what we should do."

My strength takes over my fear, "Mom, it is okay. Do you have a towel on it?"

"Yes."

"Okay, good. Is the blood coming through?"

"No, the towel is holding it." I could hear Annika's crying and through the phone her voice sounded even younger than it did in person.

I wanted nothing more than to hold her in my arms. I love you, Annika, I thought so hard I could feel it. "I love you Mama." I heard her voice answer me through the background noise.

"I am on my way to get y'all. I want you to wait on the porch for me, okay?"

"Okay, Natalie, I am so, so sorry."

When I pull up to my mom's house, Roxy, my sister, is holding Annika. She is not crying anymore, but I can see the blood-filled towel held close to her head. My mom and Roxy jump in the car without a word, and we take off to the hospital. We wait in the waiting room to go back, which seems like hours. They finally call her name over the intercom, and we follow a nurse that looks more like a supermodel to a room. She takes Annika's vitals and asks the same questions the receptionist asked. After stating all the same answers again, we are taken back to a room and told the doctor will be with us shortly.

"Mama, I okay." Annika keeps grabbing my face and meeting my eyes with hers. She knows I am worried and is trying to comfort me. My baby is trying to comfort me.

"Oh my God! This is taking forever! Don't they know she is little?" Yep, that's my eighteen-year-old little sister, Roxy. She has short hair with black and blonde stripes, shaved over one ear, my mother's huge marble green eyes, big lips filled in with maroon lipstick, and a piercing through her nose.

"Roxy, I am sure they are working as fast as they can to get to us." She rolls her eyes and kisses Annika on her forehead.

"I love you too, Aunt WoxWox, always and fo-eva." Annika giggles as if she knows what we are all thinking.

And she probably does, I tell myself.

Finally, the doctor walks in. "Hello there, I am Dr. Richards." A tall man that looks too young to be a doctor walks in. He has earnest, brown eyes and dirty blonde hair. "You must be Annika." He winks at Annika and grabs her hand before looking at any of us. He looks up and asks if I am the mother. As our eyes meet, a memory is passed between us. I nod silently and immediately hand him Annika as if begging for an all clear. Although the pass wasn't expected, he grabs her naturally and sets her on the patient's cot, ready to get started. He pulls down a lamp from overhead and examines the cut. "Well, she looks just fine. The bleeding has stopped on its own and although it looks like a pretty good nick, I do not believe stitches are necessary. We could do a cat scan to double check for a concussion, but she's not showing any signs of one. I will leave the final decision up to you, but she seems to be just fine, probably more of a scare than anything else."

I stop to think as my sister begins twirling her hair. I want to know 100% that she is okay, but it may cause more harm than good. What if there is something there, something that shows up that isn't from the injury? What if something shows up that proves she has some kind of different brain activity and questions begin to arise? "If you think she is okay, then we will leave it alone." The words spill from my mouth faster than I had anticipated.

He smiles a genuine smile, and his straight, white teeth show behind his full lips. "I think she is just fine," he replies. But then he looks at me. "Are you okay?" I am taken aback by his sincere concern.

"Yes, I was just worried she was really hurt."

He pulls some stickers and a couple of suckers down from one of the cabinets. Annika reaches out for the red sticker, but he stops her and says, "You were so brave. I want you to have all of this."

Annika smiles. "Thank you, Docta Wichards."

He seems surprised at the recognition and pauses for a second. "You have a smart little girl here."

"Thank you," I reply with a smile. He closes the door behind him, and we are left in the room, waiting for the dismissal paperwork.

"Dr. Richards and Natalie sitting in a tree," Roxy begins. I can feel my face turn ten shades of red.

"He did seem rather interested in you, Natalie," My mother chimes in.

"Oh my goodness, really you two? That is enough, the nurses will hear you."

"He likes you, Mommy." Annika smiles. Sometimes it is hard to understand if she knows the things she implies or if she is merely sharing her thoughts.

"Well, I am just ecstatic that my little sunshine is okay. Isn't that right, sweetheart?" My mom rubs Annika's back. The same nurse that looks like she belongs on a daytime soap opera walks in and goes over all the dos and don'ts for head injuries. Then with the signing of my name, we are free to go. Dr. Richards smiles and waves to us on our way out, and my sister makes an I-told-you-so face as she smiles back at me. I roll my eyes back at her.

The tall, handsome doctor flashes through my mind. Scott, my first crush, and nobody even knew. I had no idea he was back here. Although we only passed that silent memory between our gaze, it was clear he remembered me the same as I remembered him. It was the summer before I met Afton. Even though it was just one summer, the memory still inflicts a shivering, hot sensation. His uncle owned the bed and breakfast, and Scott had come to help him with construction and maintenance, one last hope to keep the B&B going. Scott could fix anything, even in his youth. Now he was fixing people. I am brought back by the stinging feeling of guilt. Afton flashes in my thoughts, and I remember how much I miss him.

"Mommy, I miss Daddy too." Annika turns away from her show. She comes up and wipes the tears I tried to hide. "It's okay Mommy. He is with angels now." These are one of the times I am unsure whether she knows or thinks, but instead of fighting for the answer, I decide to fall into the comfort of her words.

As I watch her turn and walk back to her purple Gobba Gobba chair and settle back into the *Gobba Gobba* episode, I see a normal two-year-old. I ache for a normal toddler, but the incidents don't even seem to catch my attention as they once did. Every day she knows something that will happen or knows what someone is thinking.

For now, I am content knowing that she knows she will get a pink swirl sucker, knowing that I am thinking of her dad, knowing that Aunt Tori bought her a new big girl car seat, knowing that I am thinking about our busy day. But I am hesitant about what the future holds, hoping for the best, but expecting the worse. As sweet and day-dreamy as thoughts can be, they can also be a dangerous place to wander; a trap that cannot be escaped.

As Annika sings along to the songs on the television, I go back to that day. The day we lost him. Tears silently, yet uncontrollably stream down my face; this time it is not for Afton, but for Annika. She knew. She knew those were her last moments with her father. The smiling eight-month-old that giggles at the nurse is unaware of the shot about to be received; and then there's my Annika that knew, that comprehended, at least in those seconds, that she was about to lose her dad. The heavy weight my heart carries aches.

I look at the clock and wonder if it is too early to try and lay down for the night. An uneasy feeling starts to pull me in. The phone interrupts my thought and in place of a name there is an unrecognizable number. I reluctantly answer, even though I usually let the machine take unknown calls.

"Ello?" A thick Mexican accent of a woman travels over the phone. "Ello, es Natalie dere?" she asks hesitantly.

Before thinking, I answer, "This is me? Who is this?"

"My name es Muneca. I know dese es soun crrazy, pero please no hang up. My daughter tol me to call dese number an ask for you. You have a daughter name Annika, no?"

Chapter 3: Never Alone

My teeth clench, and the recognizable sensation of goosebumps start to pucker my cheeks and stroll down my right side, eventually covering my whole body. The shivers shake them off. My mind races, but I am at loss for what to say. My voice whispers through the phone, "Yes, my daughter's name is Annika." I hear a sigh followed by a little girl's giggle.

"My daughter, er name es Karisa; she es deferent. She as, I no know en engles, pero she tell me what happen before it happen. She see things dat are dere but no whun else see. She want me to call you porque she alone, and she need someone like er, you know?"

I remember when I went to school the first time, and I was the only shy and quiet child there. I did not have any friends, and I felt alone. Then one day there she was, Anna. Anna was quiet and shy just like me. Her dad had left when she was little, and it was just her and her mom. Anna and I understood each other. I didn't feel alone anymore, and I even felt freed in a sense.

Maybe this is just what Annika needs. Maybe Annika needs Karisa even more than I needed Anna. Questions race through my head. When will we meet? Where will we meet? Would we meet? Do they live close?

"Natalie, Karisa say no worry. She say we meet soon, when the time es right. She say tell Annika she no alone, never es alone."

I pause and want to at least know where they live, but before I can ask the phone beeps off. It always seems to beep off at all the wrong moments but trying to get steady service in my house proves difficult. I think about calling her back, but I do not want to seem obsessive. I almost push send, but my finger moves to save contact. As I save the name, I replay what just happened, and there is an overwhelming feeling of did-that-really-just-happen.

I think about her last words, and my first response is comforting. Annika will never be alone. She has someone like her, and they will have each other. Then the heavy sadness in my heart falls to the ground. Annika will never be alone in another aspect as well. It seems she will always have these thoughts and premonitions hiding behind her blue eyes. Hopefully she will have this little girl forever because my Anna was taken away from me. I shudder as I remember the flashing sirens and blaring echo. I look at Annika and fear strikes that she might read into my thoughts. So I quickly dismiss them and focus on the present.

What can I think about? Bedtime. Yes, it is late enough now to go to sleep. I pick up Annika out of the chair. Her eyelids are heavy, and she is fussing. "I don't want sleep now!" She is such a precious, easy-going baby. She has an amazing temperament for a toddler, but she still has her moments.

"Yes, my sweet girl, it is time for bed. We can play tomorrow." It seems she is too tired to fight because she puts her head on my shoulder and pulls her hand around my neck, holding onto her cuppy. By the time we make it to the bed, she is already asleep.

I have not told a soul about her, and I will not tell a soul. If we meet up with Muneca and her daughter, I do not have to say anything about Annika. I have an urge to tell someone about the strange phone call I received, but then I would have to tell them about Annika. Annika's confidentiality is more to me than the brief relief of telling someone else. I push the thought of telling out of my mind.

I wake up thinking about Mr. Collins and how lonely he must feel after losing his dog. I wake Annika up, and we soak in the morning together. I love morning snuggles with her and would not trade them for the world. She is getting so much older and growing so quickly. I wish I could hit a pause button and hold onto her a little longer. After relaxing, playing, sharing morning coffee and chocolate milk, the thought of Mr. Collins still rests heavily on my mind.

"Chocolate, Mama!"

"You want more chocolate milk?"

"No, chocolate!!"

Hmm, I wonder if Mr. Collins would like some chocolate?

Not at all expecting a response, Annika replies, "YES, chocolate!" She smiles a big smile and is very pleased she was understood. I do not feel the heavy weight I usually feel when she reads me and so I decide, *Okay, chocolate.* A smile makes its way across my face as well.

At the store, I wave to Missy and speak briefly to Mr. Tom, one of our customers from work. Annika and I find our way to the chocolate section, and I choose a box of chocolate. I let Annika finger paint earlier and decided we would go with that over a store-bought card. I've been carrying her this whole time, and as we walk to the checkout, she pulls her arm around my neck and starts to play with my hair. She lays her head down on my shoulder and gets still. *It must be naptime*, I think to myself.

By the time we get to the car she is fast asleep. I try to put her in the car seat as gently as I can without waking her. She falls back asleep, and I decide to go lay her down at Tori's before we go to see Mr. Collins. That way she can get her nap out.

Tori is in the kitchen and uses her hand to direct me to her room. I lay Annika in the middle of her California king and put pillows all around her. I gaze at her until I am staring into her. I am concentrating on her so much that it startles me when Tori grabs my shoulder. "Hmmph!" I let out a startled sound. Tori silently giggles. She points to the camera baby monitor in her hand and motions for me to follow her out. I send a kiss to Annika, and then follow my sister.

"So, I heard from mom that the new doctor has the hots for you?"

I roll my eyes before I even realize what I am doing. "I would not call it that."

"It is Scott. Isn't it?" Her eyes are even smiling. Before I even knew what I was doing, I could feel my eyes turning the size of my Nanny's saucers.

"Yes, his name is Scott Richards."

"The same Scott Richards you snuck out with in eighth grade?" Her eyes are squinted, but they are still smiling.

"How do you know about that?!" I say louder and faster than I meant.

"Big sisters see a lot and hear a lot." She is waiting for something juicy, but unfortunately (and fortunately) for her, I don't have much.

"We were obviously young (he was older than me) and carefree. He was probably just bored." Her eyes beg me to keep going. "We never even officially went out. We hung out some, and he walked me home from the store a couple times. The night you're talking about was the second to last night he was going to be here before going back home. It was also the last time I would be able to see him. At first we were just talking, but then we found ourselves walking. I didn't want the night to end. We found ourselves at the park. Before we knew it, we were sitting on the bench next to the shore. We fell silent. It was dark. The stars were our only light. The breeze sparked a wave of goosebumps on my arm." I am deep in thought, almost as if I am reliving the moment itself, a memory I didn't even know I had. "He pushed my hair behind my ear, gently touched the side of my face, and then he pulled me in for a..."

"Mommy?" Braiden flashes on one of the baby monitors. Now he is in the camera waving and flashing a giant smile.

"That nap did him good." I laugh as Tori snaps from me to the camera.

Tori then grabs me by both my shoulders. "Well, did y'all? Did you? Did he kiss you?" I burst out laughing, as the moment fades into a distant memory now and much less real. She frowns and puts her hands on her hips. "Mommy's coming Braiden." She says into an intercom. Then she glares at me.

"Yes, he kissed me." I shrug more amused with her enthralled state than the actual answer.

"I knew it!" She releases.

"Yes, but please don't tell Mama or Roxy. I do not need them coming up with any ideas. I don't even know if he remembers me. Please, Tori."

She smiles and says, "Okay, okay." She turns to get Braiden, and I notice Annika starting to stir on the other baby monitor. I try to figure out the intercom system and decide I could probably get to Annika by the time I figured out the buttons.

We both meet with the babies in the living room, and my sister takes some blocks down for them to play with. Braiden is my sister's baby, and he eats that up. Even so, he is very good with Annika, and they play very well together. Braiden runs up to me and gives me a big hug. I take a piece of the brownies that Tori just pulled out of the oven, and he looks at me with tempting eyes. I break it in two, and I put a piece in my mouth and hand him the other. He starts to smile, and then he stuffs it in his face. "Are y'all getting into my fresh baked brownies? Those are for the church, and they are not gluten free, and they..." I push some in her mouth. She starts to laugh, Braiden starts to laugh, I start to laugh, and then Annika starts to laugh.

"Brownie, me too, Mama!" Tori pulls up Annika and then plops her into her lap at the table (only after putting a full sized bib on her) and feeds her a gluten-filled chocolate brownie.

"Brownies are not really a good snack to have after a nap," she starts to say.

I look at Braiden. "They are when Aunt Nat is here," I reply with a smile. My smile is returned with a chocolate grin from my favorite little boy.

We are disturbed by the sound of keys at the back door. My brother-in-law Brandon comes in with Brianna. "Aunt Nat! Annika!" Brianna squeals.

"Hey, sweet girl," I say.

"Bwi!!!" Annika climbs out of Tori's lap to fall into Brianna's hug.

"How were swim lessons, honey?"

"They were great." Brianna smiles so big I can easily see all the black spaces where several teeth used to be. Brandon is in the background giving a very concerned look and shaking his head **NO**. I start to laugh.

"So what are on your plans today, Natalie?" Brandon asks.

"I think I am going to head over to see Mr. Collins and take him some chocolate. His dog passed away, and that dog was all he had."

Brandon hangs his key under the small sign that says "HIS" and walks over to kiss Tori on her cheek. "Tori, why don't you take the kids and go with her?"

Tori thinks for a moment and then says, "Okay, that's a good idea. I'll grab some tea, and we will walk over with you."

I can see Mr. Collins tending to some of his plants as we approach the side of his house from the sidewalk. He sees us too, and he starts to stand. He is an average man with kind eyes and gray hair. Annika waves to him, and he replies to her wave, "Well, hello there, Annika. What a nice surprise! Natalie, Tori."

Tori passes him the tea. His mouth turns up, forming a smile, but his eyes are still sad. "We are truly sorry for your loss, Mr. Collins. I brought you some chocolate, and Annika made you a painting."

His eyes get a little brighter, "Well, thank you, thank you, I really appreciate it." He winks at Annika and says, "Chocolate is my favorite." He turns and ushers us to follow him. "You know I just planted some pansies, but I bet I still have a couple in the garage." He motions over to his car. "I'd love to give them to the kids. If you have any questions about how to best care for them, I can answer them. I always wanted to open up a nursery, and I am not sure what held me back." His voice gets softer. "Life, maybe just life."

Brianna starts to jump up and down when he pulls the pansies off a shelf, so of course Braiden follows her lead. Before I know it, Annika is sliding off my hip to join them. "Thank you so much, Mr. Collins, you sure made their day." Tori smiles.

"Yes, thank you, Mr. Collins," I say.

"You know, I sure miss sweet Betsey." He pauses and wipes his eyes. "I could never replace her, but I think I'll start looking for another dog soon. It's funny. At first, I wanted nothing of the sort, but I've since warmed up to the idea."

Tori pats him on the shoulder. "You know, I volunteer at the dog shelter every Wednesday. I can start looking for you."

"That'd be real nice. Thank you all so much for coming by. It sure means an awful lot. Remember, if you have any questions about the pansies, you just ask, ya' hear?"

"Yes, Mista Cowins."

He pats Annika on the head. "You all stop by anytime you like."

It is quiet on the first part of the way back to Tori's house, but I break the silence. "I feel so bad for him. He must feel so lonely."

"Poor, Mr. Collins." Tori shakes her head, but then her face lights up. "We had an older dog brought in last week, and I just think it would be perfect for him. I'll go up to the shelter tomorrow and see if I can get it worked out."

With that, we walk back up to their entryway. Brandon meets us at the door with his kiss-the-cook apron on. "Who wants to stay for a cookout?"

That means I won't have to think about dinner. Win for me. "Yes, please."

Annika starts to laugh. "Yum, yum, yay!"

Chapter 4: My Secret No More

Most nights I do not feel scared or paranoid about being alone in this old house. Tori urges me to leave and stay in their guest house to ensure our safety, and my mom still does not understand why we don't just move back in with her, but I like my independence. I like that it's just Annika and me, and we make it on our own. But tonight, I feel apprehensive.

I know I am dreaming because I have seen this all before. Anna is at my house, and we are playing tea party and dress up in Tori's clothes, but Tori doesn't care. Then the years jump, and we are sneaking out to spy on Tori. Then our seventh grade English teacher, Mrs. Postle (except her head is bigger than her body, and it doesn't really look like her) is telling my mom how inseparable we are (and it almost looks like we are really joined at the hip). Then in a flash, I am blinded by the police sirens, the ambulance, and detective in my face. Not the real detective, but a generic one that you see on all the crime shows. Then I see it, what I never saw, but was only told about. Anna's body is tangled and her clothes torn, her lifeless face lying on a cold floor. A light is flashing every so often over the scene.

"UH!" I wake myself up trying to familiarize my settings. I see Annika on the bed, and she is still asleep. Even though my room is warm, I have a chill I cannot shake. I sit up and try to calm myself. I turn on the light next to my bed and grab my phone. There's nothing to do, and it's too late to call anybody for a phone call that would not spark suspicion. I would never admit to Tori or my mom about these kinds of times anyway.

Yes, it is too late to call them, but not Roxy. I don't care if she knows how I am feeling. She won't tell unless I tick her off, but I haven't ticked her off since we were kids.

"Hello?" Music is blaring, and I can hardly hear my sister's voice.

"Can you come spend the night with me?"

"What?" she shouts.

"Can you come spend the night with me?" I can tell she is walking outside because the music begins to fade. "Can you come spend the night with us?"

"Is everything okay?"

"Yes, everything is okay, I just had a bad dream." She pauses, and I know Jace is the reason.

"Okay, Jace is being an ass anyway. Let me grab my things, and I will be over."

Roxy owes it to come stay with me when I need her, as many times as Annika and I have woken up and been greeted by her soundly sleeping on my couch with about every snack food I have opened, out and laying around her. I have woken up in the middle of the night with her letting me know she was about to crawl in the bed with us. My baby sister got my mom's impulsiveness and taste in men. She is the definition of wild and free. She is beautiful and stronger than I could ever be.

I turn on almost every light and start one of Annika's children's movies. I usually enjoy them as much as she does, but I am having trouble focusing. I finally see headlights hit the back wall and glide across until they disappear. A car door slams shut, and a knock that sounds more like an intentional rhythm quietly meets my front door. I open it quickly and pull her in. She doesn't ask me questions. I'm not sure if it is because she has Jace on her mind or if it is because she senses I am bound to my silence, but I am grateful. She lays her head in my lap, and I play with her hair while we finish up the movie, the same movie we watched as kids over and over again. By the time the movie is over, I am centered in the feelings of my childhood. It's almost as if I was back in time, and I feel comfortable and sleepy, not tired, just sleepy. It feels good. We climb in bed with Annika. I kiss both their foreheads, and we all sleep soundly until the next morning.

I usually make breakfast for Roxy when she stays with us, but I wake up still feeling tired. I make coffee and try to decide if I want to give in and call my mom to make us breakfast. The thought of her homemade biscuits and gravy is my breaking point, and I grab the phone to call her.

Sometimes she acts like making breakfast for us is a chore, but I know she secretly loves it. I am relieved today. She sounded inviting. We finally get Roxy up and all three of us, still in pajamas, load up and head to my mom's. The fog is hanging thick outside the windows, and I can barely see two feet ahead of me. It looks still and grey. The inside of the car matches the outside, silent and still. We drive over a little bridge with running water, and the movement seems to spring the feeling of life back into the car. I turn on the radio and a nostalgic acoustic song is playing. The song seems to soak into the thick fog. The trees we pass seem to breathe in the music the fog has consumed. The song ends, and a fun beat begins to play. The surreal emotions in the car evaporate, and the whole mood is lost.

Annika starts to giggle. Roxy looks sick, and I get scared she might be hung over, even though she is well under drinking age.

"Aunt Wox Wox baby sick."

At this point Roxy's phone goes off, and it is Jace. I was looking forward to her having breakfast with us, but I'm pretty sure this phone call will end that idea. Sure enough, she asks me to drop her off at his place on the way to my mom's.

"There is my sweet baby!" My mom grabs Annika, and Annika flies into her arms. "Nat, go ahead and make your plates while I make Annika some chocolate milk. Have you talked to Tori?" I grab a plate and start pinching up a biscuit for Annika.

"Yes, I think she is taking Bri to her piano lesson, and then Braiden has a playdate with someone's kid. Oh, I know. It is Mallory's son, Benjamin." My mom shakes Annika's cup and hands it to her as she sits her down.

"Did you know that Missy still has not invited Macy to her Christmas party?" I start to answer, but Annika startles me as she stands up and starts jumping up and down.

She is so out of control that I cannot embrace her. She is starting to turn red, and it seems she cannot grasp her breath. My mom turns white and drops her plate. It shatters on the floor, but we could not hear it break because Annika had started shouting, "Aunt Wox Wox blood, Aunt Wox Wox, blood, blood, blood. BLOOD, BLOOD, BL "

My phone goes off, and I answer it. Before it even registers, my sister's voice shakes on the other end. "Where are you?!! Roxy, where are you?!?!" I hang up the phone. My mom is staring at me and looking at Annika, and I can tell she is in shock.

"Mom! Mom! We have to go. Come on! We have to go get Roxy. She has been in an accident." Annika has calmed down, and although she still has tears in her eyes, she is letting me hold her. She seems calm. She is the complete opposite of the fit she just had. My mom, usually a strong woman, begins to bawl. I give her a quick hug and whisper, "Mama, come on. We have to go get Roxy." She snaps out of it, wipes her eyes, and follows me to the car.

Jace lives about fifteen minutes from my mother's place. At first, we are silent. I am hoping that we stay silent, but I'm also not that naive.

My mom breaks the silence with dreaded words, "Natalie, Annika called out 'Roxy blood' before Roxy called you. Natalie, Annika knew what was going to happen before it happened."

To think it is one thing, but to actually hear it out loud, to hear it stated matter of factly, seemed to make it so much more concrete. It could not be taken back. It confirmed what I had been trying to hide.

Ten words, ten words that hit me like a bat to the stomach. Ten words and all I could do was cry.

As I pull up to the edge of Jace's land, I see Roxy pacing back and forth next to a car that is crashed into a tree. Jace is inside, slumped over his steering wheel.

31 My Side of Her Story

"Stay in the car with Annika!" I do not give my mom a chance to answer. I jump out and run to my sister. I parked far enough away from them because I do not want Annika to see too much. As I get closer, I can see blood coming from my sister's head. Anger and sadness engulf me, and I race to her. She has her hand over her forehead.

"What happened? Is he okay?" She falls into my arms but says nothing. I hold her for a moment, take off my shirt, leaving me only wearing an undershirt, and hold it to her head. I check Jace. He is breathing and looks to be okay. It just seems he is passed out. "Have you called an ambulance? Roxy?!? Have you called an ambulance?" She shakes her head no. I call for an ambulance. I tell them my sister is bleeding from her head, Jace is passed out in the car, but is breathing, and there is no blood. They have an ambulance five minutes away.

Jace is loaded into the ambulance, and I am to follow. As soon as Roxy sits down, my mom starts in. "Roxy, what happened?" she asks, with the voice of a mother bear.

"Jace wrecked into the tree, and I guess I hit my head."

"Jace hit Aunt Wox Wox with bat."

Now, Roxy goes white. "Annika, what did you say?" she spatters.

"Bat," Annika answers.

Roxy looks at me. I cannot help but scream, "He hit you with a bat! Roxy, what the heck?"

There is no denying that Jace hit Roxy with a bat. Roxy knows we know. "It wasn't a real bat…" She trails off, so we ride in silence to the ER.

My mom and now Roxy too, they know that Annika knows things. They know she sees things. They know that this baby, my baby, is dealing with a huge burden, something so deep and so complicated, something so complex, something we cannot even understand as adults. Something I know is referred to as a gift, but from up close seems much more like a curse. Something I tried with every ounce of my might to keep bottled tight. Something I tried to make disappear.

And now it is staring me in my face, a secret no more.

Chapter 5: The Unexpected

I drop my mom and Roxy off at the emergency entrance and then pull into a front row parking space. The emergency entrance is actually the only entrance to the small hospital, anything serious gets sent a town over. It's a wonder that this little place sees enough patients to stay in business. *Funny that my little family has been here twice in such a short time when I am not sure any of us have ever even been to the ER before.*

When Annika and I get in, we are sent immediately back to a room. The magazine worthy nurse must not be on duty because I am greeted by a thin, tall man with glasses that seems to talk more with his nose than his mouth. He asks us to follow him and then trips on his own feet. He lets out a nervous laugh. "Right this way to room 302." By the time we make it back, Dr. Richards is already cleaning the wound. Roxy, teeth clenched, is turning red and muttering something under her breath.

"A mantra, huh?"

Roxy's jaw relaxes, and she looks at Dr. Richards. "You study metaphysical philosophy?"

Dr. Richards talks fast enough to keep her attention, but steady enough to make his point clear, "Well, I have dabbled in readings from Hinduism and Buddhism, but I am more of a church boy with an open mind. I know mental can be just as-you're going to feel a slight pinch-you know mental health can be just as crucial, sometimes more so, than physical health. If you feel anything more than pressure now, just let me know. You see, I take on an integrative medicine approach. Okay, you're good as a new."

Roxy looks surprised. My mom is looking a little green. Annika has her gaze on the cabinet with the suckers.

"That's it?"

"That's it for the wound." Dr. Richards smiles. "Due to some of the answers on your entrance paperwork, I'd like to collect a urine sample and run some bloodwork."

"Is something wrong?" my mom asks.

"Well, no, not necessarily. I just want to make sure we cover all our bases before I send her on her way. We want to monitor her for a little while anyway. I'll get the nurse back in here to help you, Roxy, and I'll come in and talk with you before you leave."

"Thank you."

The same nurse that walked me down the hall, comes in to escort Roxy to the restroom and labs. He looks at my mom. "Don't worry, ma'am. I'll stay with her the whole time in case she displays any signs of vertigo."

"She's a leo," my mom answers.

"I think he means in case she gets dizzy, Mom."

"Ah, well that makes more sense. Sorry, it's been a long day." My mom pauses and rubs her forehead with both hands. I would have felt embarrassed for my mom, but the thing about my mom is, she doesn't get embarrassed.

They aren't gone long. "Okay, I'd like to show one of you how to properly care for the stitches."

My mom looks at me with raised eyebrows, and I can almost hear her saying, "You want to do it?"

"I'll do it," I volunteer.

"Great. Okay, just show me how you would unroll the gauze to cover the affected area."

"Um, okay." I start and right as I grab the bandage.

"No, no, no!" He pushes his glasses back up on his nose. "You've just conta-mi-NATED the bandAGE!"

I can feel my face start to turn red. "Oh, I'm sorry," I whisper.

"No, no, it is fine. Here I'll show you how to do it. Remember, you only want to cover it during times it needs extra protection, not all the time."

"Okay, got it," I say.

"Alright, that is all I have for you today folks." He gives a wave and leaves the room.

Immediately the conversation rises louder and louder until we are all almost shouting, trying to talk over the other. "Roxy, you have to press charges," my mother exclaims.

"No, I am not pressing charges. I'll just leave him."

"Roxy, I usually don't like to intervene, but I am scared if you don't press some kind of charges, he might do this again."

"No, I AM NOT PRESSING CHAR..."

We all notice Dr. Richards at the same time, and then, boom, you could hear a pin drop.

"Sorry," I start.

"No, no need to apologize, but I have some news that might sway your view. Roxy, nothing to be alarmed about, but I got your test results. Just like I presumed, Roxy, did you know that you're pregnant?"

35 My Side of Her Story

I look at Roxy, and she turns paler than she already was. Then my gaze darts to my mom. Her jaw is on the floor.

"Are, are you sure?" my mom manages to get out.

He nods his head. "Yes, I can confidently say that Roxy is pregnant. Roxy's head drops into her hands. "Now Roxy, there are many options as I am sure you are aware, but I would like to refer you to Dr. Basil before you make any decisions. She's the best OB I know."

I put an arm around Roxy and send eye motions to my mom telling her to stop tapping her foot irritably on the floor. "I would also like to let you know that there is someone from the police station waiting to speak with you. Off the record, and as one of Natalie's friends, I think you might want to think hard about what to do, you know, after being presented with this new information."

My mom, although still very wrapped up in the current situation, somehow managed to catch it. "Natalie's friend?"

"Oh yeah, Natalie and I go way back. Right, Nat?"

My mom snaps back to me, and I shrug. "Yeah, way back." I smile. My mom's eyes are scheming, and I can hear their words loudly.

However, we are all brought back to the moment as Dr. Richards begins, "Hey, Roxy, you need anything before you get in with Dr. Basil, you just give my office a call." Roxy nods. My mom and I thank him. Then he turns to walk out the door. "Annika, you are welcome to pick a sucker and a sticker. Do you think you could keep the rest of these Haven women out of the ER for a while?" He winks and turns to leave.

The room is heavy. "Pregnant. I cannot be pregnant. I am on the pill, and I take it just like I am supposed to. I just had my monthly!"

"The pill is not 100% effective. You've just ruined your whole future! Your whole future, the *reeest ..of..your..LIFE!*

What were you think--ing?!?" Roxy begins to bawl. Then my mom goes from one extreme to the other. She jumps up and holds her. "There, there, it is going to be okay. You hear me? We will all be there for you, and we love you so much. Just look at Annika. This really will turn out to be a blessing." She grabs Roxy's face. "Everything is going to be just fine. We'll get it all figured out. There, there."

We compose ourselves and get ready to walk out, forgetting what was waiting for us on the other side of the door.

"Ms. Haven."

"Yes," we all three reply simultaneously to a man in a police uniform.

"Roxy Haven?" Roxy gives a one-way, windshield-wiper wave. "Hello there, my name is Officer Rey. I need to ask you a few questions."

I grab my mom's arm. "Alright, Roxy, we will be waiting outside when you're ready."

I am thankful to know my mother has forgotten all about Scott, me, and going "way back". If she had remembered, she couldn't have helped but to slam me with the question as soon as we stepped out into the cool air. We walk the sidewalk that circles the hospital, following Annika's steps. By the time we make it around a second time, Roxy meets us at the exit. I give her a huge hug and an honest smile but no words. Then we all walk to the car.

Sometimes saying everything without words is more impactful than trying to find the words that would fail to carry the same meaning altogether. I knew in this moment I could say much more to my sister without the heavy anchor of speech. Unfortunately for me, my mom needed words, and those words were directed at me.

"Natalie, what was that with Annika? Back at my house, she knew that Roxy had blood. *Aunt Wox Wox blood*."

37 My Side of Her Story

Fortunately, Annika was now fast asleep. "Yeah, and she knew *what* had hit me," Roxy chimes in. I focus on the road and try to drown them out, but I know we still have a fifteen minute drive. I picture myself pushing them out the door but am quickly brought back by my own laugh at the thought.

"Nat, we can tell this is hard for you," Roxy says. "The same way you feel about being here for me and my situation is the same way we feel about you and your situation." Those words, right there, were exactly the words I needed to hear. The words I needed to feel. They resonated with me. I felt a huge release and a powerful awakening that Annika and I had never been alone. Our family was there the whole time. The more I start to fill them in, the easier the words spill from my mouth, coming from my soul and filtering through my heart.

Roxy wants to stay with my mom, but I think it's best if Annika and I go home and let them have some time. Annika always sleeps better at home anyway. I am emotionally drained, and I throw my own little fit when I realize I need gas. Reluctantly, I pull into the gas station. There isn't any money on my card, so now we have to get out. I put my head on the steering wheel and let out a sigh. "It's okay, Mama. It's okay." I can't help but to smile at the sweet sound of her little voice. I get out of the car, and we make our way to the inside of the store. I'm indecisively checking out the candy. *Sweet or sour, or sweet and sour?*

Annika pushes to get off my hip. She starts walking away from me. "Annika, what are you doing? Hey, where are you going?" She ignores my call and is not at all acting like herself as she keeps walking away from my voice.

"Annika!" A little girl around six, with a thick black braid and huge eyes embraces Annika. My thoughts are racing. I'm confused while at the same time everything seems to make more sense than ever.

Then I hear someone call, "Karisa, dónde estás, mija?"

Chapter 6: The Forbidden Questions

A woman with the same thick, black braid and huge eyes turns the corner of the aisle. She has long eyelashes and a petite figure. She has an apron on covering her jeans and what seems to be a plain, white t-shirt, matching her plain, white tennis shoes. She is absolutely beautiful, not beautiful like the nurse at the doctor's office. She is imperfectly beautiful, genuinely beautiful. She looks like she is probably in her late twenties, but something tells me she is in her early thirties. Annika and Karisa are still wrapped close when she holds out a strong arm. Her bold smile exposes her perfectly straight and bright, white teeth.

"Hola, I am Muneca and dese"-she grabs onto Karisa's shoulders- "es my daughter, Karisa." Karisa giggles and waves.

As I am standing here, blinking my eyes, with my head tilted, an overwhelming amount of love at first sight takes over. I take in Karisa, and I just love her. When I love, I love strongly. I love her so much. She is absolutely adorable, and I feel like I've known her forever. "Hi Karisa, you are so kind, and it is very nice to meet you."

"It's nice to see you too." She gives me a big hug.

The phrase is innocent enough, but I immediately wonder. *It's nice to **see** you too?*

I look back at Muneca. I'm about to hold my hand out to her again, so I can properly introduce myself instead of standing there like a person in a ridiculously uncanny trance. However, I quickly find myself in a tight hug. Muneca pulls away, and then Karisa says, "See Mami, I told you we would find them when the time was right." She smiles.

Muneca laughs and then shrugs. "Sí, mi amor."

Okay, so what now? If we go our separate ways at this point it will feel abrupt, but do I invite them back to my house? It's too late to go anywhere.

"Natalie, I *am* six years old, and if you'd like us to come over, we can, right Mami?" Karisa looks to her mom with those big eyes.

"Of course, mija, but only if we are invited."

"We were Mami, right, Natalie?" Now those big, beautiful eyes are anticipating my response.

"Yes, you were."

"Thank you." She grabs Annika's hands, and they jump up and down.

"Okay, why don't you both go ahead and pick out a snack too." Karisa skips, and Annika follows behind.

As we get ready to load into the cars, Karisa pauses and says, "I've met you before already, Natalie, so it is nice to *see* you." She laughs. My mind almost begins to race, trying to recall a time when I would have met her.

Muneca must pick up on my puzzled face. "She no mean, you meet er before. She mean she see you in vision before. She does not always understand how explain." I nod and smile because even though this all sounds completely crazy, it makes complete sense.

Muneca follows me into the driveway. The heavy tiredness I had felt earlier was gone. I'm not sure if I am running on adrenaline or if I caught a second wind, but I am thankful either way. We all meet at the front door. I walk in and find the light. Then they both follow, a little more timidly than their extroverted behavior at the store.

Annika leads Karisa to her toys, and I bring Muneca a glass of tea. "They no talk tonight. They play." I look puzzled because at that exact moment, I was wondering if I should be concerned. "I no get visions like Karisa, I just know you worry how I worry. Today they play only. Karisa tell me in car, 'Mami, we will just play.' She say, 'You and Natalie talk,' es what she tell me."

I don't really know how to respond, and I am very thankful that Muneca just laughs, a kind laugh that breaks the awkward silence. She has a very charismatic personality and a sense of euphoria and charm seems to follow her.

"Well, I am very happy you are here." I look over to Annika and Karisa playing. Annika is having so much fun. Karisa, still young herself, is being very helpful and playing with Annika so well. Muneca follows my gaze, and we both stare with love at our daughters playing like typical kids. These are the moments I yearn for.

"So, do you live close?"

"No, we live one hour away, but we pass through here much on way to see my brother. We left fiesta tonight and go home now."

"Oh, you are leaving now?" My heart starts to sink.

"Ah, no, sorry, we leave my brother to go home. Now we here. My inglés no es perfect, but I understand, como se dice...ah, everything."

"I think your English is perfect." I smile. "I am so happy you are here because I have felt like Annika has been alone for so long, and I am so happy that now she has someone that will be here for her. I did not even realize how nice it would be to be able to talk to you. I have so many questions. I didn't realize how alone I was feeling too. I've been trying to keep it a secret this whole time, and it was excruciating." Muneca is listening, and she starts shaking her head quicker and quicker. "Oh, I am sorry, I am just rambling on and on. It's just, this is so nice."

"You keep secret?" she asks, surprised. I nod my head. "That must be real hard. I never keep secret. Everybody know."

"But didn't you think you needed to protect her?" I ask earnestly and not accusingly.

"No, rituals are part of Mexican culture, chants, ojo, una limpia, my family know. No harm come." She smiles.

"Do friends and strangers know?"

She thinks for a moment. "No, I do not think, that is er choice. When she older, not time now. Your family no know?"

"Well, my mom and one of my sisters just found out, but I am not ready to tell my other sister. Like you, I don't really want other people to know unless she decides to tell them when she is older. It did feel better telling my family though, and once I told them I realized we had never been alone, just like Karisa told you to tell me."

She nods her head. "Karisa is smart girl." She smiles and we both get quiet. "You ask me what you want. Karisa tell me you have questions, and that why we here tonight."

My heart gets heavy because the questions pulling at my heart are deep. "Are you sure?" I ask.

She pats my shoulder and says, "I have many question when Karisa visions came first times. I have someone answer my questions, and now I answer you questions." She smiles, looks to Karisa, and I can see the same love in her eyes that spills from mine when I soak in Annika. I take a deep breath and a sigh accidentally slips. She nods her head and says, "Go on now, ask. I am here."

"Okay, aren't you scared that she is going to hear your thoughts all the time. I mean we are adults, and there are some things I think that I would not want my daughter to know. From things like, not having money for the electric bill, to things like, thinking a man is attractive." For some reason, well, I probably have a good idea what that reason is, Scott pops in my mind. "You know, things that they shouldn't know."

"Oh, yes! I think same thing, like oh my God, she going to know all adult things, inappropriate things, but Karisa no, she do not. Maybe her head filters it out before it goes to er heart because her mind know she too young to understand or see, or maybe she never see at all. Maybe God protect her from that part."

"Oh, that is really reassuring to hear. I hope Annika is the same way. That would be a huge relief. Wait, how do you know for sure she does not know certain things?"

"We are mothers, maybe we no have gift, pero we are mothers. Mothers know our babies. We jus do."

I do not think I have ever heard truer words spoken. "A mother's intuition," I proudly state.

She raises her cup of tea to mine. "A mother's intuition, salud," she parrots back to me.

So I parrot back to her, "Salud," and our glasses cling.

Then she lets out a deep sigh, and I jump.

She looks distressed, which even though I've only known her for about two hours, I can tell it is not an emotion that visits her frequently. My stomach drops.

"I no want to worry you, but there are times, and maybe Annika es deferent, pero, there are times that Karisa see things when people allow her look for things. She see things, and it is hard for me to see her see things." I can see her trying to shake the uneasy feeling, pleading for her relaxed optimism to return. "But, when she, I don't really know how say, when she wake up, She no remember nothing, nada."

She smiles a true smile. Then I pat her back and smile. "Thank you for sharing with me. I have had all these questions, and they have stolen away my happiness many times. I have longed to know the answers, at the same time, not wanting to hear the answers. But, this, everything you have shared, is so much better than I had anticipated. I really appreciate you taking this time and sharing your much needed insight. I think I might have needed you as much as Annika needed Karisa."

Muneca's yawn is interrupted by her cell phone. "Excuse me please. Hola, mi amor. Estamos en la casa de Annika. Sí, están jugando." She looks over at Annika and Karisa. "Mi amor, ello?"

"Oh, sometimes the service is not great in here. You should be able to hear better from the porch though."

"Oh, yes, Karisa es okay here?"

"Oh yeah." I smile. "No problem."

Muneca comes back in just as Annika starts to yawn. "I sorry, pero I do not realize the time. My husband es worry, and I think it is time for us go." The tiredness from earlier hits into me.

"Oh, yes, it is getting really late." I try to think of something to give them as a gift.

"Karisa, we going."

"Buuuuuuut Maaaaaami, I want to play dolls with Annika. We just started a new game," she whines.

"Ah, Ah, Karisa, I say is time to go. Ya vamanos. Tu Papi está esperando. Okay, dile a tu amiga hasta luego y ya."

"Annika, I'm sorry, but it is time for me to go. My dad is waiting for us. My mom wants me to tell you I'll see you later. I know you are getting tired." Karisa starts to whisper and looks back over her shoulder at her mom. "I am too, shhhh, I don't want my mom to hear."

Annika goes to give Karisa a hug, and Karisa kisses Annika's cheek. "Buh bye." Annika says.

"Bye, Annika. Remember, you're never alone." She looks at me to make sure I am listening too. "I'm going to be your friend forever and ever, and your family is always going to be here for you too." These sweet babies being concerned for adults always leaves me melancholy. I know Karisa is saying this mainly for me.

I notice the extra saucer set, and even though it is one of the only things I have left to cherish from my nanny, I feel something tug at me. "Wait, Muneca, Karisa? I would like you to take this teacup and saucer set with you. Words cannot express how thankful I am that you came over and shared so many things with me."

"But that was your Nanny's!" Karisa says, eyes wide open.

I am not sure if it is because I am tired or because the unbelievable is becoming my new reality, but I just calmly respond, "Yes, I know sweet girl, but I'll still have a pair. I want to give you something with meaning."

"Thank you, Natalie."

They are about to walk out the door, and then Karisa pulls on Muneca's apron. "Natalie, Karisa say me to tell you that I am going to be with you. Rodriguez and Haven till end of time." She waves her hand as if motioning eternity and shows her perfect white teeth as she smiles behind big red lips. Then she adds, "She say next time we talk to someone." Karisa pulls on her mom and whispers in her ear. "Ah, yes, someone name Anna."

That familiar prickle in my cheek, followed by goosebumps transferring over from one side of my body to the other, from top to bottom, greets me, and my hand goes over my mouth. I start to feel sick. "Only if you want," Karisa quickly adds. "She loves you. She is good. She is happy. Do not worry." She gives me a reassuring hug.

Chapter 7: The Christmas Party

"Natalie, hun, on your way to the Christmas party could you stop by and grab my green bean casserole? I don't think I'll have room for it in the car," Caroline says as she buzzes around the office. Caroline always brings at least three casseroles and every kind of homemade pie you can think of. There's never anything more than a few crumbs left of each. It's actually pretty amazing Rob stays as thin as he does with such a chef for a wife.

"Sure, Caroline." I smile. "I just have to pick up some tea and ice, so I'll swing by your place on my way."

"Okay, dear, we appreciate it. Why don't you go ahead and head on home, and we'll see you tonight."

"Are you sure?"

"Yes, dear, Rob and I will follow you out. It's too close to Christmas to work too hard." She laughs and throws her hands up. "The only person that should be working now is good ol' Saint Nick." She winks. Christmas time is Caroline's favorite. They always set up their jobs so that there is at least a week off for Christmas. I love that too because if I ever just had two days off it wouldn't even feel like Christmas. I am a lot like Caroline. I can smell, taste, and even feel Christmas. I love Christmas time. I don't go crazy with decorations like my mom and Tori, but I put out just enough to make it cozy.

As I am putting Annika in the car my phone goes off. "Hello? Oh, hey Mama."

"Hey, Nat, I don't have any gas in the car, and I don't get my check for another week. I was wondering if Roxy and I could just ride with you?"

"Sure, Mama." I pause so I can put the phone on my shoulder and hold it with my ear. I finish snapping Annika's car seat. "I have to stop by Caroline's, and then I'll head your way."

"Okay, and on the master list I saw you were supposed to be bringing the tea and ice. I made up plenty of tea, so we'll just have to stop for ice."

"Okay, sounds good, Mama, thank you." She is always prepared, and when she is in a good mood, selflessly helpful.

Caroline holds the dish as she carefully makes her way down her front steps. She has a Santa mitt on each hand and is carefully coming out to the car with a huge smile. Her hair is on rollers, but she has a full face of make-up on, including bright red lipstick. She has ornament replicas dangling from her ears, just as big too. She looks beautiful and so festive. She could almost pass for Mrs. Claus. Rob sends a wave from the front door and smirks. He teased her all day at the office, just like he does every year, for making so much food. However, I can tell from his smirk that he is actually pretty proud of her. It's sweet how he is admiring her from her afar. "Thank you, sweetheart. I hate to just run back in, but I have got to get these rollers and the last pie out within 10 minutes." She throws her hands up then winks. "I've done it in less." Then she scurries back in the house.

I pull up my mom's driveway, and I see Roxy open the door. She calls back into the house, probably letting Mama know we're here. Then I see my mom come out with two jugs of tea. She looks mad and sets one down and points inside. *She is probably telling me to get out and come get the rest.* I start walking up, and she has already walked back in. "I can't carry all this by myself." She sounds aggravated.

"Okay, well, I'll help."

Her demeanor changes. "Thank you, it's just you're always late, Natalie, and we can't be late today."

"Okay, I think we are doing just fine on time, Mama." I check my phone for the time to make sure I didn't fall behind schedule. Then I catch a glimpse of Roxy's scheming eyes. "What are y'all up to?"

Roxy looks surprised. "Huh? What? She never likes to be late." She shrugs, and she is right. Mama never likes to be late.

We pull up to the Christmas party, and my mom is almost climbing over the backseat (Annika wanted to sit by Nana). "Is that Macy? I can't see it's so dark out here. They should really get some more outside lighting. It sure looks like Macy." She squints and nudges my shoulder. "Natalie, is that Macy?"

I pull my shoulder away from her. "I am not sure, Mama. I am trying to park." The cars always get packed on their lawn like sardines. I am trying to park straight, so I can get out if I decide to leave early.

"Roxy, is that Macy?!?"

"Goooooo-lly, Mama. I think so." Roxy looks over at me with squinted eyes, letting me know she is annoyed. I smile back.

"I just can't believe Macy is here. Missy must have broken down and invited her."

"Mama, I don't really think that is any of our business," I say.

"Nonsense, if they didn't want it to be our business the whole town wouldn't know about it. Come on, Ms. Annika. Let's go strut our stuff. You look absolutely adorable in your Rudolph dress, and I would hate for anyone to miss it."

Inside the party, I find a cozy corner in the back of the room. I watch everyone greet and chat. The guys gather around a fire in the back, and the women go to the old garage that Missy had turned into a commercial kitchen. They all grab wine and go to decorate cookies. Macy stops and waves at me. I wave back to her, and then she comes up to me and gives me a hug. People usually open up to me easily, but there isn't even a hesitation. "I have missed my sister so much. Sure we still talked"-she raises her shoulders-"but it wasn't like it used to be. But I am here now." I can smell the wine on her breath.

"Well, I am sure Missy is just as happy, and it is really good to see you. I am glad you came."

"Thank you, beautiful." She kisses me on my cheek.

Tori comes and grabs Macy by the hand and looks at me with a smile. Tori's eyes tell me she is keeping a close eye on Macy, who already seems really pretty tipsy. "Natalie, you don't want to come decorate? Mama and Roxy are over there."

"No, I am going to keep an eye on Annika and the others." I smile.

"They'll be fine, Nat." Tori rolls her eyes. "Geez, we will be right here."

"I know, but I like it over here."

Macy chimes in. "Well, if you change your mind"-hiccup- "just come on o'er." I watch Tori walk away in a leather pencil skirt. Of course, to embrace her conservative side, it is almost swallowed by an oversized Christmas sweater. Her hair is pinned back perfectly, and she moves swiftly. Macy has on an ugly Christmas sweater over some tights and some funky Frosty socks pulled up over the bottom of the tights. She walks away with a little more zig and zag, as she tries to keep up with Tori's graceful steps.

It's only Annika, Bri, Braiden, and Benjamin. They are all playing great. I see my mom and Roxy walk into the kitchen in the house to pour another glass of wine. Roxy is wearing a tight and short little dress that I wouldn't wear any other way than a shirt. My mom looks nothing less than a famous movie star.

"Roxy, you better keep on with the ginger ale."

Roxy rolls her eyes. "Do you think we were too late? I haven't seen the doctor."

"No, we were on time. When Tori told me that that doctor was going to be here, I sure was wanting to make sure Natalie crossed his path." Their voices fade as they walk back to the commercial kitchen full of women scurrying around.

That's why Roxy looked up to something when she got in the car.

"Hey, Natalie."

I look up and get butterflies in my stomach. It's Scott. He is by himself and carrying a gift that is wrapped so elegantly that it definitely had to be professionally done. I can feel myself turn red when I notice how he looks even more handsome in regular clothes than hospital attire. *How he could get even more handsome? I'm not sure.* I try to shake the thoughts.

"We sure have been seeing a lot of each other lately."

I just smile. "I am glad that this time we aren't in the office. I mean, not that I don't like seeing you in the office, but the change of scenery is nice." I smile again. I can't find my words. "Um, all the guys are out around the fire," I manage.

"Oh, I see. You're trying to get rid of me."

I laugh. "No, but it's probably a little boring in here. It is **nice** to see you too."

Did he mean it was nice to see me or was he just being polite? Should I have added too at the end? He didn't exactly say it was nice to see me. Why do I do this to myself?!? Stop overthinking and pull yourself together, geez Natalie. You're blowing this.

"Okay, I guess I'll head over to the fire."

Finally the right words find me, "Would you like me to take the present to the table for you?"

"Sure," he says and he smiles, "thanks."

Thank God for that save because the whole rest of my side of the conversation was awfully awkward. I grab the present and smile. "No problem."

The whole time he was talking to me I couldn't wait for him to just leave, but now that he has left I have this burning desire to run back into him. I distract myself with the kids and go ahead and make their plates before the adults come in to eat. Everyone makes their way back inside the huge living room/dining room area. Missy's husband, Edward, says the blessing. I see my mom see Scott, and I pray she doesn't try to pull a fast one. After the blessing, everyone makes their plate. Mallory and Tori are relieved that all the kids have already been fed.

"Where's Aunt Macy, Mom?"

"She is asleep in the guest bedroom. That merlot did her in." She giggles.

The kids get into the cookies. Then some of the adults follow, although most choose the pies that Caroline brought.

The kids do a gift exchange, and they all get the same thing they do each year. Mr. Tom always gives them a bear, Mr. Collins gives them a pouch of flower seeds, Missy puts in something different each year, but always something expensive, Mallory usually puts in a puzzle, Tori puts in a book, and I put in some candy.

Then the adults always play White Elephant. I always find an excuse not to play. This year I give my gift to my mom, so she can play. I would never want to take a gift from someone, and I always felt awkward when someone took a gift from me. Anyway, it was a fun game to watch. I started feeling even more fondly toward Scott when I realized he didn't steal from anyone even though he ended up with a floral scented spray and lotion gift set. I noticed when it was over he secretly handed it to his mom, Rhonda, and kissed her on the cheek. He was too good to be true.

"I wanted that designer handbag. I cannot believe that sleezy Susy stole it from me, and I ended up with this stupid ornament." My mom holds the bobble-head Santa up higher so that it is in the direct view of my eyes. My mom was never happy with what she got and there was no arguing with her when she was in a mood. I just smile and shrug.

I notice Missy sternly talking to Edward. She is pointing at a paper with a pen and then to the clock. Edward smiles and tells her something, but then she starts tapping her foot. Then Edward sighs and lets out a laugh. "Okay everyone, according to the master schedule, it is the exact time for the outside festivities to begin." With that, he props open the back doors.

The kids run out the door, and it isn't long until they find the new dog to play with that Mr. Collins brought to the party. Tori matched him with the best dog. It's older than a puppy, so it has already gone through the puppy stage. Even though it's an older dog, it still has enough spunk to keep the kids busy for at least a little while. The new/old dog called Foxy goes to lay down after being worn out from the kids. That's when I notice Benjamin yawn. Then Annika yawns. Yawns always seem to be contagious. I find myself thinking of Scott, and my heart sinks at the thought he might have already left.

I see Roxy go behind the house, and I can hear her throw up. I've got Benjamin on one hip and Annika on the other. "Rox, you okay?"

"Yeah," she says with tears in her eyes, "it always just seems to hit after dinner."

"I know, I know." I try to console her. She composes herself, and then grabs Annika. "I think they're ready to lay down."

"Okay, I'll help. Come on Bri. Come on Braiden. Let's go watch a movie."

"Okay, Aunt Rox Rox."

On our way in I see Scott, and I feel myself get flushed. Then I realize he has about three young single ladies around him. I scold myself for thinking he'd ever be interested in me. I laugh out loud and roll my eyes at myself.

It isn't long before they are all out, even Roxy. I decide to walk outside and watch the fire alone from the playground. My mom hates that I'm not more social, but large groups overwhelm me. It seems the party's just really getting started. Rob and Caroline hear a song they both must love because Caroline grabs Rob's hand and leads him to the concrete dance floor. I am so far away that I can only vaguely make out the words of the song. I see Mr. Tom getting groovy with it. *Is that Macy awake and back out there dancing with Mr. Tom?* My mom is dancing by herself, a little provocative for a woman her age if I have any say about it. Missy and Edward are barely rocking back and forth, and you could almost fit a whole other couple between them. The fire is going strong, and I see a couple of the younger couples sitting around and holding hands. I'm really soaking up everyone and enjoying the party. I think one of the younger guys just kissed one of the younger girls. I lean closer.

Pat. Pat. I jump up, startled, from the touch on my shoulder. I turn around to see who it is, expecting Roxy, and I am surprised that I find myself hoping it was Scott.

Then, there he is. My blue eyes meet his deep, brown eyes, and I blush. I look away. "So how have you been Natalie? It has been a long time hasn't it?" I shake my head yes. "Annika is a great kid. She is really smart for her age."

I love the way he always focuses on Annika, even with her absence he recognizes her. That makes my heart ache even more. "Thank you."

"So, I talked with your mom earlier."

"Oh no!" I let out, as if it were a reflex.

He laughs. "She has a strong personality doesn't she? But, she is pretty cool too." He nods in her direction, a sly smile appears across his perfect face. I smile as I find her out there still shaking it, comparable to an exotic dancer, and roll my eyes. I put my forehead in my hands.

"Yeah, she wanted to know how we met."

"I bet she did," I say.

"I told her you were my first crush, but I have to say, it hurt my feelings a little that she didn't already know."

I stay quiet, unsure of what to say. The only words that fill my head: *I was his first crush? I thought he was just bored. I don't even know how much he remembers. Maybe I really was his first crush.* Then those young ladies flash in my mind "Well, I might have been your first, but you're pretty popular with the girls these days." That sounded way more jealous than I had anticipated it sounding, another epic fail. "I mean…"

He laughs. "That was my cousin and her entourage. You remember Becky, don't you?"

"That's Becky? Of course, I remember her, but I didn't know she still lived here."

"She moved back a couple of months ago. A bad break up I think."

Before I realize it, we are walking away from the party. Scott breaks a long silence. "How is Roxy doing?"

"We haven't talked much about the baby, but she did press charges."

"That is good to hear. The last thing I'd want to do is push something on someone, especially when I'm on the job, but I really think that will help protect the baby."

"Me too, we were really relieved she did."

"What is your other sister's name? Does she know?"

"Tori, no we haven't told Tori yet. She tends to freak out about stuff like that. We will when it is the right time though. We are all really close."

He nods his head. "You know, Natalie, you look the exact same. You haven't changed a bit." I stay quiet. "You're really beautiful too, you know?"

I shake my head, "Me?"

"Yeah, and I think it makes you even more attractive that you don't realize how beautiful you are." I look down. His hand brushes my cheek. Caught off guard, I look up. Then, just like all those years ago, he kisses me. Even though the air around us has become chilly, heat stirs within. This time the kiss is real. It's sensual, long, and I find myself not wanting it to stop.

Chapter 8: What's Mine Is Yours

We make our way back to the party and just as we walk up my phone goes off. It's a text, "Please tell Annika hi. I know it is late. We can talk later." It is from Karisa. She must have Muneca's phone. It's around midnight, and the party is starting to settle down.

My thoughts fly to Annika, but then I remember Roxy is with them. "I have to go," I say, " I need to take my mom and Roxy home, and Annika really needs to be in her bed." I quickly add, "I had fun tonight." I wince at the word, "fun." *Why don't my words work around him?*

"I hope to see you again, Nat, and preferably not at the office." He smiles.

As we walk back up to the house I notice my mom and Roxy. I break away from Scott before giving them anything to see worth prying over.

"Hey, who is with the kids, Roxy?"

"They all left with Tori and Brandon."

"Annika?"

"Yea, she went too. Mallory took Benjamin to the bedroom Missy made for him. Brandon grabbed up Annika, so she wouldn't be left alone, and I wouldn't have to cart her around." I frown and then Roxy adds, "They called when they got home and said she was still fast asleep. They played hard and apparently all three of them are out."

I start to feel angry that Annika left and nobody even let me know. Then again, I probably would have done the same thing if it was my niece and nephew. They really are like second moms to Annika.

"Where were you anyway? We tried to call you. You must not have had service."

"Um, just walking." *Well, they did try to call me anyway.* "I want to go get her tonight though. Even though she can obviously sleep without me, I don't think I can sleep without her."

"Well, take me home first, and then you just stay over there. There's no point to keep dragging her all around."

"Mama's right."

"Okay, that sounds good. Roxy, you want to stay with me at Tori's?"

She shrugs. "I guess."

As we are walking in, we hear Tori quietly grasping quick breaths through her nose. "Is she crying?" Roxy whispers. "It sounds like it." We are already inside but knock quietly on the closing door behind us.

"Oh hey," Tori says. I notice the almost empty wine bottle about the same time as Roxy. Tori wipes her eyes quickly and fakes a smile. Tori usually doesn't drink.

"Where are the kids?" Tori knows I am just wondering about Annika.

"I laid Annika down in Bri's trundle bed." *Ah, so that's where I'll be sleeping.*

"Are you okay, Tori?" I am surprised at Roxy's sincere concern. She usually isn't sensitive to other people's needs like I am. I was so worried about getting to Annika that I skipped over the most important thing at this moment, my sister.

"Oh, nothing, I'll be fine." I can tell she isn't going to be fine. Something is stirring inside her, and I hurt for her. It's like I can feel her heart breaking.

"Tori, it's us," Roxy says. Tori looks up, and my first thoughts of her being drunk are second guessed. She maybe a little buzzed, but she definitely isn't drunk.

"I never told y'all, but about a year ago, I had some complications and had to have one of my fallopian tubes removed." Tori has always kept her private business very guarded. "The doctors told me I could still get pregnant, but I have not been able to conceive. I had already started ordering things to turn the guest room into a nursery. When I pulled out the blankets for Annika, I saw a lamp I had ordered. I guess that mixed with the wine. I know I have two beautiful, healthy children, and I am so thankful. Maybe I am just being selfish."

"No, you aren't being selfish, not at all. Just because you want another baby doesn't mean you aren't thankful for the two you have."

She smiles kindly at my attempt to console her, but then she goes on, "I didn't even think I wanted more kids, but when I missed my monthly menstrual cycle I felt a tug of excitement. When I took the test and saw it was positive, I made this great little surprise for Brandon. He was ecstatic. Of course, we wanted to wait until the first doctor's appointment to tell the kids. I had already found the best way to surprise them, but that surprise never happened. Brandon stood holding my hand. We anticipated hearing the little heartbeat for the first time, but the anticipation turned into…" Tori can't speak through the tears.

I get up and grab her hands. She shakes her head and stops reliving the moment, instead we just get an answer, "It was an ectopic pregnancy."

"That's why your fallopian tube was removed?"

She shakes her head yes. "Then, I wanted a baby so bad. So we started trying. I know in my heart that another baby will never replace *that* baby, but after picturing us a family of five and getting so excited, watching some of the things I ordered for the nursery come in." She shrugs her shoulders.

Roxy chimes in, "Why didn't you tell us? How did you even hide a whole surgery from us?"

"Mom knew." Then it was silent.

I look at Roxy, and she sees me. *You have to tell her now,* I think. Almost as if she can hear me she shakes her head no. "Yes, Roxy," I say out loud. I just have this powerful feeling. It is an emotion I cannot describe. I know that even though it doesn't seem like the *best* time for Roxy to tell Tori she is with child, it is the *right* time.

"What?" Tori looks desperately at me. "What?"

"It is not mine to tell. Roxy, you need to tell her."

"Are you shitting me, Nat?!?"

"No, Roxy, please tell her."

"I don't even know what I am going to do. I have not even thought about my choices."

Tori is turning from me to Roxy and back again, trying to make sense of the situation. "What is going on?" Tori demands.

Roxy lets out a loud growl, "I have no damn idea. What in the world makes Natalie think this is the best time to tell you, but..." Roxy continues, but her tone goes from harsh to sensitive, "Tori, I'm pregnant."

We wait for Tori's reaction, and her initial statement could have been guessed by anyone that knows her. "You're not married, Roxy. You can't be pregnant!"

"Tori it doesn't take a ring on your finger to get you pregnant." Roxy says seriously, "It happens when..."

Tori and I look at each other. Is *she about to really go there?* We know she is and probably with the most vulgar language too. Then we all three look at each other and burst out in laughter.

Then Roxy looks overwhelmed. "I don't even think I want to keep it."

"You cannot get an abortion, Roxy. You just can't," Tori says, her eyes starting to swell again.

"No, I am not going to get an abortion, but that is all I know. I know I don't really want a kid. I can't even take care of myself."

"But, just look at Natalie and Annika. She was young, and they are okay. In fact, because of how Natalie and Annika are, I am not completely losing it after learning my only other sister will also be a teen mother out of wedlock."

I smile at the compliment and then shudder because I am in the middle of two polar extremes.

"I am not Natalie though, Tori." Roxy gets quieter with each word, so quiet that by the time she gets to Tori, we have to read her lips. We sit there in silence for a moment.

Roxy starts to cry. I am starting to feel like maybe the feeling I had was just anticipation, and I start regretting that I made Roxy tell Tori tonight.

"Roxy, why are you crying? Is it because you're scared? Because you know you have me, Natalie, and Mama."

"I'm not scared. I really just don't want a baby. I don't want to have an abortion, but I just wish I could make this all go away. The dad, Jace, I had a restraining order put on him. He is in jail now for hitting me on the head."

"Hitting her on the head with a bat!" Roxy shoots me a glare. "Sorry."

"You mean all this was going on, and I had no idea?"

"Well, it was not mine to tell," I say.

Roxy follows with, "Mama knew." Then it goes silent again.

"I wonder how much Mama knows? I always thought she would be the first one to tell, but apparently she keeps secrets better than we do." After the words pour from my mouth I realize I am the only one still sitting here with a secret. "Tori, there's something else I need to tell you. One more secret." Then I tell her about Annika from the very beginning.

As I wrap up everything, Tori cuts in, "That just doesn't seem real, Natalie. How would she? Why would she be able to do that? And that girl, Karisa, there are con artists out there, Natalie."

"No, it's fucking real Tori. I was in the car with her when Annika told them that I had been hit in the head with a bat."

"Roxy, language."

"Oh, my bad. But, it is real Tori, and it is freaking crazy." I wince at the word crazy. "Well, not crazy, but definitely bad ass."

My mind starts to roll, "Roxy, have you thought about giving the baby up for adoption?"

"Well, yeah, I guess those are really my only two options. Grow up and keep it or give it up for adoption. It is just I hate the thought of giving it to strangers. I had trouble giving Tomcat's kittens away, remember?"

"Oh yeah, who knew Tomcat would turn out to be a girl, and a pregnant one on top of that?" Tori laughs.

Then I chime back in, "Tori have you thought about adopting?"

"Brandon and I started, but it is a long legal roller coaster. I just think I am too sensitive to take it on."

Roxy starts to see where I am going with this, and I start to recognize that strong feeling that is almost like a new emotion growing from within.

Tori's lip has started to quiver again. Roxy gets up and sits in front of her. "Tori, don't cry. Tori, listen, this baby that I'm carrying, is your baby." Tori looks confused. "Tori, I want to carry this baby for you and Brandon. I am in no position to care for this baby like it deserves. I'm sure I'll grow to love it, but I cannot raise it. You and Brandon are perfect parents, and I know it will be raised in the best environment. Can you take this baby for me?"

"Roxy, you're going to change your mind."

"No, Tori, I cannot do this. I am not Natalie."

"Roxy, if this is how you truly feel, of course I will take this baby. I already love it so much."

***

I finally make my way to Bri's bedroom around 3 a.m. The carousel night light gives off just enough light so I can see Bri sleeping in her oversized bed in her comfy linens that perfectly match the night light. She looks so beautiful and peaceful. I love her so much. Then I see Annika, my baby. She is as perfect now as the first time I ever saw her. Her blonde hair falling around her, her eyelashes, her little hands. I feel such an overwhelming love for her. I do not worry as much as I did before I met Karisa and Muneca, but oh, do I still worry. I love her so much, and I would do anything for her. I say a prayer that she will be able to hold onto her innocence as long as possible. I kiss her cheek and get as close to her as I can. My sweet, precious baby.

The night jumped from one thing to the next so fast, but as I get still and replay what just happened in Tori's living room over and over, I feel something else tugging at me. Scott. A hot sensation runs through my body as I recall the details from earlier this same evening. I hastily check my phone and Muneca's message is still last. No new text from Scott. I feel a little disappointed. I feel like I already miss him. Did he really kiss me? I wonder if he is really attracted to me, and if so, why? He works with that gorgeous nurse, and Becky's friends were basically drooling over him. But it does feel like no time has passed since all those years ago. It is like time stopped in that moment all those years ago and picks right back up in the same spot every new time we meet. He is kind, intelligent, patient, and he is as handsome as ever. I fall asleep with Scott, his jawline, and his soft lips on my mind and in my heart.

Chapter 9: The Fiesta

"Afton!" I wake up and check my phone. It is only 5:00 a.m. I've only been asleep about two hours. I can't remember my dream at all, but it must've been about Afton because he is the only thing on my heavy, half-asleep mind. As I start to wake up more, I wonder how I could fall asleep in such deep thought over Scott and wake up calling out for Afton. Annika turns over. I curl up next to her and fall back asleep easier than I thought. Annika wakes me up, and it feels like it is around 10:00 a.m. I check my phone, and it is 10:11. I feel an emotion nagging, and I realize I am feeling down. The forgotten dream leaves me missing Afton very much. There is some guilt there too.

***

"Natalie, grab the bananas and that sweater by the front door," my mom is shouting from her room. Roxy is running around turning off lights and lugging around a suitcase. "Oh, and Natalie…"

"Yes, Mama?"

"There's a special gift for you by the front door. Don't forget to grab that too."

I have a good feeling that it is my favorite seasonal candy. We all pile into the car. Annika pouts. "I want Aunt Rox Rox."

"Wow, her Rs are perfect now, Nat." My mom sighs. "She is growing up so fast."

Roxy smiles, "You want me? Okay, I call sitting by my girl." Annika kicks her legs and smiles, pulling Roxy's face in by her cheeks. Then Annika kisses her.

We pull up to Tori's just like we have done every Christmas Eve since she has been married to Brandon. We unload my car, which my mom has filled to the brim. It doesn't get too cold here, and we almost never have snow, but I see some flurries start to fall as we pull the last things into the house. It is Christmas magic. I can smell it, see it, and I feel it. The kids play, and Tori helps them make cookies for Santa. They drink Brandon's homemade hot chocolate with extra marshmallows. Brandon takes them outside to leave carrots and reindeer food for all the reindeer. Roxy reads them a Christmas book, and then it is time to lay them down. I know they are having trouble going to sleep. They each have Christmas morning fantasies running through their little minds. We all go and tuck them in with a kiss for each. When we get back into the living room, I notice my mother digging through all the things we carried in. I'm thinking she is getting ready to do Santa, but then she says, "Natalie, where is it? Where is that little package?"

The little package? I think to myself. "Oh! The candy?"

My mom stands, puts a hand on her hip, and looks a little bewildered, "Candy? No, that special little gift that was by the door."

"Yeah, my candy." I think she is going mad, well madder than she already is. I smile at the thought of my mother as the mad hatter.

"That wasn't your candy."

Genuinely disappointed, I let out a whine, "You didn't get me the Santa candy this year?"

She relaxes. "Yes, sweetheart, I got you the candy, but that's in the bag with all the other candy. The present Natalie, where is it?"

Confused, I look around, "Here it is." I hold it up.

"That's a gift from Scott Richards to you."

My heart flutters.

I don't know how I am able to get out of opening the present in front of everyone that second, but I do.

At exactly midnight I get a text, and then right after I get another. One is from Muneca, "Feliz Navidad, Merry Christmas."

I reply, "Merry Christmas."

The next one is from an unknown number, "Merry Christmas." I don't reply.

Two days after Christmas my phone goes off. I get an overwhelming feeling out of the ordinary. I find myself curious to see who texted because that feeling makes me wonder if it was someone besides Mama, Tori, or Rox. It is from Muneca. She is inviting us to a party at her house. She says she is making a party for her father.

The thought of a party full of strangers stresses me out, but after all she has done for me, it's the least I can do. The party is tomorrow, and I tell her we'll be there.

Tomorrow is today before I know it. I get Annika ready and pack her some snacks and a cuppy for the long ride. We stop at the gas station and fill up the car. Mr. Collins is inside drinking coffee with another local. He smiles and waves me over. "Hey, Mr. Collins, how are you?"

"I am doing really good. Tori did pretty good matching me to Foxy. She is a really good dog."

"I'm glad, Mr. Collins."

"You know, Mr. Roverts don't ya, Natalie?"

The name sounds awfully familiar. "You're Becky's dad?"

"Yes, ma'am, I am." He nods. "I hear you know my nephew, Scott."

I smile. "Dr. Richards. Yes, I know him." Annika tugs at my hand, and I look down at her. The tug has a domino effect, so Mr. Collins and Mr. Roverts are looking at her now too.

"Well, hello there, Annika. How are your pansies doing?"

"Hi, Mr. Cowins. They are pretty."

"Pretty just like you," Mr. Collins says and pats her head.

"Thank you."

"Well, we are going to a party, so we better get going. Bye, Mr. Collins. It was good to see you, Mr. Roverts."

"Bye, girls, y'all be careful now, ya hear?"

"Yes, sir."

Annika and I listen to her special CD that has her name in each song. Then we pull over at a rest stop and pick some flowers, get some fresh air, and I change her diaper in the car. We get back on the road. The closer I get to Muneca's, the slower I go, dreading the actual arrival. Eventually, we make it to Muneca's house. It is a trailer house out in the middle of a large piece of land. She has all kinds of flowers and plants around the front. There is a big garden on the side, and goats, chickens, and a donkey roam around at the back. It feels homey and welcoming. There are already a lot of cars pulled up to the side fence. I can see a bunch of kids jumping in a large bounce house on the opposite side of the garden. There's a group of men around a barbecue pit, and I can see women coming in and out of the house. I take a deep breath. *Here we go.*

I pull Annika out of her car seat, and we head up to the front. I am unsuccessful at finding Muneca, and I can feel my shyness starting to take over. I see an older man getting all kinds of attention and realize that must be Muneca's dad. A man starts to approach us. "Annika and Natalia." He holds out a hand, so I shake it. "I am Raul, Muneca's husband.

"Oh, hello. Yes, I am Natalie, and this is Annika. You have a very lovely home." I smile and shake his hand.

"I'll go get Muneca. She will be happy you are here." Some women walk by, smile, and wave timidly. Annika pulls at me and points to the bounce house.

"I play with Karisa." She starts to jump up and down.

"Okay, Okay," I say.

We walk over to the bounce house. Karisa squeals, "Annika!" and climbs out. "Can I take Annika in with me, Natalie?"

"Sure, be careful, Annika." I can hear murmur coming from the party, but I am unsuccessful in making out the words. Everyone is speaking Spanish. I am relieved for Annika that the kids seem to mostly speak English. It feels very weird to not be able to understand what is going on. I feel very welcomed, but at the same time, somewhat isolated. I am a guest at a friend's house and not being able to understand makes me feel this uneasy. It makes me think of what happens when someone that doesn't understand English has to get out into the world or take care of business over the phone. It must be extremely intimidating.

My thoughts are interrupted by a familiar voice. Muneca pulls me in with a hug and even her eyes are smiling. "Natalie, I am so happy you come. Come with me. We go to the kitchen. I am cooking pozole and tortillas."

"Hey, I am so happy to see you! Maybe I should stay here with Annika though." I turn my head and nod in Annika's direction.

Muneca dismisses that comment with her hand. "See that big girl there? She is my, how you say, niece. She has 16 years. She will watch them, no problem." She points to the girl. The girl seems much different from other girls I have seen her age. They can't keep their eyes off their phone screen, but I don't think she even has a phone. She is in the bounce house, and she is already holding onto one hand of Karisa's and one of Annika's. "Consuela, mija, cuídalas. Por favor, la chiqueta es Annika, okay, mija?"

"Sí, Tía."

"She really loves kids. They will be okay." I hesitate, but before I know it, she smiles and pulls me by my wrist. Muneca's English is much more clear than the last time I spoke with her.

I find myself in a kitchen filled with women slapping dough in their hands and then placing it on a flat pan they call a comal. Spanish fills the air. It's weird because although I don't understand the words, I can understand the conversations. There is laughter, joking and a delicious smell rising into the air. It feels comforting and welcoming.

Muneca goes out to call the guys, and everyone comes in and sits around set up tables that fill the small living room and dining room. Raul brings in a pan and the smell escaping from under the foil is tempting. Two women link an arm around the older man's arms and walk him to a spot right in the middle.

He gets a kiss on the cheek from each of them before they go on their way. There's a variety of salsas covering the tables, ranging in all different shades of red. There's two different green salsas, and the tables are also adorned with cilantro, onions, limes, and the fresh tortillas. The women start preparing the dishes in an assembly line sort of way. The way they are working together, so in tune and in rhythm, reminds me of a train chugging along on the tracks.

I stand aside watching. One of the women brings me a bowl and a plate of the meat. Consuela grabs three plates of rice and takes them to Annika, Karisa, and another little girl. The woman gestures for me to sit down and pulls a hand to her mouth. "Es good." She smiles and goes back to her spot in the line. I find a chair in a corner and wait for the other women to make their own plates. The food smells delicious, and I am anticipating the first taste. It seems like forever before Muneca sits down to eat. Finally, I take my first bite. The food is as delicious as it smells. A red soup with hominy and meat topped with cabbage, the homemade tortilla, the meat, and the rice, I feel as though I'm flashing through generations with each bite.

The deep, red salsa is extremely spicy. I get embarrassed when my nose starts to run. However, the green salsa is amazing and has just the right heat for me. I watch Muneca pour the deep, red salsa all over her plate. She eats it as if it is nothing. I see Annika and the other little girls talking and laughing. Annika has cleaned her plate. She loves rice. I hear some Mexican music start outside, and most of the men and children slowly start filing out. A woman stays behind, and Muneca motions for Karisa. She tells Karisa something in Spanish. Then Karisa takes the lady into a bedroom.

"The woman is sick," Muneca fills me in. "Karisa makes her medicine and will rub her sickness away. Come." I follow Muneca. We stand on the outskirts of the room. Karisa takes some herbs and plants that I recognize from her garden. She mixes them in a small bowl, pours boiling water over them, and chants something in Spanish. While it cools, she rubs the lady's feet with some kind of lotion.

Consuela comes up from behind us carrying Annika and explains, "It's *brujeria*. It translates to witchcraft, but she is quite the opposite. Karisa is a healer and a viewer. She sees things and uses her powers to help and heal." Consuela is whispering, and she puts one finger over Annika's lips. I get a vibe from Annika that she already knew she should be quiet. Karisa tests the concoction. I'm certain she is checking to make sure it has cooled. Then she puts some into her fingertips and starts at the lady's temples. Next, she pulls back into the lady's hair, rubbing her head all the way back.

Other women that have stayed in the common area are throwing away red plastic cups, beer bottles, and clearing the tables. Every once in a while, they look over this way, but nobody interferes. There isn't any discussion over it. I start to realize that this is their normal. When everything is done, Karisa helps the woman lay down on a cot and starts some type of natural incense. Then she walks out. She pulls Annika down from Consuela, starts giggling, and says, "Let's go back out and jump." Just like that, she went from performing some type of healing seance to being a typical six-year-old little girl.

Muneca puts a finger to her lips, closes the door, and leaves the woman asleep in the room. "She will wake up in one hour." I follow Muneca to the living room, and we start helping clean everything. Everyone works together until every job is finished. The house is cleaner than when I arrived. I text my mom to tell her I am still at the party. All the parties I have been to only last about two hours, but this one seems to be never-ending. As the night goes on, people slowly start leaving. When there's only a couple people left, Muneca pulls me into the room that the lady was in. Karisa is sitting across the cot in a chair. Consuela is feeding Annika some cake called tres leches in the kitchen. Muneca closes the door this time and tells me to sit with my back to the chair and lay my head back into Karisa's lap. Karisa also lays out her hands for me to place my hands in.

"Anna is here." The persistent tingles start in my spine this time because I can feel her here, and then my arms and legs start to tingle with goosebumps. "Close your eyes, Natalie, it is okay." I close my eyes. And then I can see her. It is Anna.

Chapter 10: The Vision

Her voice is an echo. "Hi, Natalie. I miss you so much." I can see myself standing with her, almost as if I was dreaming. I wave to her. "You want to play?" And she motions for me to follow her. She starts to skip quickly, so I start running after her. I'm scared to lose her. I can feel my cheeks twinge. The goosebumps seem here to stay. I'm trying to keep up. The sky starts to turn grey. It gets cold, rain starts to fall, and clouds swirl in the sky until it turns pitch black. Then I see a light. Just like in my dream. The light shines. Then it's gone. Again, the light shines, and then it's gone. I can still hear Anna's voice, so I push against the harsh wind. I keep running harder and harder. Out of breath I am stopped in my tracks. Goosebumps have consumed me at this point, and I cannot shake them. I am in front of a lighthouse. The light goes by once and then back around again, and then back again.

"You were in the lighthouse." I shiver, and then we are both back in the sunlight.

"It is okay, Natalie. I am okay now. I have to go, but I'll see you again."

I start to cry. "Anna, don't go. Don't leave me." But she was gone.

I feel someone lift my head. It is Muneca. She is in front of me, and she is coaxing me back. I familiarize myself with my surroundings.

Then I hear Karisa crying. Muneca grabs her up. "Estás bien, mi vida. Hermosa, estás bien. Niña, mirame." She holds onto Karisa tightly and rocks her back and forth. I've grown accustomed to having my heart break twice in one day. After breaking for Anna all over again, now it breaks for Karisa and her mom.

"Okay, Mami, okay. I am okay. Anna is okay too, Natalie. This is good. It isn't bad, okay? She holds a secret. It is our job to learn it, so that she can be even happier and free."

"I am so sorry. I am so sorry," I keep repeating.

Karisa comes and gives me a hug. Then Muneca cuts in, "We know what will happen. We know Karisa see and feel with you, but now she feels nothing. She was in the moment, like how I tell you at your house, but now she good."

"Mami, can I have a big piece of Buelo's cake?"

"Sí, mija."

We all walk back into the living room. Consuela applauds her aunt. "Tía your English is a lot more clear. Our lessons are working." She smiles.

"You've been giving her lessons?" I ask and look to Consuela. She shakes her head yes. "As soon as I arrived here today, I noticed her English had improved."

Muneca proudly smiles. "Really?"

"Yes, I promise! As soon as I got here I could tell you must be practicing. Now I need to practice Spanish." I look at Consuela. "You are very helpful."

"I like helping. It is how I was raised. We just do it. You know, familia." She smiles and shrugs.

My phone goes off. I expect to see my mom responding to the text I sent a while ago. Instead, it is an unsaved number.

"Hey, Nat. I was wondering if you and Annika had plans for New Year's. I was supposed to be on call at the hospital, but a resident took my spot. Now I am free." It is the same number that texted Merry Christmas at midnight.

I text back, "Scott?"

"Yeah, I guess I could have started with that. :) I hope it's okay I got your number from your mother."

"Ah, my lovely mother. I would love to meet up with you, but I already promised my sisters and mom I would spend New Year's with them." I grab the silver N charm that hangs from the necklace, my gift from Scott. I feel guilty for not reaching out to him yet. I continue "Thank you for the necklace. It's perfect. I really love it."

"You are welcome. I thought it looked like you. Dissed by Natalie Haven. Ouch!"

"No, I really would love to hang out, but I already promised them. I am sorry."

"Okay, but I'll take that raincheck."

"Of course :)"

"Guy trouble?" Muneca looks at me with raised eyebrows and a smile. "How did you know?"

"Your face says it all." I look over at Annika. She is having another helping of cake. Meanwhile, Karisa is dipping her finger in icing and licking it off.

"It's just there's this doctor that I like, and I think he likes me, but…"

"Is he handsome?"

"Yeah, but…"

"A handsome doctor doesn't sound like guy trouble to me." She smiles deviously.

"Well, it is just that I lost Annika's father, so I feel guilty when I think about Scott. I start to miss Afton so bad it hurts because I'm in love with him, but I really like Scott. It's just really confusing and overwhelming. It's like bittersweet. The bitter part is Afton, and it is harshly bitter. The sweet part is Scott and his smile."

Muneca is following me and sighs when I am finished. "Ah, sí, es una novela."

I'm brought back to the conversation, out of my deep thoughts. "Huh?"

"It is, how you say, soap opry?"

"Oh, a soap opera. Yes, it is like a soap opera, hopelessly devastating." I sigh, and Scott's smile is still dancing in my mind.

We find Annika and Karissa outside dancing with Buelo. He is spinning each of them around to the music and their dresses are twirling with them. "Annika, it is time to go."

"Mommy, I want to stay longer."

"I know, baby, but we still have a long drive. If we don't get home soon, Nana will worry." I look at her and then to Muneca.

"Muneca?"

"Sí?"

"How do you say, happy birthday?"

"Feliz cumpleaños."

I turn to Muneca's dad, "Feleece cumpleeanos." Her dad smiles, nods, and grabs my hand to shake it. He waves bye to Annika. There's still a few couples outside dancing, and there were a few relatives passed out in the living room I notice on my way out. *This really is a never-ending party,* I think to myself.

Muneca, Raul, and Karisa all walk us to the car. "Thank you so much for inviting us, Muneca. This was an amazing day, and Annika and I both had so much fun. It was almost whimsical, and I feel so peaceful."

"Gracias por venir. Thank you for coming." They stand there waving until we pull out to go home.

Annika falls asleep fast. She had another day of playing hard, just like a little girl her age should. I find myself smiling as I replay the night. Then an eerie feeling creeps in and steals my happiness. It's Anna. In my dream a light flashed, was gone, and then flashed again. It was just like the lighthouse light that Anna showed me in the vision Karisa shared with me. The only thing I can make sense of is that Anna must have been murdered in a lighthouse. My mom would know, and I could not wait to ask her.

"Mama?"

"Oh, good are y'all home?"

"No, I was calling because, well, it is about Anna."

"Anna?" My mom sounds caught off guard.

"Yea, Mama, did Anna pass away in a lighthouse?"

"Natalie, where are you?"

"I'm about twenty minutes from the edge of town. Mama, tell me. Was she found in a lighthouse?"

"Natalie, you need to pull over." I put on my blinker and pull off the two lane country road.

"Mama, it was in a lighthouse. Wasn't it?"

"It was Natalie. It was in the old lighthouse on the outside of town."

There is a long pause. "Natalie, why do you ask?"

"Because I dreamed it."

Chapter 11: New Year's

I pull up to my mom's house, and Roxy runs out to the car. My mom follows with an oversized box. I can see all kinds of horns and streamers sticking out the top of the box. "Hey y'all."

"Next stop, Aunt Tori's." Annika says with a big cheese face.

My mom and Roxy look at each other. "Guys, she knows we are going to Tori's. We have gone there every year since she was born on New Year's, and I've been talking about it all day." They both relax and giggle.

"Well, I was hoping that you, Natalie, would be going out on a date."

"Hmmm...what would ever give you that idea?"

"Well, Scott asked for your number."

Roxy's eyebrows raise. I give in. "He did text me, but I told him I had plans with y'all already."

"Natalie Rose! We didn't have this planned until yesterday."

"Yeah, but I am a creature of habit and sentimental with traditions. We all three go to Tori's every year. It wouldn't feel like New Year's if I wasn't with y'all, Tori, and the kids."

"So, it had nothing to do with Afton." Roxy isn't asking; she is implying.

"Maybe a little." My mom sighs and rolls her eyes, but then I sense her body language change. She is feeling sympathetic. "Natalie, you know you can't wait for Afton forever. You don't deserve to be miserable the rest of your life, Nat."

I can't talk about this right now. Since Roxy doesn't give one of her signature snarky comments, I know that they are both sympathizing. Although their mouths are watering for some gossipy news, they are kind enough to ride the rest of the way to Tori's without insisting I share anymore than I already had.

When we pull up, we all three see Mallory crying on the front steps. Mallory is one of Tori's best friends, and it looks like Tori is trying her best to soothe her. They see us pull in. Mallory lets herself into the house. I wonder what is wrong. Mallory has never been here on New Year's before. Then my ears prickle, and I feel tense. I'm pretty sure the whole car feels the tension. Then it happens, and it comes from Annika's lips. "Benjamin's dad is with someone else, really pretty."

There is time for us to process it. Then Roxy lets out, "That fucker is cheating on Mallory!"

In sync with my mom we scold, "Language!"

"Oops, sorry Annika."

Just like that, the tension is gone. Annika is swinging her feet and playing with a fly away streamer like nothing has happened.

"Wow," slips from my lips. "Well, okay, let's do this." We walk in together.

Tori looks to make sure that Mallory is in the bathroom. Then she pulls me and Tori into the kitchen. Roxy crosses her arms and confidently lets out, "He's cheating on her."

Tori's hands go straight to her cheeks, "Oh God, please tell me it wasn't you?"

Roxy's jaw drops, and she frowns. She lightly pushes Tori back. "What?! No, of course not." Then Roxy thinks for a minute, as Tori and I watch her remember the time we opened the door to a screaming girl, rightfully accusing Roxy of getting a little too cozy with her *fiancé*. "Oh yeahhhhhh, but NO!" Her demeanor turns pretty cocky. She places a hand on her hip and shrugs the other shoulder as she matter of factly says, "Annika told us."

"No way!" Tori let's out. I can tell from Tori's reaction that she still doesn't believe Annika has a gift. We all three hear the bathroom door open, so we quickly break apart and act normal.

I find my mother in the living room with Braiden, Benjamin, and Annika. She has given all three of them the number blocks, but her focus is 100 percent on Annika. "Go ahead, Annika. Pick them for Nana. You just concentrate real hard. Then hand them to me." My mom jumps as she sees me.

I immediately know what she is doing. I look to the kitchen where Mallory has joined Tori. I growl out in a whisper, "Mom, are you serious right now, lottery numbers?!?"

I grab Annika up. "Well," my mom says innocently, "I thought it was worth a try." I roll my eyes and take Annika to unpack the New Year's goodies. My heart hurts for Mallory. She is trying to compose herself and act as normally as she can for her son. It's like I am feeling her pain with her. I think of how she is trying so hard for Benjamin even though she is falling apart on the inside. A mother's love is a powerful thing. In fact, I can honestly say that I think a mother's love for her child is the most powerful thing in this whole earthly world.

Mallory and Benjamin fit right in. Without any deep conversations, we make it to the countdown and surprisingly all the kids have made it. 10-9-8-7-6-5-4-3-2-1 Happy New Year's! The horns blare, and streamers leap in the air. I get a slobbery New Year's kiss from my sweet baby, followed by hugs and kisses from everyone else. I love my family so much, and I am so thankful for them everyday. Then all of the sudden, in the midst of everything, I think about Scott. I wonder, with a little jealousy, if he had a New Year's kiss. I pull out my phone and start a text. "Happy New Year's Kiss." *No.* "Happy New Year's!" *No.* "Happy New Year's <3" Without giving myself second thoughts, I press send.

Chapter 12: The Gift That Keeps On Giving

I mark my calendar and set it in my phone as soon as I get off the phone with Tori. I cannot forget about Bri's recital. I would never forgive myself, and Tori wouldn't either for that matter. A week from today we will get to watch Bri take center stage as she shows off her hard work. It is gratifying and intriguing to watch her. To be so young, she has such poise and discipline. The best part is she thoroughly enjoys it.

Annika walks into the room. She has brought her finger painting with her. "What do you have, sweet girl?" I smile and then, here comes the familiar prickle of tingles.

"Bri, ballerina." There is what looks to be a ballerina alone, center stage. Annika proudly points to it, and I stop and take her in for a minute. She looks more like a baby today than she has lately, probably because she is still in her footsie pajamas. Her ringlets are falling around her just so, and her blue eyes are looking up to me for approval of her precious drawing.

"Bri," she says, and I know this is her gift talking. There is no way she could have known about the upcoming recital and Bri's special part because Tori hadn't even known.

Tori called me so excited because Bri's part was just made official. These are the rare moments I can smile and accept this *gift*. It is so complicated, but the ballerina painting is innocent. So I smile, and I do not let myself begin to overthink. "It is beautiful, Annika. I love it. Let's put it on the refrigerator." It soothes me to see Annika get so excited at my reaction.

I smell the thick smell of rain hanging in the air. I look outside into the grey day. Just then rain starts to lightly fall. I can hear it hitting the roof. It is cooler than usual outside, and it feels heavy. I start thinking about how the weather can affect your mood and how heavy and solemn I start to feel, mirroring the weather. The trees seem alive but sad. Their leaves sway in the wind. I watch as the plants and rain seem to tell a sad story, and my heart opens up to listen.

My phone goes off, but I feel more connected to the weather at this moment. A phone call would interrupt the emotion this kind of weather brings with it. I ignore the call. Annika walks in again. This time she has something to say. "Benjamin stay with Granny. Mallory is gone." I shudder and try not to jump to any conclusions. I have a bad feeling, but not a heart-sinking feeling. I try to analyze the words and remind myself that she hasn't even turned three yet. The words, "Mallory is gone," ring in my ears, but I just keep pushing the horrible thought of death out of my mind.

I grasp onto an idea and run with it. Maybe she is gone from home. Maybe she is at Missy's with Benjamin. I find myself pleading and look to my toddler for an answer, "Is Mallory with Granny?" She shakes her head yes. I let out a big sigh of relief.

I get the coffee I just made and sit in the window seat with Annika. She starts swirling her finger around making designs in the condensation. When the rain stops and the sun starts to peak back out, I grab my phone. The missed call was Tori, so I call her back.

"Hey, did you mean to call me again?" Then I get the whole story, and it is awfully surprising. I call Roxy as soon as I get off the phone with Tori.

"Apparently, Ben cheated on Mallory with Becky. You know Becky. That's Scott's cousin." I wait for her response. "See Scott told me that Becky had moved back because she and her boyfriend had a bad break up, but Becky's boyfriend broke up with her because he found out that Becky had reconnected with her high school sweetheart through social media. It turns out that her high school sweetheart is Ben. I just feel so bad for Mallory because they seemed so happy. They were like the perfect couple. Ben practically worshiped the ground Mallory walked on. I just don't understand how something could have broken that up. That is all Tori told me. But the reason I am even telling you all this is because right before Tori called Annika came in and told me that Mallory and Benjamin were with Granny. So I am assuming that Mallory and Benjamin have moved back in with Missy. Hey, hold on, I have another call coming in. I'll text you later. Love you too, bye."

It is my mom, and she is calling to tell me about Ben. She is obviously foaming at the mouth to spill the newest juicy gossip of our small town, so I don't interrupt her. When she finishes, I tell her I love her and let her go.

My phone rings, and Annika holds her hand out for it. For some reason unknown to myself, I follow her lead and hand it to her. "Aunt Tori! I love you too, always and forever. Yes, right here. Hold on. Aunt Tori, tell Mallory to look in the little door in the car." I wince at all the information Annika must have spinning in her mind. But then I feel a presence and the paralyzing feeling rises from my shoulders. Annika is looking slightly above my head and giggles.

"Natalie!" I am pulled back to the phone call.

"Huh? Yeah, sorry."

"Annika, what did Annika say?"

"I think she wants Mallory to look into her glove compartment."

"Why?" I find myself getting agitated. A year ago I never thought I would find myself getting defensive over the fact that Tori doesn't believe that Annika does in fact have this *gift*. Even though I cannot fully accept calling it that, I know that is what is bothering me. It's that Tori still doesn't believe. "I don't know, Tori. She just knows things."

The frustration is heard in my voice, and Tori hesitates. I can tell she is wanting to start accepting that Annika may in fact have this *gift*. Her voice is quiet and easy, "Well, how can I tell her to look into the glove compartment without sounding completely out of my mind?" Then I realize she is thinking about telling Mallory about Annika.

"No, Tori, no, please do not tell her about Annika. I do not want anyone else to know."

"Oh, okay." I can tell she is as relieved as I am. "But what can I say."

"I don't know." I really don't, but she is creative. I know she will figure it out on her own.

Well, in the last hour, Annika predicted Bri's recital, Mallory moving in with Missy, and now apparently, there is something that probably has a lot to do with Ben's affair in Mallory's glove box.

My phone goes off again. I am expecting it to be my mom or one of my sisters, but Annika shouts out, "Dr. Richards!" To my surprise, it is Scott. This kid is three for three. Maybe I should call my mom over here with her number blocks. I laugh to myself and shake up Annika's hair with my hand.

"You little stinker." I kiss her neck over and over.

"Answer, Mommy." So I do.

He texted me back on New Year's, but just that, "Happy New Year's." I hadn't heard from him since.

"Hello."

"Natalie, hey wow, I've really missed your voice." I can feel him second guess letting that slip, thinking he might have overshared, and that could be a weakness. At that my heart skips a beat, which makes my knees go weak.

I answer, "Hey, I was kinda worried when I didn't ever really hear back from you."

"Well, we are usually pretty busy at the office around holidays, and then I had to get my mom packed and to the airport to get back home." I hear his pager go off, and he pauses. "I'm sorry I can't talk longer. I've got to get back, but I was wondering if maybe we could hang out. I'm on call this week, but seven days from now, I am free." I feel bad for turning him down on New Year's. I really would love to hang out with him. I feel the butterflies in my stomach, and my face flushes.

"Okay, that sounds good."

"Okay, great, I'll get back with you on the details, but I have to go now. I'll talk to you later."

"Bye."

Annika is smiling at me. I smile back at her. It's probably a goofy smile because I am on cloud nine. I thank God that nobody else is here to witness my dumbfounded smile. Then she says, "Dr. Richards watch Bri." That is when it hits me. A week from now I have to be at Bri's recital. I think about texting Scott back, but he seemed really busy. I'll just talk to him about it later. My heart tugs, *Oh my precious Annika.*

I go back to Annika, and we both finger paint until her naptime. I try to walk lightly across the old wood floors, but it still growls at me with a creak every other step I take. I lay Annika down softly. Pushing my luck, chancing to sabotage my success, I push my lips to her plump little cheek. She stirs but rolls over and stays asleep.

As soon as I get to the living room, there is a light knock on the door. It isn't Roxy's rhythmic knock, and I can't think of who it could be.

I open the door, and it is Tori. I tilt my head to the side and look at her puzzled. "A bracelet. A gold bracelet."

"Huh?"

"In the glove box." She looks at me like I should know what she is talking about. "Oh my God, Natalie, Annika has a gift. She really does, but it isn't really a gift. Is it?" She starts to cry. I realize that it is just hitting her, like it used to hit me over and over and over. I hug her, and she lets out words between sniffles. I try my hardest to make it out. "I am"-sniffle, sniffle-"so sorry, Natalie!"-sniffle, sniffle, sniffle-"I am sorry that I didn't believe you. I am really sorry." She starts to cry again. Sniffle. Sniffle. "I am so sorry that you had to hide this for so long. You must have just felt so alone and scared, and I wasn't there." I know she loves Annika as much as one of her own, and I know she is easily putting herself in my shoes. Although I felt all these exact feelings at one time, they are just barreling into her for the very first time ever.

Suddenly, I realize just how much Muneca really helped me. I am so much more at peace now. I send Karisa a hard hug with my mind. Then I hug Tori super tight. "It is okay. It's okay, Tori. It was hard for me to believe at first and even harder for me to accept. I was scared, but I've learned that we were never alone and will never be alone. We have you, Mama, and Roxy, and we always will. Is it a gift? I cannot really bring myself to call it that, but it is quite something. Isn't it? Now tell me about the bracelet."

I get a text and notice it's from Muneca. "Karisa says she loves you and Annika and to tell you right now." It must have been the hug I sent her when I was talking to Tori. I bet she felt it.

"Please tell her we love her too, and we cannot wait to see y'all again."

We both notice someone pulling in the driveway. I kick myself. I hate how I can be so forgetful.

After my mom called to spill the beans, she told me that she and Roxy were on their way over to drop off some chili and cornbread. I look at Tori as if to say sorry. She shrugs, "Well, they already know about Mallory, so I guess it is better to just get it out all at once."

I hear Annika wake up. Her naps are getting fewer and farther in between. When she does nap, she doesn't sleep as long. I pull her onto my hip and stand with her in the living room. My mom touches her back and Roxy kisses her. We all keep our voices to a whisper because we can tell she is waking up. Even though sometimes I think she loves my mom even more than she loves me, in this moment, anyway, it is clear to see she just wants her mommy. As her head rests on my shoulder, I slow down time and soak her and this moment in. I can smell the baby shampoo on her head and feel her warmth and weight in my arms.

"Okay, so Annika tells me to tell Mallory to look in her glove compartment." Roxy smiles an I-told-ya-so smile. Tori shrugs but keeps going. "So, I tell Mallory that maybe she should check her car for something. She calls me back and says that in her car in the glove compartment there is a bracelet and engraved on the inner part, there is a B & B. So of course, she is thinking Becky and Ben, right? She doesn't know for sure."

I sigh. "I just feel so bad for her, and I feel guilty that we are talking about her life." I think about how people used to hush their conversations when Annika and I would walk by after Afton. They were getting some type of satisfaction from letting my story spill from their lips. Meanwhile, that same story was a nightmare I couldn't wake up from.

As if she knows what I am thinking, Tori goes on, "No, she knows y'all know." Tori looks at me. "Mallory and I have been friends so long, she considers y'all little sisters too."

Annika picks up her head. "Ben and Benjamin." We smile, and I decide it is time to change the subject, if not for my own guilt, but for Annika's listening ears.

"Okay, there is something that I really don't want to tell y'all, but I have run into some complications. So now I have no choice but to tell you," I say teasingly. Annika wants down, and she goes to sit in my mom's lap. My mom hands her the tablet, and Annika sings along with the screen. As far as my mother's intuition reads, she is completely focused on the color song flashing on the screen.

"Well, go ahead, now you have to tell us."

"Okay, okay. The night of the Christmas party I had walked off with Scott." My mom looks satisfied, and Roxy looks like she is checking off a confirmed box in her mind. I look away. "Well, we walked and talked. After that, he apparently got my number from Mama." I look sternly at my mom. She shrugs as if she doesn't know what I am talking about, but her facial expression gives it away. "He has texted a couple times."

"Don't forget about the Christmas gift, Natalie, and that makes me think there was a little more than walking and talking going on to get a necklace like that." My mom is interrupted by Tori's hand.

"Please Mother, it is not appropriate to assume that Natalie would do something completely inappropriate at a friend's Christmas party."

I had no intention of telling them about the kiss, but I can feel myself starting to blush. My mother is leading everyone down the road that suggests we did much more than kiss. Roxy stares down my blushing face. She knows better than anyone that I'm not as conservative as Tori is expecting me to be, but she also knows that I would not have done anything as provocative as my mother is implying.

My mom starts again, "Nat, we know." She looks at all three of us and continues, "Girls, we all know that men don't just hand out gifts, especially jewelry."

Roxy interrupts right after the smile breaks across her face as she self confirms her reading from my blushed face, "Oh my God! Y'all kissed!?!"

I am more worried about Tori's reaction than my mother's, so I look to her as I hesitantly nod my head yes. "Anyway, the only reason I am telling y'all this is because, yes, he did ask me out for New Year's"

Roxy lets out a "Yeah, yeah, yeah," letting me know to get to the point because she already knew that.

I continue to fill Tori in. "Well, I turned him down then, but we rescheduled." My mom throws up her hands as if saying *hallelujah*. I get serious because something about her reaction is bugging me. "The only reason I am telling y'all is because the day we hang out is going to have to be the day of Bri's recital." I get it out as fast as I can.

Roxy claps her hands together. "I knew he liked you."

Tori is following along. She isn't disapproving, but she isn't jumping out of her seat with excitement either.

"There, that's it."

My mom still looks a little too amused. "And I expect best behavior, especially from you." I point to my mother. She doesn't like being told what to do. I can tell she doesn't appreciate my tone, so I change it pleading, "Mama, please, just don't push things, okay? It isn't even an official date. He just asked to hang out."

"Me, push things?" She lets out a yeah-right kind of sigh as she crosses her legs.

My sisters and I share a *really?*-stare at the fact our mother seems to honestly not even realize how pushy she is. Then it hits me out of nowhere. Annika's tiny voice and what she said earlier, how the timing really went right with the conversation, the goosebumps creep in once again.

"Tori," I say a little uneasily. I can tell she is sensing my vibe. "Ben and Benjamin." Everyone looks puzzled. I emphasize the beginning, "**B**en and **B**enjamin, like Annika told us earlier. B & B."

All three of them stare blankly back at me, except Annika. She looks up and says it again very proudly, "**B**-en and **B**-enjamin."

Chapter 13: Ice Cream, Stars, and Annika Too

Friday morning Caroline comes in looking frazzled. She is busy messing in the drawers and frantically pulling out papers. She sits down in the office chair and shuffles her feet across the floor, sending the chair around the room as if it were a skating rink. A pencil is sticking up from the back of her hair. Her glasses are on the very tip of her nose. She looks up over them at me and says, "Natalie, honey."

"Yes?"

She looks back down and starts filing through more papers. "You haven't seen that invoice for the Roverts have you?" Caroline never has been the best organizer. I can usually keep all of our ducks in a row, but since coming back from Christmas, we are trying to get back on track. It is amazing how easy it is to forget office procedures after being out just one week.

I tell her the truth, "I haven't seen it, and I am pretty sure I didn't get it entered in the computer before Christmas."

She blows air straight up and starts to tap her foot. She starts talking to herself, "They come in with all their fanciness and business talk and large vocabulary and now, just like that, she snaps her fingers. They *need* the invoice today. Today! They know it is our first day back. Rob always gets so frustrated when I haven't kept up with the filing, and he is really going to...Wait a minute." She pulls a paper close to her face and squints hard. She lets out a heavy sigh. "Nope, this isn't it either. Well, it is no use Natalie, I just can't find it." She falls into her chair and rubs her temples.

All of the sudden I get an urge to check the top of the bookshelf that sits behind her desk. She has started searching our digital invoice system, but I know I did not enter it. It did not come in until right before I left early for the Christmas party. Full of hope and anticipation I run my hand across the top. Nothing. But then, something on the windowsill next to the bookshelf catches my eye.

"I found it, Caroline."

"Did you really?" She turns around with wide eyes.

"I think so. Look." I hand her the paper.

She takes the paper and then hops up. Her arms are around me before I can blink. "Oh, Natalie, what would I ever do without you? This is it!" Then she kisses me on the cheek. She bustles out the door with the invoice waving high up in the air. "I found it, ROB! I FOUND IT!"

Rob cups his hand over his ear as he walks up closer, trying to make out what she is saying over the loud machines. "What, dear?"

"I found it, the invoice, the one for Mr. Roverts. I found it. Well, Natalie found it, but it is right here."

She proudly waves it in his face. Although he is smiling, he lets out a sigh. "Caroline, you know I love you honey, and just about everything about you, but if I have told you once, I have told you a hundred times. You have to create and stick with a system when you are at the office. Honey, you know, stay organized."

She smiles. "Well, we found it." She sticks her tongue out.

"Well, that is true. Thank you, Natalie." He winks at me. I just smile and wave.

Caroline steps back in. "Well, I'll make him some chocolate chips cookies. He can't stay mad when he is eating those, and I'll make enough so that you and Ms. Annika can take some home tomorrow." Her cookies are the best and make having to come in half a day on a Saturday not so bad.

"That old Mr. Roverts thinks he just owns this whole town. He thinks if he likes it, he has to have it." She rolls her eyes and her bracelets jingle as she talks with her hands. "You didn't hear it from me, but rumor has it that the whole reason he has us building a guest house behind his lot is because that daughter of his, you know Becky..." She starts to whisper, even though we are the only two in the office. "Well, I heard she is a homewrecker, and she cheated on her boyfriend. They say she got to that nice young man that is married to Mandy. No, that's not right. You know her, Tori's friend, Missy's daughter." She pauses, and I know she is waiting for me to answer.

"Mallory."

"That's it! Mallory! Isn't that a shame?" She doesn't give me a chance to answer. "That's why he is building that guest house for his daughter." She nods her head. "I guess if she likes something, she just feels like she can take it. Like father, like daughter, I guess."

The phone rings. "Robert's Construction. Mr. Rovert, oh hello there." Her best phone voice floats through the air. "Yes sir, Rob should be on his way over now with the invoice for your last job and an estimate for the new one. Yes, sir, thank you, sir. Now you have a good day now, hun." She gets off the phone and does the gag motion with her finger. "The saddest part is, the last I heard anyway, Mallory, bless her heart, and that poor sweet baby are living back at Missy's." She does a tsk-tsk click with her tongue. The gold bracelet pops in my mind. I realize, just like Caroline, the last thing I had heard was that Mallory and Benjamin were still at Missy's.

"I know. I feel bad for her. She has always been there for Tori, and she really is a good person. She was even there for me when Annika was born."

I start to wonder how Becky's dad could be related to Scott's other uncle, the one he used to come here to work for, and Scott's mother. They are both saints. Caroline usually doesn't judge. She is one of those people that just loves everybody, but there is something about Mr. Rovert's. He just has that greedy look. You can even read it in his eyes.

My mom is at my house, and I am not surprised I find Roxy there too. My mom already has Annika all dolled up in one of the outfits that Tori has bought her, and the matching headband is already placed just so on her head. My mom has a little, black dress laid out on my couch. She points to it and tells me to go get dressed. I pick up the little dress. It is tight fitted, and it is way too short. "It looks like something Roxy would wear on a wild night out. Yeah, I am not wearing that." I wrinkle my nose. "Look how short it is!"

"You could put tights under it."

"No, Mom, no way!"

Roxy frowns and cuts in, "You don't wear tights under that, and it is something I'd wear because **it is *mine***." She goes to the hall closet and swings open the door. "Anyway, I thought you might say that, so I also brought this." Roxy pulls out another black dress, but this one is a lot more me.

"Thank you, Rox." I smile.

"Well, that looks fitting, Natalie. I like it even better."

I was really hoping that Tori could do my make-up for the recital tonight, but I already know from all my years attending recitals that Tori is going to be crazy busy with Bri's hair, make-up, and costume changes. I walk to the bathroom to just put on the usual mascara, and then to spice it up a bit, I grab a light-colored lipstick.

"No, no, no Natalie. This is a for-mal recital. Your dress is beautiful, but you need to put make-up on."

"I have make-up on."

My mom rolls her eyes and starts to say something, but Roxy gets excited, "Ooh, ooh, ooh, I'll do your make-up." Roxy is wearing a tight shirt that is cut down low, but she has a modest skirt pulled up over the shirt and really cute wedge shoes. She has on her usual full face of make-up.

My mom grabs Annika. "Well, we are going to go ahead and head over to Tori's, so we can see the star of the show and wish her luck. Also, you're going to just love this, we are going to take some pictures of Braiden and Annika because her outfit matches his bow tie and socks. Oh, and don't worry about finding us at the recital. I'll just keep Annika with me." My mom doesn't even wait for my answer.

Roxy has make-up bag after make-up bag lined up. My face is being squeezed together, so I couldn't have objected even if I wanted to. After at least a good thirty minutes, Roxy looks very pleased with herself and hands me the mirror. I am scared to look.

"Hey, Rox. I really like it. You did a really good job." I was expecting to see the same bright and loud colors she paints on her face on me. Instead of looking vibrantly cool like her, I would have looked like a clown. But she just added a little color to my cheeks, lined and added a darker shade to my lips, put on some light eyeshadow, went over my mascara with her fancy one, and filled in my eyebrows. It looked subtle but beautiful.

She smiles. "I got you," she says. She really did. If it wasn't for her, I wouldn't even have anything to wear.

On the way to the recital, her phone goes off. I hear her say, "Okay, bet." She turns to me. "There is only one spot left with Tori and Mom."

So, that means that Scott and I won't have a seat. "I know what y'all are doing."

"Yeah, there wasn't really a way to play it cool," she says, "but at least now you'll be alone with Dr. Hot Stuff." She makes a kissy face, and I laugh.

"Away from Mama, which I am thankful for, but not alone, dork. We will still be in an auditorium full of people watching a ballet recital."

Roxy glides across the parking lot. Her bob haircut slings as she walks. I wonder what other people see when they see her. She is gorgeous, but she is edgy. She seems so mysterious. I walk into the lobby, and I pull my phone to check it. Someone grabs my wrist instead. Expecting to see Scott, I look up. It's Mallory, "Hey Nat. Do you know where we're sitting?"

"I think they said third row on the left, but I am meeting someone here. I think we are going to grab some other seats."

"Oh, yeah," she says in a spunky voice and smiles mischievously. She glances at her watch and takes quick and tiny steps down the long aisle.

Scott was not even upset that we were going to have to start our hang out day at the recital. I start to get worried that maybe he had something come up. From the tall windows, I see an old Chevrolet truck from the 1950s pull in. Since it catches my attention, I watch it until it parks. To my amazement, Scott gets out.

He looks really nice. He is wearing a button-up shirt over some jeans. He shuffles across the parking lot, waves at a car that has stopped to let him go across, and then the butterflies come. He walks in and sees me right away. "Hey, Nat."

"Hey, Scott, you look really nice." I notice some young girls gawking at him as they walk by.

"So do you, beautiful," the words roll off his lips. The same lips that kissed me so many nights ago. He grabs my hand, and I freeze up. I try to pretend I'm Roxy so that I can chill and play it cool, but I'm still stiff as a board as we walk in and look for empty seats. We find two seats in just about the very middle of the audience. He holds my hand the whole time.

I get really excited and feel so proud when Bri comes on. I point to her and whisper, "That one is mine." He smiles back. We watch Bri as she glides across the stage. The music that carries her dance number is dramatic and tears start to fall from my eyes. I am embarrassed when I realize that Scott has noticed that I am crying. I am so sensitive, so it doesn't take much for me to cry. But he just takes his hand and wipes my face. I have decided he is just too good to be true and find myself worrying what strings are attached with him.

After the recital, we meet back up with everyone outside the lobby, just like we had planned. Scott says he has to run to his truck to grab something. He comes back with flowers.

Not really being a person that gets excited over bouquets, I think, *This is kind of cliche.* Then I start to overthink, *Now my whole family is going to see me get these flowers. What should I do when he hands?* Then he hands the bouquet to Bri.

Now I feel rather stupid. Bri does one of her famous squeals. "Thank you, Dr. Richards."

"Please, call me Scott. You did really well, Brianna. I've seen many ballets and your performance is a hard one to beat."

Tori smiles and thanks him for the flowers. Brandon holds out a hand for Scott to shake. "Long time, no see man."

"Yeah, it has been awhile. I guess the last time you came down to work for your uncle was, what about ten years ago?"

"Yeah, it was about seven years ago. Do y'all want to go grab ice cream from the Coffee Cafe? It's on me." He smiles. The kids jump up and down. My mom is being peculiarly quiet, maybe she really is trying. "Is that a yes?" I shake my head yes and Scott holds up a hand for Annika to high five.

Scott fits in beautifully. Everything seems to go perfectly, and I find myself searching for the catch. Scott and Brandon talk and play with all three of the kids. Our floats, dipped cones, kid scoops, and my mom's banana split all come out. The conversation is nice, and the ice cream is just what we needed.

"Hey, Nat. Why don't you let me take your car back to Mama's?" Roxy gleams at me.

My mom smiles and adds, "Yeah, and I have Annika's carseat in my car, so I'll just take Annika. Why don't you ride with Scott?"

I look at Scott, and he smiles. "We can take Annika, no problem."

"Really?" I say.

"Yeah, of course." Annika goes to him and raises her arms. He picks her up. My mom notices, so does Roxy, but most importantly, I notice. Annika wraps her arms around his neck and yawns.

"Well, y'all are still more than welcome to come over. Roxy and I could use some visitors."

I smile. "Okay, then Roxy, will you still drive my car over to Mama's? We will meet ya'll there."

Scott tries to put the car seat in his truck, but he doesn't quite get it. I only show him once, and then he secures it perfectly. Annika talks about ballet on the way to my Mom's. We listen and answer when she asks a question.

When we get to my mom's, she serves us tea. We all sit in the living room and mainly just watch Annika dance around until she falls asleep. We keep the conversation light. My mom is doing a great job of listening and not overstepping. She asks about his mom and work, but she doesn't push or bring up anything awkward. I just knew she was going to pry into his past, present, and even future love life. But she didn't. After the conversation dies down, Scott whispers to me, "Do you want to go walk with me, Natalie?"

"Okay." Louder I announce, "Scott and I are going to go for a walk." I catch the satisfied glimpse my mom and Roxy pass, but if Scott did, you couldn't tell.

We start walking and his voice interrupts the quiet, "You are pretty shy. Aren't you?"

"Yes, I have always been shy. My mom is the complete opposite, so I am not sure where I get it from."

"I think it's cute."

I can't help but to ask something that has been on my mind. "Do you ever talk to your Uncle Roverts, Becky's dad?"

"Well, sure, he is my uncle. I am not as close to him as I am to Uncle Ro." That's what he used to call his uncle. "Why do you ask?"

"I ran into him the other day at the Coffee Cafe when I was getting gas, and I was just wondering." I bite my lip.

The coolness of the air gives me a chill, and I shiver. "You want to sit in my truck? I can turn on the heat."

"Sure." We go to his truck like two teenagers hiding out from their parents. I think I notice someone peek through the blinds and if I had money, my bet would be on my mother. We walk to his truck. He grabs my hand, and we just sit quietly looking up at the stars. My hands start to feel a little clammy. It is then I realize that he never even turned on the truck. The heater is not even needed. Just being near him is enough.

"Well, I guess it is about time for me to go. It is getting pretty late." I feel a sudden sadness realizing this has to come to an end. He puts a hand to my cheek and kisses me. I find myself wishing that he wouldn't stop. The kiss goes on, and I envision myself moving into his lap, facing him. I feel the heat rising on my cheeks, and I feel dirty for thinking that thought, so I shake it. Maybe that is what Roxy would do, but I am me. I pull away from the kiss. "Goodnight Scott, I had a great time. Thank you for everything." Then I wave as he pulls away into the night.

Chapter 14: Mallory's Side

As I walk back into my mom's house I get "Wooooo ooooo!" I just roll my eyes. Then all the questions I was so proud of my mom from restraining come pouring out. "Has he been married?" I shrug. She looks aggravated. "Well, does he have kids?"

"No, he doesn't have any kids."

"Did he kiss you?"

"Mooo-om."

"Oh, they totally kissed," Roxy smirks. "Did he say anything about Becky?"

"No."

They both sit back disappointedly in their seats. "Well, what did y'all talk about then?"

I tell the truth, "Nothing, really, I just like being around him."

"Well, it is apparent we aren't getting anything else out of her," my mom says to Roxy. Roxy just laughs.

Then I notice Roxy walk into her restroom. It feels like deja vu, but then I can see her reaching in a drawer for something. I can feel her contemplating something. I hear her sigh and throw something into the toilet. It is like deja vu, but instead of just a familiar feeling, the feeling overlaps itself, solidifies, and takes off. I know what she is about to do. I follow her just in time to hear the toilet flush. It faintly smells like a skunk, and Roxy looks startled.

"Does it smell like a skunk in here to you?" After the words come from my mouth, I realize what she was doing. I don't say anything because I can gather from her expression that she saw me figure it out.

She just shrugs. "One of the other great perks of carrying this baby, I can't even smoke pot to chill out." She leaves me in the hallway as she walks back to the living room. I stand there thinking about everything that just happened. *Roxy smokes pot? Weed is illegal. How did she not find smoking scary? It's against the law. Okay, after looking back it does make sense. How did I never realize she was smoking?*

"Well, I guess I am going to go ahead and go lay down with Annika, so I can wake up for work in the morning."

"Okay, Nat. Hey, I think we are going over to Tori's so call when you get off, so you know where to pick up Annika from."

"Okay, Mama."

By the time I get to the office Caroline has already started filing the invoices we had got behind on. I start entering the remaining ones into the computer. We dust and make a list of materials that need to be ordered on Monday. We have gotten so good at working together that we can move together without words. We end up finishing way before noon, and I got two full bags of her best cookies out of the deal.

As I pull up to Tori's, my phone goes off. It is from Scott. It is short, but sweet. "Thinking of you." I don't know how to reply. I am not ready to give into him yet. I am not playing hard to get. It is just I have walls that I am not ready to let fall yet. I decide to just send a heart back. That'll take care of that for a while. I feel satisfied. I notice Mallory's car in the drive-way as I walk up.

Mama, Tori, Mallory, and Roxy are all in the kitchen around the breakfast table. Annika is outside with Brandon and the kids. I go straight to her. She sees me and runs up to me with excitement. When I left this morning, she was still fast asleep. "Mommy!"

"Hey, baby." I pick her up into my arms and soak her in, just as I always do, her smell, her touch, her feel. She touches both of my cheeks and kisses me.

"I go swing, Mama." She points to the swing that Bri had been pushing her on.

"Okay, baby."

Brandon has the picnic tables loaded with sliced fruit, juice boxes, and gummies. He waves to me. "How was work, Nat?"

"It was pretty good. I got cookies."

"Caroline cookies?"

"Oh yeah."

"I call some!" he says. I stick up a thumb as I walk back inside. I have to step over the big collection of cars and trucks that Braiden and Benjamin have laid out.

I catch the tail end of the conversation. Tori is talking, "...and that is when Annika said, 'Benjamin and Ben.'" Tori looks at me sincerely. Mallory looks at me too. And I know. It hits me hard. They told her. I asked them not to tell anybody. I asked Tori specifically not to tell Mallory, but she knows about Annika. Anger is not an emotion that finds me often, especially in front of others, but I can feel the anger starting to swell. My face must tell because Mallory starts talking and the words pour out so fast, I can hardly keep up. Tori gives me a look to let me know she didn't have a choice other than to tell, and that if I listen I'll understand why.

"Ben is, was, I don't even know what words to use." She starts again, "...my best friend." I nod, but she doesn't even catch a breath to notice, she flies on, battling the tears that fill her eyes. My mom, Tori, Roxy, and myself silently follow. "Okay, I felt like something was off, but I wasn't sure what. I kept getting this bad feeling, and then it was like I knew. He's cheating, I told myself. He had been distant and had been working late. When his phone would go off, he would act suspicious. But Ben just never was the type. It was not his character. It just wasn't him at all. So I second guessed myself. But then one day I accidentally logged onto his messenger. I saw some messages from Becky to him. He would reply, but he wouldn't give her much. He even mentioned me in some of the replies, and I even started feeling guilty for thinking he could have done such a thing. Just then a video message popped up from Becky." She winces and holds her stomach. She cannot hold back the tears. "I clicked on it, and at first I just saw a kitchen counter. Then I see Ben, and she pushes him to the counter. I can see her smiling at the camera seductively. At this point, I don't even know why I continued to put myself through that, but I kept watching. I didn't want to watch, but I didn't want to stop either, so I sat there paralyzed. Becky pulled her shirt off her shoulders, undid her bra, pulled up her skirt and then she got on top of him." She starts crying harder. "And throughout the whole thing she would look up and into the camera, almost as if she knew I was watching, almost as if she was saying, 'Look, Mallory, look at this.'"

My heart breaks for her. I feel so in tune with her pain and wish I could take it away. My mom just shakes her head, and Tori has tears in her own eyes. Roxy is twirling her hair and smacking her gum. Mallory only pauses long enough for me to take all that in before starting again. "So there wasn't any denying the truth. I had seen it with my own eyes, but why and how? How could he do this to us? I started trying to find even more evidence, and that is when Tori told me to check my glove compartment in the car. I was confused, but I did it. That is when I found the bracelet. It had the B & B, so I just figure it probably stands for Ben and Becky. Anyway, I just don't know what we are going to do. I feel so confused because even though Ben is still here, it is like I don't even know him or who he is. We had never even spent a night away from each other. Then, that bitch..." Tori and I wince. "Sorry, *Becky* breaks up with her boyfriend and moves back here."

Roxy adds, "Yeah and she had the nerve to show up to your mother's Christmas party."

Mallory is taken aback. Her voice whistles out, "You know, I've been so wrapped up in all of this. I completely forgot about that. She is relentless and absolutely vile. The nerve!!!"

Bri comes in to go to the bathroom, so we quickly change the subject. "Hey Aunt Nat, Scott and Daddy want to know if you can send out the Caroline cookies?"

I frown and my neck sends my head back, "Scott?"

"Yeah, Daddy called him so that he would have company since 'all of the girls would be in the house for a good while talking about some deep stuff.' I told him I was a girl, but he just smiled. Now Scott is here." She gestures to the backyard. There he is, as handsome as ever, helping Benjamin piece together his car track.

"Aw!" Mallory lets out, "He is really good with the kids, Natalie."

"Yeah, I guess he is."

After the back door closes behind Bri, Mallory takes off again, "Okay, so I started feeling low, like really low. It was hitting me hard. You know, trying to make sense of the situation, trying to get those images of Becky and my Ben out of my mind, listening to my mother's daily nagging about why I should file for full custody and never give Ben the time of day. I don't even know why I get defensive when she tells me that. I know she is looking out for me because she loves me, but it makes me so angry. Then I get mad at her, but she is the last person I should be mad at. Anyway, I am just a mess. One day after having a meltdown on the phone with Tori, she asked me if I had considered that the B & B on the bracelet might stand for Ben and Benjamin. But, without a doubt, I knew that it stood for Becky. Tori tried to bring me around, but I wasn't having it. That is when she told me about Annika and the glove compartment leading up to the B & B, '**B**-en and **B**-enjamin', but I don't even know why it really matters what the B's stand for. I saw what I saw." Her words slow down and get quieter and quieter. Then she says something that grabs my attention like a magnet. "Also, I already knew about Annika, Natalie. I really did, and I would never tell a soul. I never have." I'm stumped.

"What? How?"

She looks at Annika out the back door and points to her, "Well, Natalie, for one, don't you think it is odd that sometimes she plays as though someone else is there with her? What about the time with my mom? She touched my mom's shirt. She said, 'Pink,' and mother corrected her, 'White, honey, it is white.' Then that night when my mom pulled her favorite white button up out of the washer, it had, in fact, turned pink. It's mostly little things, but I'm observant."

I go deep into my thoughts for a moment. Annika does play and talk by herself. I know exactly what Mallory is describing. "I thought she did that because she was an only child."

Mallory shakes her head. "Not the way she does, Natalie."

You think I would become immune to goosebumps as often as they visit me. But I get a hard chill, followed by the ruthless goosebumps.

The back door opens, and we all kind of jump, startled. This time it is Benjamin. "Mommy, I hold you."

"He wants in my lap." Mallory pulls him to her, and she kisses him, filtering her love into him. *A mother's love,* I think, and it is a bittersweet moment.

It hits me. "Mallory, maybe Annika can help even more. I am not sure if it will work. But Karisa, this other little girl with a gift, helped me get a vision of Anna." At the sound of her name escaping from my lips, I pause. Gosh, I miss Anna, and my heart aches thinking about the way she died.

Tori puts her hand up, "I told you there are con artists out there, Natalie."

I shake my head, "No, Tori, it was real, just like Annika." Tori softens. I go on, "Anyway, maybe Annika can help you see the vision you need to see, Mallory. I don't know if it'll work, but it might."

She doesn't even hesitate, "Okay."

We decide that tonight at my house is the best time and place. I can tell Mallory is trying to suppress her impatience.

Mallory gets up to go outside, and we all follow. Annika runs to me, and I place her on my hip. Then she holds out her arms for Roxy.

I walk up to Scott. "Hey."

"Hey," he says, but I can tell he isn't as open as he usually is.

"You okay?"

"Yeah." He smiles. "Those cookies are really delicious. I think they're the best ones I've ever had. Just don't tell my mom."

I laugh. "They are good. I had to go in today, and those cookies were enough to get me to the office without complaints."

Brandon cuts in, "Hey, now that y'all are out with the kids, I am going to walk Scott over to the garage, okay? Man, I just got the body of a 1951 Ford yesterday. Come check it out."

"Sure." Scott grabs me around my waist and gives me a hug, maybe he isn't being distant after all.

"Maybe we can catch a movie tonight?" he stops and thinks, "Will Annika sit through a movie?"

My heart drops. I know I have walls up. I know I have to take whatever this is super slow. I also know that if I keep my walls as thick and tall as they are and keep dissing him, he is going to get tired of the chase. I'm not trying to make him chase me. I still don't even know where he is wanting this to go. My mom brought to my attention that neither one of us have discussed much. So far, each time we have been together, we share a few words then kiss. I know part of me is holding back because of Annika too. It's always been just me and her. She is my whole life. At times, I have been lonely, but those moments visit rarely and pass quickly. I hadn't even had the desire to try to meet someone new.

He interrupts my thoughts, "What's wrong?"

"It is just that I have plans tonight with Mallory." I nod my head in her direction. "She has some stuff going on, and we really need to be there for her now."

"Yeah, I've kinda heard," he whispers. "No problem, next time." I shake my head yes.

As I walk back up the playground area, everyone else has already started heading back inside for cookies. "Grab Annika on your way in, Nat." I see her back by the fence, and then I'm frozen in my tracks. I watch the same thing I've watched her do more than a hundred times, but this time Mallory's words replay in my mind, "Don't you think it is odd that sometimes she plays as though someone else is there with her?" Except this time as I watch her, it is like I am watching her for the very first time. She isn't playing and talking to herself. There is someone else there.

Chapter 15: Where There's A Will There's A Way

Annika and I are on the front porch counting bugs when Mallory and Roxy pull in. I can see Roxy's phone light, and then Mallory hops out of the car leaving Roxy behind. "Hey, Nat. Hi, Annika." I pick up Annika, and it feels like I have a bowling ball in my stomach and a lump just as big in my throat. I am regretting offering to try this out. Not only will it be Annika's first time, but I'm still not even sure how much she'll see. She is so young, and I never even asked Muneca when Karisa started. *Why didn't I think to ask that?*

As I replay Mallory's x-rated story, I cringe. "Hey, Mallory." Annika waves.

"Heeeeey, her Rs are getting a lot better! That was perfect." Mallory smiles at Annika. "You are such a smart cookie."

I smile, and then I watch Mallory's sincere smile turn to a worrisome glare. "Hey, I was thinking, this might be too much for Annika. I think I've actually changed my mind. Roxy pushed me to keep driving over, but…" She looks back to the car, slowly crosses her arms, and pulls back a little. "I just think this is too much for her." Annika holds out her hand, and Mallory rubs her cheek, then the top of her head, and lovingly smiles into Annika's eyes.

I know what she is doing. She is seeing Benjamin in Annika, just like when I am out without Annika and I see another baby around her age. I see Annika in them. Then I miss her so much it is overwhelming. Not only is Mallory seeing Benjamin, but I know she is seeing Annika there as well. It hurts her motherly heart to think about going through with this.

I begin to speak without thinking, "Mallory, we are doing this. It is going to be okay." I hear myself for the first time with her, and the words startle me. *What am I doing?!* But the words keep coming, "She won't see anything she shouldn't, and when it is over, it'll be like it never even happened." And then, either by coincidence or by a force greater that I can fathom, Annika shakes her head yes.

Mallory reluctantly comes in. My thoughts that had deserted me in the moment before return. "I would like to wait for Roxy though. If this goes the same way as when I was under, then Annika will support you. However, since this is our first time, I'm going to need someone to support me." I smile to let her know I haven't changed my mind, and we are going to at least attempt this. "Just come in and have a seat. I'll get you some tea. You prefer lemon, right?"

Roxy walks in and seems lovestruck. Her face looks about the same as I know mine did that rainy day with Annika when Scott called. But my mind and heart are completely focused on Annika and what might be about to happen. I don't even think twice about it.

I just want to get this over with, and I know Mallory does too. Annika's calm and comforting demeanor is the only thing that pushes me along. Roxy starts lighting candles. Then she takes out something and starts burning it. I look at her, "What are *you **dooooing**?!!*"

She shrugs. "I am setting the mood. I brought lavender and my amethyst necklace to help with anxiety. Now I am just finishing up using this sage to smudge your house."

"To what?"

"You know, a cleansing of bad energies and shit." She shrugs again.

Mallory and I share a quick glance of uncertainty. "Yeah, okay, Rox, thanks," I say, a little more baffled than appreciative.

"Okay, Mallory, you're just going to lay your head back into Annika's lap, and then I'll give you her hands for you to place yours in." I go to grab Annika to plop her in the chair, but she walks over to the chair without a word, sits in it, and motions for Mallory to come to her. Roxy and I both shake chills, but Mallory's adrenaline must already be chaotically bouncing around inside because she goes right to Annika without even a shudder and has a seat. Annika grabs one of Mallory's hands and places it on hers. Then she holds out her other hand so that Mallory can place hers on top. Roxy and I, both baffled, are left gawking.

Roxy holds me and puts her necklace into my hands. Then we just wait and watch. It is actually pretty boring, and besides the fact that Annika looks like she is zoned out. It doesn't even seem as if anything is going on. Until it is over.

Mallory still looks like she is sleeping, and Annika is still just sitting quietly and looks zoned out. But I notice that Mallory's cheeks are starting to turn red. She starts stirring a little like she is having a bad dream. Then she opens her eyes, and tears start streaming. *Roxy needs to go to Mallory, and I need Annika.* As if she knows what I am thinking, Roxy looks to me, and then goes to Mallory's side. I rush to Annika and pick her up. I remember how Karisa had cried, but Annika isn't even phased. Annika grabs both my cheeks, like she sometimes does, and kisses me.

"It's all better now," she says. She wants down, but I try to hold on tight. She is persistent, so I put her down. When her feet touch the floor, she looks up to me and says, "Thank you, Mommy." Something from within tells me she isn't thanking me for putting her down.

Annika grabs her small box of toys I keep in the living room and pulls out her crayons and coloring book. "TV please, Mommy." The thoughts flying through my mind almost pulling me into a whole other world with them start to fade. "Mommy, TV!" Now she is up and tugging on me. I come back to the present moment escaping the grasping hold of my thoughts.

"Huh? Oh yes, TV." I turn it on, and she watches as she colors. I go to Roxy and Mallory.

Mallory is wiping her face. Roxy is just there, just being, but I can tell her presence is helping Mallory immensely. I quietly sit down on the floor beside them. Mallory's crying subsides, and then she begins.

"Natalie, Annika has an incredible gift. I saw everything. I did. I really did. I know it sounds crazy. It was as if I was in a dream. Voices were echoes. I could see myself," she continues sputtering out details that align perfectly with the same details I recall from my vision with Karisa. "I knew where to go even though at times it went black." She sighs, and then I notice her desperately searching the room for Annika. I see her find her at the table coloring and watching TV. She is relieved and smiles.

"Well? Did he cheat on you?"

"Roxy!!"

"What?!? You know that's what you're thinking." I give her a disapproving glance.

"Mallory, my only business is Annika, and Annika seems to be doing fine," I say.

She interrupts me with big eyes filled with a little guilt, "Are you sure?"

"Yes." I point in Annika's direction. "You see her coloring, and I'm pretty sure she even thanked me for letting her help you after it was all done. So, like I was saying, this is not our business." I cut eyes at Roxy. "If you do not want to share, you absolutely do not have to."

Mallory shoulders go up and then fall down hard with a huge sigh. "It is okay. I would actually rather talk it out, if you're willing to listen."

Roxy gleams and purses her lips trying her best to conceal the smile that's creeping in, and her ears perk with curiosity.

"So, I saw Becky, and she was coming onto Ben. Ben tried to push her away. He really did. I felt it and saw the messages, the same messages I had already read. But then, Becky got pushy. She started sending him pictures of herself." She pauses and looks at me, quickly adding, "Nothing inappropriate was visible. It is like those are the moments it would go black. Anyway, she was like telling him he was her hero and how she couldn't live without him. Then she told him her boyfriend had found their messages and was leaving her. She went on about how she didn't have anybody and felt as if she just couldn't go on. Then she apologized for not taking his subtle hints that he was happily married, and she just needed someone, anyone, to talk to. She knew he would probably have great advice for her on relationships and maybe even know how she could fix the breakup with her boyfriend.

So, Ben, my caring Ben, tries to go to help her because he is scared for her to be alone, and she was saying some pretty deep things. Then it blacks out again. I'm assuming that this is where the sex scene comes in to play. Which let me tell you"-her voice gets a little weak-"I saw that with my own two eyes on Messenger, and he definitely wanted it. Then in the vision just now, when it was blacked out, I could sense that he didn't want whatever was going on to stop. He was in his right mind, and he thoroughly enjoyed it. I could just feel it, like I could feel his emotions and mindset." She quickly adds, "There was nothing sexual there at all, no physical feelings, just a sense that he knew what he was doing and that he wanted it to continue. He could have just been eating a bag of potato chips for all I know."

She takes a moment and lets the silence fill her as I can see her trying to sort all this out and find her own emotions about the situation. She starts again quietly, "But then the bracelet flashes, and it wasn't for Becky. Annika was right. It was made for him and Benjamin. There is another one in my car that I must have missed that says, 'Ben and Mallory - forever and always-.' Anyway, he felt guilty, and he really loves me and Benjamin with his whole heart. He has also ignored Becky since. Those last parts all kind of spun out fast and all at once. I just don't know what to do."

She thinks for a minute, "But I am forever thankful to Annika because she showed me something that I would never have been able to believe from Ben's words alone. And I thank you, Natalie, for allowing me to try this with Annika. It really has given me a lot to consider, and I can try to start understanding all of this now."

She grabs me into a hard hug and then gives Roxy a side hug that lasts a long minute. "Thank you so much." Mallory gets up and stretches, giving her legs some time to adjust after sitting for so long, walks across the room, reaches into her bag, and pulls out a small wad of money. She puts it in my hands. I look at it. There's two hundred-dollar bills rolled up around what looks to be small bills inside. I'm startled.

"Mallory, I can't take this. I'm not going to take this, " I say and hand it back out to her.

"I want you to have it, Natalie. I want Annika to have it. Please, it would make me feel better, and I'm staying with my mom. Lord knows 200 dollars won't hurt her pocketbook. I really need you to take this."

I feel uncertain and don't really want to take it, so my hand just dangles there. She grabs my hand and closes it, pushing it back to my chest. "Really, Natalie. I have been a single mom for such a short time, and this is hard, extremely hard, the hardest thing I've ever done in my life. I honestly don't know how you do it, and I am even staying with my mother. Annika did something for me that nobody else would have ever been able to do. She showed me the truth." She goes and kisses Annika on top of her head.

We finish our tea with light conversation. We even laugh some as we reminisce. Mallory colors a page with Annika, and then it is finally late and time for them to go.

On their way out Roxy holds back, "You know, Natalie, if you don't want that money..." I squint my eyes at her. "Kidding!" she says, "just kidding, gosh." She holds up both hands as if surrendering. Annika follows us to the porch. Roxy grabs her up, "You're my special girl. You know that right?" Annika shakes her head. Then she grabs both of Roxy's cheeks and pulls her in for a kiss. Mallory holds out her arms for a hug, and Annika hugs her from Roxy's arms. Then, Mallory kisses the top of her head. Annika comes back to me, and we watch them get in the car and pull away.

When we walk back into the house, I'm greeted with the strong aroma of sage. It's actually not bad. I laugh to myself as I remember Roxy, coming in with her little seance kit. Come to think of it, the smell is familiar. I think sage must have been the incense that Karisa had burning that day. I start to use my hands to push the air up towards my nose and take it in. I really think it was.

I need to remember to ask Muneca how old Karisa was when she started doing readings. I wonder if that lady paid Muneca. I need to remember to ask Muneca if she was paid, not that I want to start a business, *Two-Year-Old Psychic*. I shutter and roll my eyes at the thought, *Just out of curiosity. No, I better not. It doesn't matter either way.*

I feel so bad taking the money. I wish I would have just given it back. It just doesn't feel right taking it. All of the sudden that same familiar presence comes over me, and the guilt seems to rise from my shoulders. Annika gets up and walks over and smiles as she looks just above my head. Mallory's words find me again, my thoughts start to spin, and I remember Annika talking to someone at Tori's.

Fear strikes me, and I almost can't even get the words out, "Who is it, Annika?" I pause and fail at trying to shake the prickle of goosebumps consuming my body.

"Who do you play with? Who is here now?"

The presence disappears, but Annika's words do not. She nonchalantly answers, "Nanny."

"Who?" I say as tears fill my eyes. Annika never got to meet my Nanny.

"Where there's a will, there's a way." She smiles as she recites my Nanny's most famous line. Then she walks back over to her toys as if nothing happened.

Chapter 16: Falling

Three ideas hit me, almost as if I can hear my Nanny speaking to me herself. First, I used to make my Nanny promise if she passed away before me she would come to visit me, and she would always answer, *"Where there's a will, there's a way."* Second, Annika tried tonight. She had the will, and she was able to give Mallory the answers she was looking for. *"Where there's a will, there's a way."* Third, Mallory wants to make it work with Ben. *"Where there's a will, there's a way."*

Mallory's going to get back with Ben. I can feel it.

***

It is pitch black. I'm falling, falling, falling, and then I jump as I wake myself up. I hate these types of dreams. I wake with a start and look around trying to stabilize myself. Annika is still sleeping next to me. I check my phone. It is 4 o'clock, but I notice a text alert from last night.

"Natalie, I'm sorry if I seemed distant earlier." It's Scott. He did seem distant at first, but then he hugged me, and I shrugged it off.

"Not at all." I answer. I close my eyes and roll over, but my phone goes off.

It's Scott. He answered right back, "I feel like you've got some type of boundary up with me. I think about you all the time, and I just need you to tell me how you feel, how you really feel. Sorry, this is long. It's 4 a.m. I'm a little out of it."

I read the message three times. While I am replying, another message comes through. "I'll tell you how I feel first. We just started talking, so I am not suggesting that we put any labels on it. I really like you though, and I'd like to be able to talk with you more. I'm probably going to hate myself for sending these when I wake up."

Oh God! I woke him up, oops. "I am so sorry I woke you up. I had a bad dream and saw your message. I really like you too, Scott. I'll let you get back to sleep."

"It's okay. I'm a light sleeper. I should have silenced my phone."

"Okay, well if you aren't able to go back to sleep, you can call me. I guess I kinda owe you one ;)" I roll over, not really thinking twice about him calling when my phone goes off. I wince as Annika stirs, but she just rolls over.

I whisper, "Hello?"

"Hey."

"Hey, I'm sorry I woke you."

"I'm sorry I sent you a whole story. I like you Natalie; I like you a lot." I get butterflies. "But, I feel like you're blocking me out."

I don't know what comes over me, but I open up. "No, it's just that...." I know I can't keep succumbing to my pride. I'm going to have to share my weaknesses with him, and I stop to think if I really want to put myself out on the line.

"What Natalie? If this is going to go anywhere, we are going to have to take steps. I can promise to take tiny steps with you the whole way, but you have to open up, at least a little."

I sigh and decide to risk my heart and my pride. "It's just that I'm just me. I am a single, young mom. I work at my cousin's construction business. My whole world and life is Annika. You are you. You are a successful doctor. You're charming." I pause. The time has to have something to do with the word-vomit fit I am having, and I empathize with the words from Scott's text about oversharing because of the time, but it feels so good to release all of this so I keep going. "All the girls like you. I watch them check you out all the time."

He stops me. "Natalie, you are a good mother. You're one of the best mother's I know. You're smart, a hard worker, and you make situations work. You problem solve, you're caring, giving, and real. Believe me, my mom brings to my attention all the girls, but you know, Natalie, your beauty mirrors your soul. It's real. The fact that you don't even see it makes you even better."

I pause before asking, "Have you been married before?"

He laughs, and I realize how impulsive and direct the words shot out. *I sound like my mother.* I frown to myself.

He laughs. "Me, no I never had time. I had a couple of steady girlfriends, but my schedule was hard on them." Then I realize I should have never asked that because now it's his turn.

Afton flashes in my mind while he continues, "You know, when I am with you, I feel like we are two young kids again, and I feel like I've known you forever. Time has stood still since that night on the shore."

He spared me, I think to myself. Then I remember. I had thought the exact same thing. *That's kind of crazy.* "I feel the exact same way." I hear an alarm.

"Hey, Natalie, that's me. I've got to get up. I'm supposed to go help Brandon with his truck today."

"Oh, Okay."

"I'm really glad that we talked, and I hope to see you again soon. I miss you."

"I miss you too." And I really do, more than I ever thought I could. His words linger.

"Natalie. Natalie. NATALIE!" I wake up to my mother standing over me, shaking my arm.

"Hmmm?"

Annika slowly sits up. It takes her a moment to verify Nana is here, but as soon as she does, "NANA!!" She wobbles to the edge of the bed, and my mom grabs her up.

"Natalie!"

"What?"

"Get up and get dressed. We are going to Tori's."

I yawn and stretch. "Tori's? I was going to garden today."

She shakes her head. "Nope, we have to go to Tori's to help her plan the Valentine's Party."

"Ugh!" I scoot over to the side of the bed, throw my legs over, and slowly sit up. "Whyyyyy?!"

She has already had enough of my whining, so she doesn't even answer me.

"Get dressed, and do not wear **those** shoes." She points to my favorite pair of tennis shoes. I roll my eyes in my mind because I can tell she is not in the mood to be challenged. She struts out of the room with Annika. I get dressed in my usual t-shirt and jeans, pull my hair back, and put on **those** tennis shoes.

I think twice and exhale a loud growl as I kick them off and grab some newer ones instead. I walk to the bathroom and grab the toothpaste. I push from the bottom up, a habit I formed as a result of one of my mother's grueling pet peeves. I watch myself in the mirror as I brush my teeth. *Scott!* Scott is going to be at Tori's today too. Warmth tingles from within, and I blush when I notice where it started from. I pull my hair back down.

I walk into Tori's, trying to hide the fact I am searching for Scott. I go to the kitchen and prepare a bowl of cereal for Annika and then grab a bagel for me.

"You like some coffee?"

"Oooh, yes please? Well, do you have milk and sugar?"

Tori nods as she pulls down a coffee cup.

"So, who all is here?" I try to hide the eagerness in my voice.

"Both kids are here and just us."

"Just us? Like, Mama, Rox, me, and you?"

She nods again. "Yep, and well, of course, Ms. Annika."

I'm shocked that I actually feel a slight twinge of disappointment. "Why, were you expecting someone, Natalie?" Roxy sings out, as she glides in with a smirk on her face.

I frown and make a face at her. "No."

"Okay, I was thinking we would do the Valentine's Party at Mr. Tom's empty shop."

I'm confused. "Mr. Tom? He doesn't even usually come to the Valentine's parties, does he?"

Tori's eyes are dancing, and she pauses, which gives me the impression she is contemplating sharing something. "Well, actually he is coming this year." She tries to contain her goofy smile.

"What's going on?" My mom says slyly.

Tori puts her hands up. "I'm not sure if it is true, and I would not tell anybody else, so y'all better keep quiet." Her stare fixates on Roxy. Roxy holds up scout's honor and then motions for her to go on. "Okay, rumor has it Tom and Macy are getting married." Her voice gets higher and higher with each word. Married almost comes out as a squeal.

"What!?" My mom's jaw drops. "Tom and Macy???"

Tori nods her head. "That's what I heard."

"Well, that was fast," my mother adds.

Tori shrugs. "I guess what's meant to be will be. I saw them pulling up to Missy's the other day. Macy comes from money. Mr. Tom has a pretty good set-up, so there isn't any suspicion that it's just for the money. It is just so strange because Macy has never been married. I don't even think I've ever seen her with a boyfriend."

My mom is pondering over something. Even though she has a dumbfounded frown on her face, she is as beautiful as ever. It is like she doesn't even age, a timeless beauty. Then she loudly let's out, "I thought Macy was gay. Hmph, I guess I read that wrong." Then she adds a heap of cream cheese to her bagel.

Macy and Mr. Tom, huh? They must be trying to keep it a secret because Caroline hasn't got a hold of it yet, and she is usually the first one to know about her clients.

The door opens, and my heart jumps into my throat. It's Brandon and behind him Scott walks in. I feel weird after our sleep-text conversation, so I just smile. He just smiles too and says, "Hello," to everybody. Tori hands them both some coffee, and they head back to the garage.

"OH MY GOD!" Roxy stares into me as she barks. Everyone looks at her.

"What?" I say completely confused.

"You're falling for him, Nat. And by the looks of it, you're falling fast *and pretty hard.*"

I shake my head. "I am not."

Everyone just gleams at me with a yeah-right expression. Tori kindly adds, "He is a nice guy, Natalie. Brandon has known him a long time, and he's a good one." She adds more coffee to her cup and then continues, "It is okay if you're attracted to him. It's not against the law," but then she rushes to add, "just take it slow."

I look at my mom, and my eyes desperately beg her not to say anything. She just smiles, closes her eyes, and shrugs her shoulders.

"I bet you think dirty thoughts about him."

"Roxy!" Tori shouts before I can even open my mouth.

Tori lightly pops Roxy on the head. "She most certainly does not, and do not talk like that in my kitchen." Then she looks to me for confirmation.

I shake my head. "No, No, of course not." A white lie slips from my lips, and my mother's eyes catch it satisfyingly.

I break away from my mother's gaze. "Where's Mallory, anyway? She's always been in on our party meetings."

"She went to talk to Ben. She found the bracelet that Annika was trying to tell her about. It was in the glove compartment right past the bracelet found first. I think she is going to try to work through things with him. Apparently the B & B wasn't just for Ben and Benjamin. He wanted to open a bed and breakfast as a family. Ben and Benjamin's B & B. See the first B stands for Ben and Bed and the second..."

My thoughts fade away from the conversation and focus on Scott. I start to daydream about him: his hands, his lips, his arms. I wonder, *Is he thinking about me too. Maybe I should go out to...*

"What do you think, Natalie?"

"I'm sorry. What?" I pull myself out of my thoughts and back into the conversation.

"Dirty thoughts, " Roxy smirks and ducks away from Tori.

Tori doesn't try to get her this time; she just rolls her eyes. "I said I think that we should do red and light pink plates instead of red and hot pink."

"Yeah, that sounds good." Not very interested, I give a half nod.

It's then when I notice Roxy's shirt. She is wearing an oversized shirt, and there's a jolt when the name on the shirt registers in my mind HIT THIS. Then all of the sudden, her love-struck face from last night comes to mind. I know I can't bring anything up in front of my mom and Tori, so I try to hold it in, even though I feel like a tea kettle about to whistle.

Annika calls for Roxy to come to the living room, and I take it as my chance. I walk to the restroom, and after I hear Annika's voice stop, I intercept Roxy and pull her into the hallway.

"Okay, What's up with you?" I get serious and my voice gets low. "Oh no," I hesitate as I double check the evidence staring me in the face. "Roxy, please tell me you're not back with Jace."

"What?! No!"

She's telling the truth. I can sense it. "It's nothing," she says defensively.

As long as it's not Jace, I think to myself.

I nod my head and turn to walk away, but she pulls me back. "It's the singer."

Chapter 17: The Appointment

"Have you lost your mind!?"

"Why are you always so like whatever with every other person, so like 'oh it is okay, oh you don't have to tell your business, oh we shouldn't talk about them,' but then when it comes to me you just don't even care about how you make me feel!"

I try to sympathize with her but thoughts are flying through my mind. I go ahead and let them spill from my lips. "Well, first of all, let's start with the restraining order you have on this singer's drummer. Then let's talk about how you went from the drummer to the lead singer. Finally, let's talk about the fact that you are pregnant!!!" My rising whisper turns back to a soft tone, and I answer her question, "It's because you're my baby sister." And I give her a hug.

"Don't tell?"

I shake my head no and give her a side smile. I do wonder to myself if this singer even knows she is pregnant, but I don't ask.

Annika crawls into my lap, and I hold her tight. I take her to the living room with Bri and Braiden. I help Annika put together a number puzzle. I watch in amazement as she does most of it by herself, only confusing 6 and 9. I watch her little hand grab a piece and correctly place it while saying the number out loud. She accidentally steps on Bri's toe, and before Bri even has time to react, Annika hugs her tight. "I'm sorry, Bri," she says. Bri kisses her, instantly forgetting about her toe.

I help Braiden with his dinosaur puzzle and Bri with her princess puzzle. Then they both help me and Annika with an alphabet one. Braiden yawns and Tori checks the time. "It's naptime."

"Please, no, Mommy, no!"

She grabs Braiden's hand, as she starts to lead him down the hall she says, "You'll feel much better when you wake up, and you'll get a yummy snack." He starts to suck his thumb. Tori lovingly picks him up and carries him the rest of the way. He pulls his other arm up around her neck and holds tight. She is back in five minutes, and he is already sleeping. She keeps them on a strict schedule.

She turns on the baby monitor. Annika yawns and then quickly covers her mouth, which sends all of us into a laughing fit. Then things get quiet again as my mom and Tori clean up the kitchen. Roxy gives her attention to her phone. Before I know it, Annika is asleep in my arms. "Why don't you lay her down in Bri's bed? She'll sleep better." Tori flashes the extra monitor and gives it a wave.

I watch her sleep and take her in. Her hair is stuck to her cheek, either from drool or sweat. I push her hair back away from her cheek and kiss her softly. She looks so peaceful. The love I have for her overwhelms me, and emotion radiates from within. For the first time, I take her in without the ache in my heart that usually follows. She is going to be okay, and she will never be alone.

After quietly stepping out of the room, I find my thoughts once again circling Scott. I go against my timid demeanor and decide to just go for it. I am going to go to the garage. I notice my mother's eyes follow me, but I don't look back at her. I put my hand on the door, hesitate, then to my surprise, I turn the knob and push.

Scott turns around and his eyes meet mine. Brandon looks up from the truck's engine. "I think it is about time for a break." He smiles, wipes his hands into a towel, and goes into the house. Since he leaves us alone, I know that means he approves and that means a lot to me. Since I am so much younger than Tori, and she got with Brandon when they were still in high school, he's more like my older brother than just a brother-in-law.

"Hey you," Scott says.

"Hey." I smile and wonder if I should go there, but my heart starts talking before my brain can overthink it, "I cringe when I think of some of the stuff I said this morning, but I am glad I shared. It's just I guess I don't have much confidence. You know, I haven't ever wanted to move on since Afton, but then you came back."

He hugs me, one of those moments when actions are needed in place of words. "I just..."

He stops me. "Natalie, Brandon has told me about Afton. You don't have to talk about it unless you want. I can't imagine what you go through with all of this because of that, but like I said, I'll take tiny steps with you."

Tears come to my eyes. I am so thankful for Brandon, and I am very thankful for Scott's acceptance of the situation and his sensitivity. It's hard to think about kissing him at this moment. I feel torn instead. As if he can read me, he just hugs me long and hard and leads me back into the house.

"Okay, so tomorrow is Roxy's first appointment with Dr. Basil, so I am going with her. Natalie, can you take Annika to work with you?"

"Mama, I am going to the appointment too."

"Oh, okay, is everybody coming then?"

"Well, of course Tori is coming," Roxy lets out, and my mom turns her head away from the conversation. I can tell my mom doesn't approve the adoption plan, but I can also tell that she will never say anything because she doesn't want to break Tori's heart.

She pulls herself together. "Well, the more the merrier." She smiles a real smile.

Scott taps my shoulder and points to the monitor. Annika is waking up. He follows me to get her. When we are out of everyone's view, he puts an arm around my waist and then pulls me so that I face him. He pulls me in close for a hug and then steps back so that I can open the door.

I grab Annika up, and she smiles at Scott. He smiles back at her. "Hey you."

She waves. I kiss her forehead. "I'm thirsty, Mommy." She grabs my cheeks and kisses me. Scott holds out his hand, and Annika high fives him.

Roxy and I decide to take the kids outside to play while Mama and Tori complete the plans for the party. As we step out the back door, Brandon and Scott step back inside the garage. Scott looks to my mom and asks, "I am invited to this party, aren't I?"

"Are you kidding? You're the reason I'm having this party," my mom answers him and then raises her eyebrows up and down while pointing to me. I can tell she is no longer going to hold the silence I begged for, but in her defense, she lasted way longer than I thought she would.

I start walking to the swings with the girls. Roxy gets on the ground with Braiden. Then she turns away from the toy car she is pushing as she says, "He doesn't know."

I'm confused and caught off guard. I give Annika another push and then Bri. "Huh?"

"Chance, he doesn't know." She points to her stomach. "I know you were wondering."

I don't know what to say. "The singer's name is Chance?"

She nods her head. "And he doesn't know you're pregnant?" She shakes her head no and gets tears in her eyes. I hug her close. "It's okay. It's okay, Rox."

Annika gets off the swing and pulls Bri over to the slide with her. "It's just that Chance is not my usual type. He is kind and considerate. He is protective. I honestly don't even know how he and Jace are members of the same band. I really feel like he is a good guy, like I might have finally broken my streak of losers, but now this." She points to her stomach. I try to find the right words to say, and then it hits me.

"Roxy, listen, you are gorgeous, mysterious, and bold. You are selfless. You are about to give the most special gift that anyone could give to your sister. If he is as good as you say he, and if he deserves you, he'll understand. If he doesn't, he never deserved you to begin with." This time she hugs me, and she starts to cry. I know part of it is the hormones. I just hold her. Then, without even realizing what she is doing, she wipes her eyes and nose on my shirt as she pulls away.

I break the silence, "You know, Annika sees Nanny."

Roxy blinks hard. "What? No way!"

"She does. After Mallory mentioned that sometimes it looks as if Annika is playing with someone when no one is there, well it happened last night. I got a strong feeling of a presence, and I could feel her looking at someone. So I asked her who it was, and she said, 'Nanny.'"

"Yeah, but do you really think?"

"Roxy, right after that, she said, 'Where there's a will, there's a way.'"

Roxy goes white. "No way!"

I nod my head yes. "She can really see Nanny and apparently hear her too."

"I miss Nanny so much."

"I know me too, and I know Mom and Tori do too. Mama's always been so independent, but part of her always needed Nanny in a way. You know, I am so opposite of you and Mama, but I just realized I am a lot like Nanny."

"You never realized that before?!?"

I shake my head. Roxy laughs. "You're just like her!"

We all meet in the house, and Brandon has his famous apron on. *Yes!* I think to myself, *I don't have to worry about dinner.*

"Who wants to stay for dinner?" Nobody turns down the offer.

After a very good barbecue dinner and some of Tori's brownies with ice cream, Scott has to leave. He tells everyone bye, but then he kisses me on the cheek in front of everyone. I don't know what to think of that, but before my thoughts get too far, he kisses Annika on her cheek, too. *How does he always seem to know just what to do?* He hugs Bri and shuffles Braiden's hair around. Before he can get out the door, my mom goes to hug him. "You smell good, Scott," she says and then smells him again. I put my head into my hands. "What is that?" He looks puzzled. "What kind of cologne are you wearing?"

He smiles. "I'm not, I'm not wearing anything actually."

My mom's mouth turns down, her eyebrows go up, and she nods her head. He laughs and waves one more time.

As soon as the door closes, there's no escaping my mother and all her awkwardness. "That man smelled delicious, Natalie. You can't let him slip away. Mmm-mmm, nope, he is a keeper." She winks, and my face turns red as I notice Brandon making a disgusted face.

Tori pats Brandon's cheek and then pinches it. "Don't worry babe, she thought you smelled good too."

"I know one thing. Scott sure is hot!" Our heads jerk to Roxy and she shrugs. "What? There's no denying it. I mean, Brandon, don't lie. He's hot, right?"

"Sure you don't want me to drive y'all home?" Mama asks with a hand on her hip.

"No, it's pretty out, and I love to walk." Mama doesn't seem thrilled with that answer. She lets out a deep sigh.

Tori comes in from the garage. "Here it is." Bri comes up, stepping between Tori and the stroller. Bri pushes it over to me.

"Thank you, Bri." Bri looks up at me and smiles. "Thanks, Tor. I love y'all always and forever."

"Love you too, Aunt Nat Nat, forever and always."

"Forever and always," Tori says as she kisses the top of Annika's head.

"Weeeeeee!"

"Do you like riding in the stroller, sweet girl?"

"I love the stroller!" She waves to anyone and everyone that is out in their yards. As we approach Mr. Collin's house, I notice a new sign in his yard, *Yard of the Month*.

"Well, hello there, Natalie." I wave. "And Annika. How are you today?"

"Hi, Mr. Collins."

"Hey, how are those pansies doing?"

I smile as I think of them, "Somehow I managed to keep them alive. Annika really enjoys watering them and watching them grow."

"Pretty Flowers!"

He frowns, as if he is pondering something, "You know those are good winter plants, but I think I've got something that would be real good for the spring." He walks over to his garage and pulls out a plant. "I was just about to plant this one. This beauty is an iris reticulata."

"Thank you, Mr. Collins." Annika smiles and holds out her arms to grab the plant.

"Yes, thank you, Mr. Collins."

"You can put it right in the ground. Just make sure to keep an eye out for weeds. You don't want them ruining this."

I nod. "How is Foxy?"

"She is doing great." He points to the well-manicured backyard, and I can see her at the fence staring us down.

"Puppy, please!"

"Can Annika pet her?"

"Of course, I bet she'd love the attention. Annika, great thinking," he says as he points to his head.

***

BADU BADU BADU BADU BADU echoes through the room. Roxy's eyes tear up. My eyes glass over too. Tears fall from Tori's face, and my mother beams. I pull Annika tight. "Baby," she proudly says and points to Roxy. We all smile through the tears in our eyes. *Yes, a baby.*

Chapter 18: My Mama

As I pull away from the doctor's office, the miracle I just witnessed replays in my mind. It was beautiful. Three sisters, our mother, Annika, and the heartbeat that filled the room and took everyone's breath away. I get tears in my eyes. There is nothing like hearing your baby's heartbeat for the first time. I still remember when I heard Annika's. It's a magical moment, a life changing moment.

My thoughts lead me to my mama. My papa and my nanny gave my mom the best life they could. They were young, but they were stable, in love, and head over heels over my mom. However, my mom was a wild child, hard to handle, controlling, but not to be controlled, so she ended up leaving home early. She got pregnant with Tori when she was seventeen and had her at eighteen. In spite of it all, my Nanny was there for her the whole time.

Tori's dad wasn't even around by the time Tori was born. From what I hear, my mom tried playing house with a lot of other guys over the years, but it never worked out. Apparently, every once in a while, she would find a good guy, a stable guy, but my mom would rock the boat, cause a scene, and shake things up. Normal bored her, and she chased after excitement. Then she met mine and Roxy's dad. He was her "soulmate."

They fought, but he knew how to give my mom just enough excitement and then pull her back in just in time to passionately make up, staying stable only long enough to keep the relationship thriving until the next explosion waiting around the corner.

You would think Tori would be the most unstable out of us three, having lived through all this. By the time Roxy and I were old enough to remember anything, our dad had already passed away. I don't even really remember him at all. Tori is so different. She is one of the exceptions, using her childhood experiences to build a life completely opposite from her own. That's one of the main reasons I look up to her.

After Rox, my mama stopped dating to focus on being a mother. Even so, she still chased the flame, and Nanny still had to put out a lot of fires. My mom could be irresponsible, irrational, and she still liked to have a good time. Overall, she was an independent woman that would do anything for her girls, and she always put us first. Even if that meant sending us to Nanny's a couple of nights at a time while she fed her need for excitement. She once went skydiving. Another time she took off to Las Vegas for the weekend. I know she drank. Whether or not she did anything else, I'm not sure, and I'd rather not know. Nevertheless, Nanny was so proud of my mom. My mom couldn't have done anything to disappoint her. Nanny only saw the good.

The day Nanny passed, something in my mom changed. She still loves excitement, but her definition of excitement changed. Now it is just being around her grandkids. She is still fun and full of fire, independent, and the strongest woman I've ever met, but she also focuses on being the best grandma she can be to her grandkids. I know no matter what I do, my mama will always stand behind me.

***

The week goes by fast, and it is already Saturday. My phone goes off. It is the same message I have gotten everyday from Scott since he has been back on call. "Good morning, beautiful. I'll text you when I get off." Then every night as Annika and I were laying down, I would get a "Goodnight, I miss you."

I replied the same everyday, "Good morning" and "Goodnight, I guess I kinda miss you too ;)"

Now my phone is ringing. It's my mom. I hesitate, "Hello?"

"Open your door." I close my eyes, wrinkle my nose, and kick my feet under the covers.

Annika hops off the bed and starts running to the door, "Nana!" I slowly open the door, and my mama catches Annika as she leaps into her arms.

My mom looks me over. "You're having a good day?"

"Excuse me?"

"Your face looks good today. You're kind of glowing. You're having a good day. You've put on a little weight too and that sadness that follows you around like a shadow, well, I haven't noticed it the last couple of times I've been with you."

Hmmm, that's not what I was expecting. "Thank you."

"Now get dressed, grab an outfit for tonight, and let's go. Natalie, you're not wearing a t-shirt, jeans, and those raggedy tennis shoes, if I have to go in there and dress you myself."

And there it is, that's what I expected.

"Mama, I was going to have coffee and take my time. Can't I just meet you at the shop later?" She gives me a look that screams no. "Okay, okay, fine," I whine and go to get dressed. I come right back out defeated. "Mama, I don't have anything besides t-shirts and jeans."

"You have to have something."

I shake my head.

She shoos me out of the way, struts to my room, and frantically goes through my clothes. She pulls a couple of things out but shoves them right back in. "Well, that settles that. Grab my purse and get in the car. We are going to Hidden Closet Resale."

"Mama, no I don't want you to buy anything."

"Too bad. I didn't ask. Anyway, when you marry Scott you can pay me back." She slaps my butt. I scoot away.

Annika holds my hand and patiently walks through the store with me. I hold up two different outfits, and my mom looks repulsively at them both. "Natalie, you haven't found anything? We are running out of time."

I look at the mannequin. "I think that looks kind of cute, but I don't even know if it is my size."

My mom goes to the little dress and looks at the size. Then to my dismay, she starts taking it off the mannequin. I look around, panicked. "Mama, you can't do that. What are you doing?"

She smiles. "Of course I can." Then she tosses it to me. "Go try it on."

Annika hasn't let go of my hand and walks with me to the dressing room. I slip the dress over my head. "Wow! Mommy you look beautiful." She looks up to me, and I can't help but to pull her up and kiss her. All of the sudden, Annika grabs my cheeks so that I'm looking into her eyes. I think she is about to kiss me, but then she speaks instead, "Mama, Macy and Delilah."

Macy and Delilah? Delilah??? Mr. Tom's sister, Delilah? Annika starts to push herself down, and then I notice the price tag, $45. That is a lot for resale. My mama cannot afford it. The little maroon dress fits me tight in all the right places. It's classy enough to satisfy Tori but sexy enough to please Roxy.

I walk out. "Oh Natalie, you look gorgeous."

I whisper to her. "Yeah, but Mama, it's 45 dollars." She checks the price tag. "Mama, it's okay I think I can just wear that first shirt you pulled out with…"

"Give me the dress, Nat."

My mom walks up to the register. "Hey there." She looks at the young cashier's name tag. "Lisa, I just noticed that this dress has a little stain and was wondering if you could take anything off the price?" My mom's eyes twinkle.

Lisa smacks her gum and looks at the dress. She sighs and then puts her cell phone down, never once smiling. "Let me see." She twirls her hair. Smack. She grabs a laminated piece of paper. Smack, smack. "I can take"-she runs her finger down the sheet-"ah there it is, 15% off."

My mom claps her hands together. "Oh, that would be just great," she says overzealously.

As we walk out of the store, my mama softly swings the bag into my chest. I sigh. "Don't worry about it, Natalie, really. I made some extra money the other night dog sitting. I'm good, and you, my dear, are going to look amazing."

"Thank you, Mama." Part of me wonders if that was her lipstick on the dress.

We all meet at the shop in casual clothes. Mallory does the streamers, Mama and Tori set up the tables, I do everything else, and Roxy isn't doing anything unless you call sneaking samples of the refreshments doing something. We finish up, gather up the kids that have been running around the place like crazy, and head to the cars. As soon as we walk out, Ben's Mercedes pulls in front of us. He rolls down the window and politely waves. All of us Haven women give him a half wave and a smile.

"Well, that happened faster than I thought," my mom is the first to speak. "I'd never take back a cheating man, once a cheater, always a cheater." My mom was true to her word too. She never had a problem breaking up and leaving a man, even if she was in love. That's one of the things Nanny admired about my mama.

"Mama, he didn't really cheat on her. I mean he did, but it wasn't really his fault. Well, it was, but I mean, I'll just tell you what happened later. It was that night Mallory came to my house." She nods her head.

The rest of us follow each other back to Tori's to get dressed. Brandon just sits back and watches with amazement as he keeps the kids busy. Make-up brushes fly, hairbrushes fly, I'm pretty sure even some eyelashes and bras fly.

Then Tori turns her focus on the kids. She already has everything laid out on Bri's bed. Roxy takes Braiden, Tori takes Bri, and I take Annika. Tori starts talking really fast, proudly walking me and Roxy through the outfits, "The skirt and shirt is for Bri, and then the dress is for Annika. See how the skirt matches Annika's dress?" She holds the skirt to the bottom of Annika's dress.

Of course it does. I smile and nod my head enthusiastically, "Yeah, it's really cute, Tori."

"And then look at Braiden's..."

"Let me guess. His bow tie and socks match the girls' outfits," Roxy continues, "Tori, every single outfit for every single holiday is the exact same."

Tori stops. "Nuh-uh, for Christmas Annika and Bri had the same dress. Last Easter, they all three had the exact same overalls, and..."

Roxy gives in. "Oh yeah, you're right. These are *way* different and very cute." I catch the sarcasm, but thankfully Tori does not.

Chapter 19: Mama Knows Best

We pull up to the shop. We are the first ones to arrive. It's a good thing Roxy and I have Mama and Tori or we would have been late to our own party. We all get busy trying to tie up all the last minute things before the guests arrive.

Caroline and Rob are the first to arrive. Caroline delicately places her cookies on the dessert table. "They're made with love." She winks and then links arms with Rob as they find a seat. After that Mallory comes in with Ben and Benjamin. Then the place quickly fills up with everyone.

I walk outside to get Annika's sippy cup and see Raul's truck pull in. *I'm so glad they were able to make it after all.*

"Hey, Muneca!" I give her a hug, and she kisses my cheek. "Raul." I smile, and he nods.

Then Karisa jumps out of the truck yelling, "Natalie!"

I grab her and hold on tight. "Hey, sweet girl. Wow, I knew I missed y'all, but now that I'm actually seeing y'all I realize how much I missed y'all. I'm so happy y'all could make it!"

"We are too," Muneca replies. She holds onto Raul's hand and guides Karisa by the shoulder, following me.

"Karisa, Annika is inside and so are my nieces and nephews. Well, Benjamin isn't my real nephew." I stop. "Anyway, there's going to be food and a lot of delicious desserts. You have to try the Caroline cookies." I smile.

"So, I'm dying to ask." Muneca smiles and gives me a sideways glance. "Is the doctor here?"

I shrug. "He might not be able to make it. He's working."

She makes a puppy dog face. As soon as we walk in, Karisa breaks away from Muneca's hold and runs to Annika. I point Muneca to a table they can sit at while I grab them drinks. Muneca's dress reveals a voluptuous woman. She looks absolutely stunning. I walk back over to the table with the drinks. We watch the kids sneak some of the Caroline cookies. "I'd like you to meet my mama and my sisters."

"Of course." She flashes a perfect Muneca smile.

Tori has put all her doubts to the side and is the first one to greet Muneca. "It's very nice to meet you. We've heard a lot about you and your daughter. Our family is extremely thankful for y'all. Words cannot even express."

"The pleasure is mine." Muneca holds out her hand and Tori shakes it.

"Natalie, you never told me she was such a babe."

Muneca waves her hand as if to disagree with the comment and laughs. "Ah, you must be Roxy." She shakes Roxy's hand.

My mom doesn't say anything, but when Muneca holds out her hand, my mama hugs her instead and pats Raul on the back. My phone goes off. It is a text from Scott saying simply, "Happy V Day." My heart sinks because it definitely sounds like he isn't going to be able to make it.

I text back, "Happy Valentine's Day."

Raul asks where the restrooms are. As I look up, I see Scott coming through the doors. I point Raul to the restrooms.

I nudge Muneca and nod my head in Scott's direction. She looks at me, her big eyes even bigger. "Is that him? That's the doctor?" I nod my head. She eyes him up and down. "You do have guy trouble." We see him greet a few people, and we both notice other girl's giving him second glances. "You better go get him, Natalie." She says seriously and a little fearfully. Then we both start to giggle, but still I get up and go to him.

"Natalie."

"Hey, I didn't think you were going to be able to make it."

"Yeah, I know." He smiles. "I wanted to surprise you. Happy Valentine's Day." He hands me a pebble. I look at it, confused. "Don't think I'm cheesy now." He looks away with a slight smirk and his jawline and full lips are enough to drive anyone mad. I shake my head no as I try not to drool. He couldn't be cheesy if he wanted to. "It's from the night of our first kiss. I grabbed it before I kissed you, and I've had it since." He whispers in my ear, "You cannot tell anyone though. It'd seriously ruin my reputation."

"Come here for a second." I walk him over to where Annika is, and Annika runs up to him. He holds his hand down for a high five, but she hugs his leg instead. I pull my bag out from behind the kids' table and reach in. I hand Scott a Valentine's drawing from Annika. It has all three of us on it, with her in the middle and what looks to be sunflowers all around. Then I hand him a keychain I made myself. "For your truck keys, I smile." I rub the pebble in my hand and smile again. Who would have ever thought the best Valentine's present I would ever get would be a small pebble?

"Hey, Annika, I've got you something in the truck." Annika's eyes light up. When we get to his truck, he pulls out a teddy bear, a small box of chocolates and a balloon.

Annika hugs his neck. "Thank you, Scott," she says. "This is the best!" He motions for me to come closer. I peek inside. He hands me a box of small teddy bears, and he grabs a box of roses. "I brought these for the other kids, and I thought your mom and sisters might like the roses."

Scott and Annika pass out the bears and roses, and it gives me enough time to rush over to Muneca. "I still haven't told Scott about Annika."

"Okay, is okay," she says.

She must be getting tired, I think to myself. Her English, although still full of a hard Mexican accent, has become 100% grammatically correct. She is extremely intelligent and a very fast learner.

"I no say nothing."

Mr. Tom clings his beer mug. Tori looks over at me, and she is about to lose it. "EEEK! This is it," she mouths in my direction.

Mr. Tom begins, "First of all, I hope everyone is enjoying the shop. It looks like this old place makes a great place for gatherings. Most importantly, I'd like to make a big announcement." Tori covers her mouth. He looks over at Delilah. "I'd like everyone to know that my baby sister has found her forever valentine. Everyone please give it up for the newlyweds, Delilah and Macy Jones."

Delilah, a very attractive woman with thick, straight black hair that hits her tiny waist, leans over and kisses Macy on her cheek. Thankfully, there's more of a younger crowd here, so there's a lot of claps. I see one older woman frown and look to the ground. She nudges her husband hard when he starts to clap, and he gives a hard shrug. I scan the room. I find Mallory and although she looks rather shocked, she's clapping. Caroline is clapping. Missy looks as white as a ghost and is not clapping. Instead, it seems Edward is kind of holding her up. Roxy lets out a loud whistle as she continues to clap. Scott has a surprised look on his face, but he is happily clapping. Then I find Annika. Although I'm not close enough to hear her words, I can make out what she is saying. "Macy and Delilah!" she says proudly, looking at Karisa and pointing at Macy.

Someone grabs me from behind, "I knew it! I called that one!"

"Mama, how did you know?"

"I just got that vibe."

Wow, she was right. "This is kind of crazy."

"Yeah, but I just think it seems crazier than it actually is because we had seen Macy with Mr. Tom and started assuming that's the direction we were going. Then we got this curveball. It is just like, wow."

"Yeah, it's not our place to say who can love who. I mean the thing about love is you can't control it. You kind of have to respect love for that. It has a mind of its own, and it does what it wants, usually taking your mind, body, and soul with it."

"Wow! Mama, that's kind of deep." And it's completely true.

As Muneca gets up to start to leave, I realize how much I enjoyed being able to just be with her and Karisa without the *gift*. We were able to just be with each other and talk about normal things. There wasn't a heaviness hanging over us like a dark cloud. It was easy, light, and just a lot of fun.

"Adios, Scott."

"Adios Raul, ten cuidado."

Raul gives a nod. I was really amazed to find out that Scott can speak Spanish, not fluently, but close. He can understand just about all of it. Karisa gets out of my lap, and I tuck some cookies in a napkin for her to take home. They wave goodbye to Scott and then to my mom and sisters.

After Muneca gets Karisa in the car, she turns to me. Her smile vanishes quickly and a look of concern finds her instead. She looks in the window, double checking that Karisa has found something to keep her busy. Karisa's attention is focused on the Valentine bear.

"Natalie, Karisa zone out the other day. When she wake up, she remember nothing. When she was out, she say, 'He killed me. He violated me and killed me. You have to know who it was, Natalie. You have to stay safe, and you have to keep Annika safe. I won't be free, not until you find him.'"

A tear rolls down Muneca's face, and she shivers, a feeling I know all too well. "It was Anna, was it? It was same girl that Karisa help take you to lighthouse, isn't it?"

I nod my head yes. "She was my best friend. We were just kids. She was only thirteen."

Muneca's train of thought finds her, "I am so sorry, Natalie, that is so sad." She gives me a hug. "Well, we have remember that when she seeks you out and communicate that even though you have grown more old, she is still child. She is still thirteen. That's one thing I have learned. This has only happened to us two times before. This is the part that scare me." She sighs. "And you have to be careful Natalie, okay, and protect Annika. She sent warning."

"I don't know who it could be. How can I protect us if I don't know who it is?" My thoughts fly to Scott, the only man I have let myself get close to.

As if Muneca tapped into my thoughts, she answers, "I know it wasn't anyone at the party tonight. Karisa would have been able to tell. So don't worry about Dr. Handsome." Her playful smile returns, and she pulls me in for a hard hug. She kisses my cheek. I open up the back door and give Karisa another hug, then I walk around and shake Raul's hand, something I saw people do at Muneca's house as they were leaving.

I wave as they pull away. I thought I would be scared to be left alone in the parking lot after Muneca shared those words, and the words do linger, but instead I get angry. I was just thinking how nice it was to be free of the *gift* and the heavy weight it carries with it, the sadness that follows it like a shadow. Then, just like that, it comes stealing it all away, pulling me back into the darkness. I hate it! I hate it!

"Natalie?" Is that you!" I jump so hard I can feel my heart jump out of my chest. I see Ben coming towards me. "Yeah, it's me."

He grabs a small box out of his car. "Are you okay?"

"Yeah, I'm fine. You just scared me."

"Look what I got Mallory." He opens the box to reveal a huge diamond ring. Diamonds aren't my thing, but it's actually pretty mesmerizing.

"It's beautiful."

"You know, I know you know everything." He looks down. I don't protest. I stay quiet instead. "But, it was a mistake, and I love Mallory more than anything. I'll never do anything like that ever again."

I put my arm around him. "I know. I know, Ben. I believe you." I smile.

I watch him from afar as he gives Mallory the gift. She hugs him around the neck and then holds his face as she pulls him in for a kiss. I look away. Then, out of the corner of my eye, I see Mallory making her way to me.

"Hey, I just wanted you to know how thankful I am that you let Annika help me get my family back." She has tears in her eyes. "If it wasn't for her gift, I don't even know where Benjamin and I would have ended up. But I would have missed out on a lifetime with my true love." She grabs my hand and holds it for a long while.

I smile back at her and then give her a hug. "Of course Mallory, I'm so happy we were able to help." And I really am.

The *gift* follows us. It haunts us. At times I feel as though I'm bound to the shackles of the deep, dark blackness of the unknown it carries, but completely contradicting and at the same exact moments, it heals us, connects us, and it even frees us.

I walk back into the party, and Scott sees me. He walks over and hands me a single rose. "There was only one yellow rose, so I saved it for you." I never thought I was into getting flowers, but the happiness this rose brings is whimsical. Because it is a single rose, it means so much more to me than a whole dozen would've. There's something so compelling and much more personnel from the simplicity and focus.

"It's perfect," I say. A slow song starts to play, he asks me to dance.

He pulls me in, and I am comforted by his strong, yet gentle grasp. "You look really beautiful, Natalie."

"Yeah, yeah, yeah," I say with a playful smile. He grabs my face and chases my eyes with his until I look into them.

"No, I mean it Natalie. You are beautiful," he says slowly.

I blush and look away. I put my head into his shoulder. My mom was right. He does smell really good. "Thank you."

"Natalie."

"Yeah."

I catch some girls around Roxy's age pointing at him and whispering. "I want to be with you, Natalie." I keep my head on his shoulder, too timid to be caught by his eyes again. "I mean I know I said we didn't have to put labels on our relationship. But I want you and only you, and I don't want to lose you to someone else."

"Okay," I say, but I keep my head down, and I don't lift it up.

Chapter 20: Within A Contradiction

As the last people linger out the door, we start throwing beer bottles away, pulling off the table covers we borrowed from Caroline, the dishes we borrowed from Missy, and start boxing up the leftovers to take to the homeless shelter. Brandon gets the industrial broom and starts sweeping. Scott folds down the tables and chairs.

My mom gives the place a final look around and seems satisfied. "Okay guys, I think that's good."

"Aunt Nat, Can I spend the night with you?" Bri looks up at me. "Please, Mommy?"

"Sure, if your mommy says yes." Tori looks concerned. "I promise, no brownies for breakfast," I say pleadingly.

"She doesn't have her clothes or her toothbrush."

"Please. Mommy, please!"

"Please, Aunt Tori, pretty please?"

Tori picks up Annika. "Okay, okay, but just because you're so cute."

"Oh, but I rode here with Mama."

My mom looks over. "Yeah, and my car is full now. Can you take them Tori?"

Scott looks up. "I can take y'all home if you'd like."

"Okay." I nod. My mom smiles, but Tori looks uneasy.

"Mommy! Mommy!" Tori is distracted by Bri. "Kisses!" They kiss. "Noses!" They eskimo kiss. "Butterfly!" They flutter their eyelashes together.

"Hey Tor," Brandon says as he stands half in the shop and half out, "I've got Braiden loaded up, and he's asleep. Are you ready to go home?"

She looks at me sternly, as if telling me to be a lady and not to do anything she wouldn't, and then she hugs me. She looks back to Brandon. "Yeah, I'm coming."

We pull up to the house and all go to the living room. We make a pallet on the floor for the girls. While we watch the movie, Annika crawls up next to Scott while I play with Bri's hair. It isn't long before Annika falls asleep on Scott, and Bri falls asleep on me. We lay them down. Scott kisses my forehead. "Well, I better go, I have to go in tomorrow."

I get up to walk him to the door and a small pop comes from my bedroom. I jump. "What was that?" I get up and go to my bedroom; Scott follows. I don't see anything noticeable.

"What's in this closet?" He points to the small utility closet.

"Um, just the AC, I think." He opens the door and the smell of burnt plastic fills the air. "What was it?"

"I think it might have been your furnace fan. My uncle knows a great HVAC tech, but he probably won't be able to come until tomorrow."

I start to fret because I only have a tiny stash of money put away. It is hard to save when you only make a little over enough to cover the bills. My face must give me away.

"What's wrong?"

A white lie speaks, "Nothing." I shake my head. The strap of my dress falls off my shoulder. Scott pulls it back up. Then he kisses me, slowly, sweetly, in a way innocently, but then it turns passionate. The heat has turned off, but again I find myself warm with him, hot actually. I'm burning up.

He slows down and pulls away. "Are you okay?"

I nod my head, and then I find myself pulling back to him like a magnet. His body language responds to mine, and he pulls me back in. The kissing gets harder, longer, and faster. His hand goes under my dress and his hand slowly starts to pull my panties down. My shoulder strap slips again, but this time instead of pulling it back up, he pulls them both down. He finds the bed, and I fall close behind. "Are you sure you're okay?" I put a finger to his beautiful lips. Then he pulls me on top of him.

It's serene laying with him. When I walk to the ocean at night and hear the waves crashing on the shore, paint the birds with my eyes, or read the light of the moon and the stars, I feel calm. I feel peaceful. I feel safe. That's how I feel now. It's safe and serene, and it feels like I'm home. I realize when I'm with Scott, it feels like I'm home. I long to be able to fall asleep next to him. But I know I can't, not just because Bri is here, but because of Annika too. He knows it as well.

"Are you okay?" he asks again.

"Yeah, I'm okay."

"That isn't something I usually do. Saying that out loud causes about a hundred movie scenes to flash in front of my eyes, but I don't Natalie. It's hard to control my feelings when I'm around you."

I nod my head, "I know, I believe you. I've never done that either. I mean not this soon."

"Well, as long as you let me in, I'll be here, Natalie. I'm not going anywhere. Natalie, I love Annika."

How did I get this man?

"Natalie..." I look up at him. "I love you." He pauses for a moment, but not long enough for a response, just enough time to get his thoughts straight. "I think I fell in love with you all those years ago, a young love, a playful love, and I did think of you from time to time but not deeply. You were my first crush, so from time to time, something would remind me of you. Coming back and seeing you again and talking to you that first day in my office, it all came back. It hit me like Cupid's arrow. Except this time, it's not a young, playful love. Natalie, I really love you."

I kiss him on the cheek and hug him hard. I think I love him too, but for some reason the words don't form. Something holds me back. Instead of responding with I love you, I just say, "I feel the same way."

We lay there for a while more, and I'm relieved when he kisses me on the forehead. I was hoping that I didn't upset him. "It's time for you to go?" I ask.

"Yeah, I better leave, so I can get a little sleep before tomorrow."

"I wish you could stay."

"I know, me too, but it's not right for the girls."

I nod. "I know this is best, but I'm going to miss you."

"I'm going to miss you more."

As soon as I close the door, the safe, peaceful feeling abandons me, and I'm slammed with guilt. Instantly, I am ashamed. Maybe a little because of what Tori would think, maybe a little because I had promised myself I would not do anything unless I got married (this time around, anyway), maybe a little because I couldn't even tell Scott I loved him back, but mostly for Afton.

Now emotions of shame and guilt flood in as though I'm cheating on Scott because I'm thinking about Afton. I know I'm still in love with Afton. I know I miss him every single day, just as though it was only yesterday I lost him. Time doesn't heal me. It teaches me to cope, but it doesn't heal. Thinking about Afton and taking in all that just happened hits me in my stomach.

I start to cry. I cry for Afton and how much I love him, how much I miss him, and how bad I feel for letting Scott in. I cry for Scott because I couldn't tell him I love him back. Even though I know we have something special, I stop myself for Afton. Then I feel as though I am leading Scott on and cheating on him for thinking about Afton. I cry for Annika because it has always just been the two of us, and the choices *I* make now will influence *her* whole life.

I cry, cry, and cry until my stomach hurts. I cry until there are no more tears left to fall and sleep finds me.

I'm dreaming of Anna again, and I know I am dreaming because I am watching myself, but I can't wake myself up. We are playing in a field of flowers. I pick a beautiful flower, but then the clouds turn dark. Anna turns arounds, her voice fills the air, "That's not a flower. That's a weed, and we can't have weeds. They're in the wrong spot. It's all wrong here, and it's invasive. It must be removed." She sounds annoyed and aggravated.

I wake up in a sweat. Something about the dream is very unsettling, and her words give me the shivers. I want to call Roxy, but she is probably asleep. I get up and get some water. Then I just go to the living room and lay down next to

Annika on the pallet. I put on a movie, but I turn the sound all the way down. Finally, I start to fall back asleep.

"Nat, wake up." Someone is tickling my nose. I push their finger away. "Nat, wake up." I push it away again, but a familiar comfort starts to engulf me. "Natalie, wake up." I open my eyes. It is still dark outside, and I can't see well. My eyes try to focus. "Natalie, come on." Someone pulls my wrist. I look and rub my eyes. It can't be. I follow as **he** leads me to the bedroom.

"Natalie, I can't stay long." The voice is something I've thirsted for but was unfairly forbidden from. The touch feels like something that used to be mine but was violently stolen away. He turns around, and my hands go over my mouth. I don't believe it. It's not possible.

"Afton?"

Chapter 21: Afton

We enter my bedroom. Even though there has been more than enough time for my eyes to adjust, everything is still made of grey pixels. I feel him pulling me towards him. It's like a sweet dream that can only end in heartache. I try my hardest to push those thoughts out of my mind and instead hold onto this moment, never letting it slip away, just staying here in this moment with him until the end of my time.

His words break the silence. Hearing the sound of his voice again after never thinking I would hear it again is like catching a shooting star. I feel numb, but at the same time all of my emotions are magnified. My physical touch intensified, like the burning sensation that's inflicted by ice instead of fire.

"Natalie?" I start to bawl. He is still holding me tight. "Natalie, It's important that you listen to me." I nod my head as it still rests on his shoulder, careful not to loosen the grip I have around him.

He has shaggy, messy brown hair, and he is only barely taller than me. He looks like the kids that hang out at the skatepark. "Natalie, Annika is different, and I am sure you have realized that by now."

He pauses and then starts again, "I don't want you to ever feel like she will see, hear, or feel something she shouldn't. I'm feeling like that's what has worried you the most. All of those parts will always be blocked out. Unless she is old enough and stable enough to see them, she won't. Ever." Those words that I wanted so badly to hear just a couple of months ago barely have an effect of relief. Instead, my heart continues to break as though someone is ripping it apart, slowly torturing me.

He grabs me by my shoulders, so my eyes look into his. Even though they're grey pixels, I see the deep ocean blue swirling outside of the yellow that surrounds the pupil. The same eyes I stared into so many times before. I keep my hold on him, even as he holds me away.

"How do you know?"

"I know because her gift mainly comes from me. The same things she can do, I did as a baby and a kid, even when I was with you."

"This is crazy. It's unbelievable."

"Natalie, it's true. I knew things. I didn't get to choose what visions would come or what people from the past I would see. It just happened. It's like getting on a merry-go-round and not knowing which way you'll face when it stops, always changing, sometimes going fast, sometimes slow, sometimes still."

I start crying again because I know he is going to be leaving again soon. I dig my nails into him. I am holding on for my life. "You can't leave me again. Afton, I can't handle you leaving me again. I can't do this. I feel like I'm being tortured. I can't breathe." I feel as though someone is holding me underwater. "Please!" Then my shout turns to a whisper, "Afton, please?" Tears run and fall, and I let them.

"I never left you, Natalie." He wipes my face. "I never will. I'll always be here, but you have to listen to me. You're my best friend, okay? But I did something that was terrible to you. I loved you and wanted you so much. I knew what was going to happen to me; I knew I would have to leave. I didn't want to hurt you, so I tried my hardest to stay away from you. I tried to stay a complete stranger, so you wouldn't feel this. When I let myself get close, I despised myself, especially when I found out you were pregnant and a baby was going to have to go through this too." He lets out a heavy sigh. "I almost told you. So many times I almost told you, but I did it anyway. I got with you, and then we even created this beautiful life." His tone gets angry, but I know it is directed only at himself. His voice softens again, "I couldn't stay away. You pulled me in, and I hurt you."

"I would do it again, Afton. I would. I love you with every ounce of me, and I wouldn't have Annika. You gave me a gift nobody else could have, and our baby is my whole world."

"Shhhhh." His hand strokes my face, and he kisses the top of my head. "The thing is, you know I have to leave, Natalie. You know I can't stay."

"But..." Thousands of hopes, thoughts, and negotiations spin violently in my head.

"Natalie, there isn't anything I can do about it, and there's nothing you or Annika can do. It's what was always meant to be, but keep listening, I am always going to watch over you and Annika, but this guy Scott..."

A blade goes through my heart at the sound of his name coming from Afton's lips. I feel like I have betrayed Afton. I feel exposed, ashamed, but at the same time, I feel another type of love, different from the love I have for Afton, tugging me in another direction.

"It's okay, Natalie. Scott, he is really good, and he is going to be great for you and Annika, okay? I can't be here for her." I see him rubbing a hand slowly down Annika's cheek and back up again, even though she is in the other room. I cry even harder than before. "But, he can. He can be here for you and her, too. Natalie, you have to let him in. I know you love me. I know you would do anything you could do to have our family back, but it's not possible. You love him. I know you do, and Annika does. It's the right thing to do."

"It doesn't feel like the right thing to do."

He lifts my chin, so I'm looking into his mysterious eyes again. "I will never be able to be with you, in this life or the next. I have chosen something, and it doesn't give me time to hold a relationship. It meant losing out on you and Annika, but it will allow me to help so many others. I will always be looking over y'all, but I'll never be able to stay. Never." Something settles in, and I'm still. My heart opens up. I'm at peace, and instead of fighting to keep him here with me and shutting everything I don't want to hear out, I open up and listen.

"Natalie, the reason you pulled me in is because you're different too."

Those words leave me puzzled and a little rattled. "What?"

"Natalie, I couldn't stay away from you. You kept pulling me back in. You're different too. You are. You're not as strong as Annika or me, but you have a gift."

"I do not." I stumble on my words, "I don't." I feel inadequate and embarrassed for him that he is overestimating me.

"Natalie, what about when you get deja vu? You can almost see what continues to happen, even after the moment of deja vu passes, right?" But he doesn't want me to answer. He is proving a point, so he goes on, "You can feel people. For example, you can tell if someone is being truthful or hiding something. You know. You suspect things before there's any real evidence to suspect anything at all. You sense the correct time before you even check the clock. There are moments your mind also tells you what to do and say before you even have time to process what you're doing. People open up to you easily. You can even communicate to people through your eyes." All of this starts sinking in and a lot of scenarios start replaying themselves in my head, as if I am watching different clips of movies from my own life.

"You have your own form of the gift, Natalie, so it probably runs in your family." I think back to Roxy, who always seems to get people to do what she wants and my mom, who gets gut feelings and always runs with them. Afton answers my thought, "Maybe they're charmers or readers, but there is something."

Running in my family, running in families, my thoughts go straight to Muneca, who always seems to answer my thoughts out loud. She must have a gift, and just like I had no idea, I know she doesn't either.

"Every single person has a gift really, at least once in a lifetime. They just have to learn to use it. There's different types, different forms."

I stop him as I remember something. "But sometimes I'm wrong, like I'll look for shoes in the closet, but they're under the bed."

He laughs. "The gift is fluid, ever changing. Sometimes it is with you, and sometimes it is not. The important thing is to figure out which is which, and if it is there, to listen because it doesn't lie." He holds me for a while longer.

In the silence, my heartache is heard once again. "I don't want you to go." My voice becomes almost angry. "I wanted Annika to know you. I wanted to be with you forever. I wanted our family. It's not fair," I plead.

"I know." He nods and kisses my forehead. "But it was never meant to be, Natalie." He rubs a hand up and down my cheek. Then again, Annika seems to appear, and he lightly kisses her on the cheek.

I hold onto him tight. "Please Afton, can you just hold me until I fall asleep."

Tears fill my eyes, and I can hear his voice tremble, "Okay, I'll stay until you're asleep. I love you."

"I love you always and forever. I always will, Natalie."

***

I wake up and the sun is shining into the room. An aching for Afton slams into me like a hangover, and I desperately search around the room for any sign of him. I get up and even look in places he couldn't possibly be. There's nothing. I start to feel sick. But then, all of the sudden, the peace that took over last night comes over me, and I feel rested and calm. *It was never meant to be.*

"Okay girls, put the chocolate chips in now! There you go. It's going to be delicious." My mother's voice travels out of the kitchen and makes its way to me. *Here we go.* I put on my slippers and slowly walk to the kitchen. I get distracted on my way because my coffee table has been moved. In addition, the artificial plant I had on my shelf has been moved to the middle of the kitchen table. My mom is filling my saltshaker as I walk in.

"Aunt Nat, we are making pancakes!"

My mama turns around. "Well, hello there, Sleeping Beauty, nice of you to join us."

I pick up my plant that now sits on the table and look at it. "It really brightens up your table huh, Natalie?"

"I liked it on the shelf."

"Nat, some canisters would look nice there, but this single plant looked silly. I fixed it for you."

"Mmmmhmmm." I point to my coffee table.

"I never thought it looked good where you had that either. See? Just by moving it there"-she waves the spatula in the direction of the table- "your whole living room was opened up."

I frown. "I liked it where it was, Mama. I could reach my drink. It was convenient."

She cuts in, "And an eye sore. It's much better now."

I let a heavy sigh escape under my breath.

"Sit, sit, sit, girls, you too, Natalie." She slides pancakes in front of all three of us. "You're welcome." She smiles expecting an answer.

"Thank you, Mama."

"Hey, I made them, Aunt Nat, and Annika helped too."

Annika nods her head. "I made them Mommy. I did it!" Annika pushes her hair away from her face and smiles proudly. "I did it!" she declares.

After swearing my life away with no brownies for breakfast, Mama swirls some whip cream up higher than the Eiffel Tower on the girls' pancakes and then tops that with syrup. Mine and hers are next, only she adds some pecans in addition to the whip cream and syrup. They are indulgent. I have two. Their sweetness eases the bitterness of my rearranged items. It actually does look better, but I'd never admit it.

"By the way, you have a message from Scott on your phone." Her eyebrows go up and a smile comes across her face.

My heart skips a beat. *Please tell me she didn't read it.* I try to grab it so fast it turns into a slippery fish, and I almost drop it. Annika and Bri find this amusing.

"Good morning, beautiful. Are you still okay?" My mom looks at me as if she is begging for all the details. I freeze. This is it. This is what Afton was talking about. I'm reading my mom. I get the shivers.

"So, what did he say?" But the smile she is still wearing across her face tells me she already read it.

"He just said, 'Good morning.'"

"Mommy, watch me! Watch me!!" Annika goes into the living room pulling Bri behind her. "Look what Bri taught me." Bri helps her do a flip on the floor.

"Good job, baby. Bri, you did a great job, too. You're a wonderful helper and teacher."

"Mommy, Mommy watch! Nana, watch! Nana!" The girls have our full attention.

I feel free, as if the new beginning that had been playfully toying with me is finally going to be indulged.

I look out the window. I almost see Afton's promise in the sky, and I listen.

Chapter 22: Thorns Come From Roses

Knock! Knock! "Are you expecting someone, Natalie?"

"No, I don't think so. Maybe it's Tori." For some reason I look to Annika for the answer, and then I realize the reason I look to her for the answer. If she knows, she doesn't share.

My mama peers out the kitchen window. "It's a younger guy, plump little fellow. He's holding a tool bag."

I open the door. "Hello, Ma'am. Dr. Richards sent me over to look at your furnace." Heat falls through my body as I wonder if I'll be able to cover the bill. "My name is Greg. Mind if I come in and take a look?"

I smile and guide him in. "Mom, this is Greg. He is going to look at the furnace."

My mom smiles. "Good morning, out and working so early on a Sunday, I bet you'd like some pancakes?"

"Sure, something in here does smell delicious."

"That'd be my pancakes." She shakes a spatula at him and smiles.

I lead him to my room and point to the closet. He looks it over, tinkers a little. "I'm going to walk to my truck to grab some things, and I'll be right back. My memory slipped me, and I'm not sure if I have the part on hand. I can always order if need be." I smile nervously.

"What's wrong, Natalie?" My mama always knows. Mother's intuition I guess.

"It's just Scott called him over, and I don't know if I have enough in my savings to cover it."

My mom looks at me and comforts me with a smile that seems to have answers. "Natalie, you know Brandon and Tori would gladly take the bill. Even if you felt like you wanted to pay them back, y'all could work out payments."

I feel so relieved. "You're right, I can just borrow the money from them and make a payment schedule. I could make monthly payments."

She looks back over her shoulder. "Or you could just let them take the bill," she says as she turns back around to flip the pancake.

There's a tap on the door, and then Greg let's himself back in. "Good news! I have the part, and it should only take me about an hour." He stops only to eat his pancakes fresh off the griddle and goes right back to work.

"Okay, Ma'am, you're good to go." He smiles.

"Thank you so much. How much do I owe you?"

"Oh, nothing. Scott took care of it. I actually owed him a favor, so now we are even."

My mom smiles deviously.

Greg continues, "And thank you for the pancakes. They were so delicious they could have been payment on their own." He winks.

My nose pulls up. *Is he flirting with my mother?*

"Oh, thank you, hun," my mom says. He packs up all his stuff and leaves with a smile and wave.

"Mama, I think he was flirting with you."

"You're surprised? I know I've still got it." She smiles. "But he was a little plump for me." She winks.

"Oh, brother!"

"I think you mean, Oh, Mama!"

"Gross."

"Speaking of gross, first jewelry, now your furnace? You can't fool your mother, Nat. What did he give you for Valentine's anway?"

I put my hand into my pocket and reveal the small pebble.

Her nose crunches up. "That's what he got you for Valentine's Day, a rock?" She isn't impressed even after I shared the story with her.

"After the silver necklace, I was expecting a diamond or some kind of stone at least, and by stone, I don't mean that kind of rock. I mean a *rock*." She wiggles her fingers.

"Mama, diamonds aren't really my thing. Honestly, I think this pebble is the best Valentine's present I've ever received."

She checks me for fever. "Are you even my daughter?"

I roll my eyes.

Annika and I wave to my mama and Bri as they pull down the driveway. I squeeze Annika before I set her down. She crosses her arms and frowns. "I wanted Bri to stay." She pouts.

"I know baby, but she has piano lessons today. It was time for her to go home and get ready."

Her frown turns to a smile. "Scott is here, Mommy."

Scott's here? I push the door back open.

"Hey, girls." He smiles as he walks up. Annika runs out into the yard to meet him, and he picks her up. My heart melts.

"Greg came by. Thank you so much for sending him, but I'd really like to pay you back."

He smiles. "No worries, it is already taken care of. Really, it's fine."

"But..."

"Natalie, really, it's fine."

"Are you sure?

"Yeah, it was no problem. He owed me one."

"Okay, thank you."

Annika gets down and goes to her table to color. "Natalie, I stopped by because I wanted to apologize to you about last night. I told you I would take tiny steps with you, and we didn't need labels. Then..."

"I love you, too, Scott."

He is taken aback. "You do?"

I nod my head. "I love you. I just had so many different thoughts going through my head, like Annika and..."

"No, I know. I completely understand."

His phone goes off. "One second." I can hear a woman's voice on the other end of the phone.

"Hello, hey, yes, yes, I am. Okay, I love you too." I find myself trying to jump to a conclusion.

"It was Rhonna," Annika says, walking over to us.

"What?" Scott asks, confused.

"It was Rhonna, your mom, Rhonna." Annika is missing the d-sound, but it's clear she knows what she is talking about. Unfortunately, I'm not the only one that notices.

Scott looks at Annika and then at me. It's happening so fast, but I feel like I'm watching it in slow motion somehow. "Annika, shhh," I plead.

I try to act normal and quickly change the conversation, "It was your mom?" I ask, trying my best to sound genuinely curious. I grab the yellow rose off the table and a thorn pricks me. "Ow!"

"Are you okay, Mommy? You okay?" Annika frowns and looks at me. She is concerned.

"I'm okay, baby." I kiss her.

"Rhonna doesn't like you, but I like you, Mommy." Scott doesn't say anything, I don't say anything, Annika inspects the tiny drop of blood on my finger. "Can you fix her, Dr. Richards?" Annika looks at him, her big blue eyes full of hope. I can hear him trying to pull himself out of his thoughts.

"Yes, of course. Do you have a first aid kit?"

I nod. "I know where the bandages are!" Annika raises her hand and pushes herself off the couch to get them. She can't get the drawer open, so Scott follows and helps her. They come back together. Scott puts some ointment on the microscopic wound.

"Alright, Dr. Annika, we need your help for the bandage." He looks at Annika, holding out the bandage.

Annika smiles, but then a look of concentration consumes her. "Thank you, Dr. Richards."

"Of course, Dr. Annika."

"Here put it on just like that. There you go. All better." Annika smiles and then kisses the top of the bandage. I smile too. Then she goes back to color.

"My mom likes you."

I nod and smile. "Your mom likes everybody. I don't know where Annika got that." I try to shove it under the rug.

"But the thing is, I do. I never would have told you in a million years. It's not like my mom at all actually. I know once my mom sees us together, she'll love you and Annika too. But honestly, she wasn't very happy when I talked to her after the Valentine's Party. She doesn't want me rushing into anything."

I start to feel something, and I listen. Before realizing what I'm doing, I start talking, "She doesn't like that I'm younger and have a baby." I smile. "It's okay. I know she only wants what is best for you. You even said that she noticed all the attention that you get from women. Just like I thought you could do better, she thinks you can do better."

He tries to speak, but trips on his words instead. "It's okay, really. We will get it figured out. All she really wants is for you to be happy."

"Well, you make me happy."

He smiles apprehensively. "But how did Annika know? She said..."

I look at Annika, my sweet baby, playing and coloring. I look at her hair and her little hands, her cheeks and her eyes, and her feet crossed so cutely under the table. I remember Afton's words. I feel Scott's questions, and I listen.

"Annika has a gift."

He nods his head but fails to conceal his puzzled expression. His eyes travel to Annika, and we both watch as she gets up and goes over to the corner of the room. She starts whispering and offering pretend tea to someone. I figure we might as well just do this if we are going to do this, so I follow my Nanny's lead, taking it as a sign. "Right now, she's talking to my Nanny." He watches in amazement. I feel him trying to fight his realist views, so that he can believe me, but I sense he is having trouble. It's not that he doesn't believe me. It's not that he doesn't want to believe me. It's that seeing isn't always believing.

I get that overwhelming feeling, and my words start talking before my mind can sort out what is going on. "I think we should make a drive to your mom's."

He looks puzzled. "Today?" I nod my head. "My mom's? That's a four hour drive, at least."

"I think we should go."

"You think that's a good idea?"

"I think it is a good idea."

He seems apprehensive, but I think he needs an outlet from everything that's playing out in front of him. "Okay, if that's what you want." Even though it's completely irrational, he chooses it over staying in our current situation.

Not really understanding what just came over me, I start to pack everything Annika would need for a day trip. *Why did I just do that? I'm already shy and reserved! Now I have to try to use Roxy's charm to try to prove myself to someone, and not just anyone, but Scott's mother!* I start to feel uneasy and start searching for an excuse to change my mind.

We switch her car seat over to his truck. I put her in, buckle the straps, and kiss her on the cheek. "I love you, Mommy, always and forever."

"I love you too, forever and always, Annika. I love you." She reaches her arms out and gives me another hug.

It isn't long before Annika falls asleep, so I start from the very beginning, just like I did with my sisters and my mom, making myself completely vulnerable.

He listens as I talk and asks questions as I go. "You know I've heard about cops hiring psychics to help with cases, and I've heard of other paranormal events, but I never gave it a second thought. I never analyzed it. I never even asked myself whether or not I believed it. I know one time, when I was a kid, I had a really bad feeling. When I got home, my mom had told me my fish died." He lets out a sigh that sounds a little like a laugh. "That actually doesn't really seem like much now, compared to Annika. I know our minds are powerful things. But I was taught to find answers, and there really isn't an answer. This is a lot to take in."

"I know."

"I believe you, Natalie, and I heard her. I was there and saw everything, but I'm still looking for an answer, something that would make all of this make sense."

"It's okay, Scott. I denied it for a long time, and Tori did too. It's okay."

He nods his head, and then to reassure me that he is still on our side, he puts his hand on my thigh.

Annika rubs her eyes. I catch her in the mirror waking up. "Hey, sweet girl, did you wake up?"

She nods, rubs her eyes some more, and then smiles. "Mommy?"

"Yes, sweet girl?"

"Scott's dad, ambulance."

Scott's phone rings. He looks at me. "It's my mom." He pulls off the road. "Hello. Hey, Mom. What happened?!? We're already on the way." He hangs up and is quiet. "They think my dad had a heart attack. They're on the way to the hospital."

Chapter 23: Another Chance

He exhales loudly, rubs his head, and debates whether or not he should drive or ask me to drive. He is having a moment, so I let him take it.

"Mommy?"

"Yes, Annika?"

"Scott?" He turns around giving her his full attention and is trying so hard to hide his own feelings to comfort her.

"Pop's okay, Scott. He is going to be okay."

He smiles and rubs her ankle. He looks at me and whispers, "Does she know that, or is she comforting me?"

I shrug. I've wondered the same thing many times. "I'm sorry, Scott, but I'm not sure."

He contemplates something, but then turns the blinker on. "That's what I call my dad."

"Huh?"

"Pops."

We pull into the hospital parking lot. Scott makes a call, and we make our way in. Rhonda is sitting beside the bed nervously when we walk in, and Scott's dad is asleep. Scott wraps his arms around Rhonda, and she falls into him.

"Scott, I'm scared."

"It's going to be okay, Mom. I've looked over everything, and I think they're leaning towards emotional stress being the culprit. I don't think it was a heart attack."

Rhonda notices us. She wipes her eyes and tries to smile. I can't read what she's thinking, and I hope Annika keeps anything she hears to herself. Annika squeezes my hand. *Did she hear me?*

"Mom, why don't you show Natalie where the vending machines are? Annika is probably ready for some food."

"My tummy is hungry," Annika says.

Rhonda hesitates. "It'll be fine, Mom. I can stay here and persuade the doctor to fill me in on every last detail when the test results come back."

Just then the doctor happens to walk in and introduces herself. Scott looks to his mom. She smiles back at him and grabs her purse. "Alright, girls, follow me." We follow her, and she leads us to the cafeteria. "The vending machines are no place for dinner. I bet the cafeteria will have something much better." She winks.

I walk through the line and pull out my card to pay for mine and Annika's. "Are you eating?"

She tries to hide her sadness and worry. "Oh, no, no, I just ate a little while ago."

I grab a muffin and an extra juice, and then I pay. When we sit down, Annika hands Rhonda the juice and muffin. She smiles. "Thank you, Annika." She looks down. "Charles is my best friend. He is. He really is, and I just don't know what I'd do without him. He is my rock." She smiles, and I watch as her eyes go back to another time. "You know his mother did not like me at first. A sweet woman with a heart of gold, but she knew her son was prestigious. I was only a young beauty operator." Her smile fades. "Oh goodness, I'm not sure why I'm all of the sudden propelled to admit this, but I was having second thoughts about you, Natalie, and I am sorry. I am very sorry. I've only seen Scott with you this past twenty minutes or so, and even though my focus was on Charles 100%, there was no denying the way y'all look at each other." She looks like she is processing what she just said and is regretting letting the confession slip.

"I'm glad you told me, Rhonda, and honestly, I felt the same way. I mean I had no idea what this handsome, charming, prestigious man wanted with me. You know, I'm a young single mother, and I just do secretary work part time. I held back for so long. I did, for Scott, for me"- I look at Annika- "for Annika."

She touches Annika's hand and then pats it. Then she looks back to me. "Natalie, darling, you are absolutely beautiful, inside and out. I know what he sees in you, dear, because I can see it myself."

We walk back up to the room. Scott's sitting beside his dad, and they're both eating jello and talking.

"Charles! How are you feeling, dear?" Rhonda walks over and grabs his hand.

"Oh, I'm fine darling. Looks like we just had a scare after all. Well, who's this pretty little thing, Scott?" He points to Annika, and Annika giggles.

"Hi, Pop." She smiles and waves.

"And wow, is this Natalie?"

Rhonda smiles and nods her head. Scott answers, "Yes, Dad, this is Natalie." Scott's eyes gaze longingly into mine before he turns back to his dad. "And this is Annika." He pats Annika on the back.

"How'd you get so lucky, son, two beautiful girls?"

"Maybe it's because I got your good looks." They both laugh.

"Well, it is certainly nice to meet you both, and I hope to see you both again soon, minus this girly gown." He tugs at the hospital gown.

I've never met Charles before. Since he owns his own company, he can't get away as easily as Rhonda. Scott reminds his parents that we have a long drive ahead of us and both have work tomorrow.

"Dad, take this as another chance. You didn't have a heart attack this time, but if you don't start taking care of yourself, it could happen." He kisses his dad on the head. "Alright, see you later, Pop." Then he gives his mom a sincere hug and a kiss on her cheek. "Love you, Mom."

"And I love you, son."

I shake Pop's hand, and he uses his free hand to pat the top of mine. Annika shakes his hand, but he pulls her in for a hug instead. "Hey Rhon, babe, pull a couple dollars out of my wallet so this baby can get an ice cream or something on the way home." He looks at Annika, "You make ol' Scott stop and get you a good treat, okay, doll?"

Annika nods her head. "Thank you."

Rhonda steps towards us and wraps us both in a big hug. "Y'all be careful on your way home, and Natalie, I'm really glad y'all came."

Everything about this evening seemed to move too fast. It was as if someone put us on fast forward. I had no intention of telling Scott about Annika, but as if Annika and my Nanny were conspiring together, it happened. I certainly had no intention of meeting with Rhonda anytime soon, and then before I even knew what I was doing, I planned for us to go straight to her. It was the gift. Afton told me to listen to it, so I did. We ended up being at all the right places at exactly the right time.

We don't pull in until around 1 a.m. Scott walks us in, and even though Annika is fast asleep, he kisses me on the forehead and turns to walk away.

"Scott?"

"Yeah."

"Hey, it's really late, why don't you stay? You could sleep on the couch."

He thinks for a minute, hesitates, and then answers, "Okay."

I bring him some extra sheets and a quilt my Nanny made that Roxy left over. I lay in my bed next to Annika and check the time. *Ugh 1:23.*

Knock! Knock! "Scott? Is that you?"

"No, someone is at your door."

At this time of night it could only be Roxy, but it wasn't her code knock. I stumble to the door in the dark. The porch light reveals a young man. A handsome, tan young man with deep, green eyes and black hair.

Chapter 24: You're So Close

"Can I help you?"

"I hope so, my name is Chance."

Scott lets me handle it and stays on the couch, but I feel him getting ready to turn to protective mode if need be.

"I'm sorry to come so late. I actually didn't even realize the time until I knocked."

I nod my head and look back to Scott. "It's fine." I reassure him; I can sense it. Then I think of something. "Chance, you're Roxy's friend." He nods his head. "Come in."

Scott watches as I pull a random guy in by his wrist. "Scott, this is Roxy's friend, Chance. He needs to talk, so I'll take him to Annika's room. Try to get some rest for tomorrow." I find myself anticipating his reaction.

He just smiles. "Okay, I can sleep through anything."

A relieved sigh escapes from my lips. "Alright, Chance, come in here. I'll go grab you a chair."

"I'm really sorry it's so late."

"It's fine. I was still awake."

"It's just that Roxy, your sister, I really like her." His smile fades. "But I can't keep up." He starts to smile again. "She is mysterious and fun. She has an intriguing personality, full of excitement. When I'm with her, I only think of that moment." The smile vanishes. "That's how she is. She doesn't think about what will come next or consequences. She lives for the moment. But being with her is like not being able to get off of a dangerous roller coaster. It spins fast, goes up, and then violently comes down. She doesn't evaluate the consequences of her actions. She's careless. It's like I've stepped into the eye of the storm, and she rages around me. It's extremely exhausting, but I'm captivated by her at the same time. I've tried to break it off with her, but it's like I'm addicted to her." I listen and know exactly what he is talking about. I empathize with everything he is saying. "The reason I came tonight is because I really tried to break things off for good, but she begged me to come and talk to you first. She said that you would have answers."

She did? "Listen, Roxy can be a lot to handle, but she is a beautiful person. She's authentic. Every guy I've seen her with jumps in and uses her personality for their benefit, to feed their own hunger. They don't evaluate the situation. Chance, Roxy needs someone to balance her. She needs someone that can help bring her back to reality. She needs someone to evaluate the situation, at the same time allowing her the freedom to explore everything that makes her so unique. You seem like you could be the balance she needs. It won't be easy all the time, and you'll have to learn that while it's okay to jump in with her at times, other times you'll have to stand back and just get your toes wet. If you want it to work, it can." I pause when we hear a knock, Roxy's knock.

I open my front door and sure enough, it's my sister. However, the confidence that usually radiates off her is missing. She's not her usual self. "Nat?" I nod my head in the direction of Annika's room. Roxy pauses and looks at the couch, noticing Scott (who is fast asleep) she raises her eyebrows up and down as she gives me a look.

"Look, y'all are more than welcome to talk in here as long as you like, but you can't stay." I look at Roxy, "Roxy, you know I don't allow guys to sleepover."

Roxy stares at me, "No Fair! You've got Hot Scott over on your couch."

I sigh, "Ro-xy, we had a long night." She looks at me accusingly and a little satisfactorily. "Not like that! We didn't get in until late, so I offered to let him sleep on the couch."

"Well, it is really late, Natalie." Roxy looks pleadingly at me.

"No, it's okay. I better go. I'm still not even sure I can do this, us." Chance looks at Roxy. I see my strong, independent, and careless sister like I've never seen her before. She is hurting. Her indestructible heart is starting to rip.

"I'm pregnant!"

He looks as though that was the answer to his question. "I knew it!" I sense excitement in his voice.

Roxy's eyes swell, and she whispers, "It's not yours."

He backs away. "You cheated on me?" She reaches out for him, but he pulls away. He's willing to listen to her, but he is hurt. His mind can't wrap around what he just heard. The only answer boldly replaying itself in his mind is that she must have cheated on him.

"I didn't cheat on you, Chance. I was pregnant when we started talking."

"Did you know?"

She breaks eye contact with him and draws her arms up around herself. "Yes, I knew. It's Jace's."

"Jace's?"

She knows she shouldn't have told him. She's risking the news getting back to Jace. "Please, you can't tell him. He's dangerous, and I don't want him to have anything to do with the baby!" She begs him with her eyes, and he nods.

"I didn't tell you that I was pregnant because I was avoiding the fact that I am pregnant. I didn't want a baby. Plus, at first I thought you were just a good fuck." I wince at hearing those words come from my baby sister's mouth. Chance turns away hurt, but Roxy grabs his face and holds it in her hand, "But then I fell for you. You're a beautiful person. You have a beautiful soul. You're intelligent and sweet. I really like you, and I don't want to lose you. I do love the baby, but I still don't want it. I mean not me personally. I'm going to let Tori adopt it."

Chance looks at her, and Roxy pleads, "Please, there's so many times that I feel like I'm spinning out of control, and I don't feel like that when I'm with you. It's like you ground me, like you balance me." Chance looks at me with wide eyes. I smile and shrug.

Then he pulls her in and kisses her forehead. Roxy looks at me with pleading eyes and sticks out her bottom lip. "Fine! But, he's making a pallet on the floor in there, and you're sleeping with Annika and me. " She bites her lip through a smile.

It seems like as soon as I close my eyes the alarm goes off. I get ready and walk to the living room. I trip over Chance and land on an empty couch, besides the blankets and sheets folded nicely at the end. Scott must have left super early.

Chance jumps up. "Sorry." He lets out a yawn. "Do you know what time it is?"

"About seven."

"Crap, I've got work."

"I'll walk you out. I'm leaving too." He looks back at the bedroom. "She'll call you when she wakes up. When she keeps Annika, I don't allow guy friends over." He nods.

***

I walk in and Caroline looks over her glasses at me, extremely giddy over something. She's busting at the seams. I think back to Saturday. *I bet it's Macy and Delilah.*

She shakes her pencil in my direction. "So, you sneaky thing you. How did you keep something so fine secret for so long?"

Fine? "Are you talking about Scott?"

She sticks the pencil back in her hair. "Am I talking about Scott?" She giggles. "Of course I'm talking about Scott. Natalie, he sure is nice to look at, and he is just as sweet as can be. You really caught a good one. You better hang on tight. I could almost see drool coming from some of those ladies." She pauses. "I might have been one of them." She laughs and waves her arm.

"I only have eyes for Rob." She smiles. "We've got a slow day today. Once you get those invoices entered in the system. You can go on home. We'll need you tomorrow though."

I start on the invoices, and she starts on the next gossip. "Can you believe about Macy? I've known Delilah since she was a little girl. It was obvious she"- she looks away from me-"you know." Then she looks back at me, "But, I had no idea about Macy. I wonder how Missy is taking the news?"

I think about Missy and Mallory and I wonder how they're both doing.

As I'm pulling away from work, my phone goes off. It's Muneca, but I don't think anything because we have become really good friends. We text, if not everyday, at least every other day. Before I go into my mom's, I check my message. The twinge hits my cheeks first. My right arm is next. Finally, the goosebumps prickle up until they have covered most of my body.

"Anna is reaching out through Karisa again, and it has happened three times today. I can't take it anymore. Can you meet us tonight?"

"I got off work early. Can I come now?"

"Perfect."

I text my mom, "Hey, Mama I got off early, but I have to run an errand. Can you keep Annika? I should get home around the same time."

"What errand?" I knew she was going to ask. "Scott? ;)"

I could have called that. "No, Mama, Karisa is going through something, and I need to go help Muneca."

"Sure, fine, go ahead. I'm making dinner, so don't worry about it."

I let out a huge sigh of relief. "Thank you, Mama."

I get to Muneca's, and she pulls me inside. She looks sick, but I know it's actually because of stress. "Karisa is okay. She doesn't remember anything. The episodes have been short, but I just feel like if she could get it all out with you, maybe they will stop. It terrifies me when it happens."

Karisa is excited to see me, and she loves the bracelet I stopped and got her on the way. It's made of colorful beads, and I was actually able to find one with her name on it. But she is also disappointed that I don't have Annika.

We go to the back room, and I know what to do this time. I just follow Karisa's lead. Then it happens. I can make out a little girl. I see Anna. There's a man, and I can feel the trust she has for him. I feel the love she has for him.

She is bobbing back and forth, up and down. She's in a boat, a small fisherman's boat. Then she is going up steps, up, up, up. I'm following her, but then it is silent, and everything blacks out. I don't fight the silence. Instead, I listen.

"Natalie, you're so close. You can see this on your own. The little girl won't see anything, but you have to keep coming with me. Follow me, Natalie. You're so close, PLEASE." The goosebumps rise from my legs, and I find it funny I am able to feel them when I am not able to physically feel anything else. I feel scared, terrified actually. I don't know if I can handle what I'm going to see if I go, but if I don't, Anna might keep calling out to Karisa. I take a deep breath, open my eyes, and listen.

She gets to the room at the top of the stairs. There's a blanket and a candle thrown on the floor.

"Are you sure you want to do this?" I hear a voice that seems familiar, but the echo distorts it enough so that I can't put my finger on it. She willingly gets down on the blanket, but she isn't expecting what's to come. It blacks in and out. All I can see are her arms, but it is apparent that someone is taking advantage of her.

She gets up. "I love you." Her statement sounds like a question. "I really *love you?*"

His body is only a shadow to me, but his voice rises, "You're not a flower, Anna. You're not my flower. You're an imposter. You're a weed, and we can't have weeds. It's all wrong here, and you're invasive." Then he picks up a blunt object and slams it. Everything goes black.

I come to in a sweat. I'm panting and shaking. Muneca is in the room, but Karisa is gone. I can hardly think or even talk. "Karisa?" I'm worried about Karisa.

Muneca gets a warm towel and rubs my face. "She is fine. She doesn't remember anything. She had no tears, nothing. She is fine. She's in the other room with Raul." I nod my head. "But I was getting worried about you. Karisa has already been in the other room for at least ten minutes. I thought something happened to you." She hugs me and keeps rubbing my face.

"I think I continued the vision on my own. Anna must have used Karisa to let me in, but then she called to me to keep following her, to keep going. I saw it, Muneca. I saw everything. I know what happened."

I start to cry as I remember the first time I saw Anna, as I recall her mother's face at the funeral, as I remember my mom pulling me into my room as she told me about Anna. I cry for the life I envisioned Anna having. I cry for the wonder of what she would be doing now. As a mother myself now, I cry for the loss of a thirteen-year-old baby. I cry for Anna.

Muneca comforts me. "There. there, you have to remember we are going to help her, okay? We are helping her. She is going to be so happy and free when all this is over.

"But what does she want from me?!? Why is she DOING THIS TO ME!?!" I look at Muneca, as she holds me in her arms, "What does she want?"

She looks me dead in my eyes. "She wants you to find him."

Chapter 25: After the Storm

Thunder rumbles, and lightning slashes through the darkness of my room. My walls surrender to the thunder's wrath as they violently shake with each *BOOM*. I can hear the rain falling fast and hard. I pull Annika close and kiss her sweetly. She doesn't even stir. The storm seems to just be rocking her as she sleeps.

I get the shivers and check the weather on my phone. We're under a tornado watch until 5 a.m. I check the time, only 45 minutes. I say a prayer, and then Anna comes to mind. It's been about a month since my last vision with Karisa. I've torn myself up trying to figure out who it could have been. I pull the blue notebook out from under my side of the bed and run my hand across the top. I don't have to open it. I have it memorized. There is a drawing of the lighthouse and some handwritten words: fishing boat, blunt object, and love. That's all I've got. I just don't know the answer, and I'm too tired to try to start the endless circle now.

My phone goes off. It's Scott. "Are you okay?"

"Yes, hopefully it'll pass soon."

"I think the worst is over."

"I hope so."

"I wish I could be there for you. I'm on call three more days. Then we should have some time."

"Okay, I'll see you soon."

It's also been about a month since I've spent time with Scott. We have got together here and there, never longer than an hour. His schedule keeps him pretty busy. Although I miss him, I also savor the fact that I still get a lot of alone time with Annika. I can't believe she is going to be three in four days.

I think about the day she was born. She was perfect. I think about the time I felt her first tooth. "Mama, feel, feel right there. Do you feel it?" My mama said she couldn't feel it, but I knew it was there. I remember the first time she crawled. She took off trying to get to Bri. Bri was so excited. I remember her first steps. Roxy wanted her first steps to happen when she was there so bad, and she was actually able to coax Annika right to her. I remember Annika the day Afton died. I remember when she started getting visions. I remember when she left Scott hanging and went in for a hug instead. I remember how much she loves my mom and our family. I remember how sweet, caring, and thoughtful she is. I remember how she becomes concerned for others, even more so than what she is feeling herself. I remember how she fell asleep last night, in my arms, just as she has always done.

Her sweet cheeks that are starting to thin out, her plump, dusty rose lips, her long eyelashes, her ever growing blonde ringlets falling around her just so. Holding her is like holding an angel. I get a little teary-eyed thinking about how fast she is growing, and I long to find a way to press pause and hold her just a little while longer.

The storm finally starts to slowly turn down the volume, fading away. Finally, the storm passes. A knock vibrates the front door. *Roxy.*

"Hey, I'm just going to watch Annika here. Mama is going to go have lunch with Bri and Braiden today." I look at my watch.

"You're early." Although it's a statement, my pitch rises at the end as though it's a question.

"Yeah, Chance had to leave for work, so he dropped me off on his way."

My eyebrows rise. "Hmmmm," slips from my lips.

"What?" She frowns.

"Nothing, it just seems like he is really good for you. He makes you a better version of yourself, not just because of this, but overall you've really changed for the better. I think he is good for you."

"Well, gee thanks, Dr. Natalie," she says sarcastically. She beams as she pushes by me and inside the house. "Hey, did the storm wake you up?"

"Yeah, it felt like a train was driving right through my living room."

"It didn't wake me up." She shrugs. "Chance couldn't sleep though. He's kind of a baby."

"Remember no candy until after lunch. She will try to manipulate you," I warn, "and no funny business."

"Fine."

"I mean it, Roxy. I don't feel comfortable with her trying to tap into the gift when I'm not here."

"Okay, okay. We'll see you later. Have a good day."

I sternly look at her. She holds up both hands. "I promise."

The weather is muggy and the broken tree limbs I pass on the way to work catch my attention. It's calm now, but the evidence of the storm lingers on. It's kind of like the gift. It comes passing through like a raging storm. Although it leaves, the leftover details continually remind you of the damage it caused. I don't know why Anna couldn't just tell me who it was. *Who was it?*

I make it to the office before Caroline and water the plants, take out the trash, and open up all the blinds by the time she walks in.

"Hey, Nat. We are going to have a busy day today. First off, Rob and his crew finished that guest house for Mr. Roverts, so we are all going out together to look at it. Rob's pretty proud of it." She doesn't even take a breath to catch up, she rattles on, "I'll need you to make the punch, and I brought my cookies." She holds up a sheet of her cookies. "These are for us. I've got theirs in the car." I smile.

"Thank you, Caroline. You know, I really think you should open a bakery."

She stops and ponders something. "You know, I always wanted to open a bakery." She pauses and shakes her head. "Who would run this place?" she says more to herself than to me.

Turning back to me, she continues, "After that we've got to go try to get Mr. Tom to sign off on the quote to turn his old shop into a dance hall." She taps her pencil on her desk. "Yep, it's going to be a busy day." She pulls out her pocket mirror and smiles, revealing some lipstick on her teeth. She wipes her teeth, uses her lipstick for blush, and then fluffs her hair. "And Natalie, I know Mr. Roverts is vile, but we are just going to kill him with kindness." She smiles and makes an okay-I-can-do-this face, as if convincing herself more than me.

I knew Mr. Roverts lived in a big house, but as we drive down the paved drive-way my mouth falls open as my eyes land on the mansion in front of me. As if right on cue, a tall, thin man with black hair and small eyes walks out the towering double front doors. There are huge plants on each side of the doors planted in pots that look like decor, very expensive decor. He makes his way to our vehicle and greets us, "Well, hello there, ladies."

"Mr. Roverts," Caroline says in her happy phone voice. She even gets a twinkle in her eye. I don't think she could be mean even if she tried. "I baked you some cookies, and Natalie ran to the store and put together some delicious punch."

Rob and Mr. Roverts shake hands. Mr. Roverts smiles a crooked smile. "You did a really nice job, yes indeed. You know, I originally had this built for my daughter, but it seems her attention span is shorter than mine. She's already been on her way. Last postcard I received came all the way from Mexico." His old southern accent is slow, drawn out, but still very proper. His laugh is unsettling. He walks us around the main house and into the backyard. We stop in front of a pavilion. "Come on in, we'll partake in these delicacies at the table." He calls out the door, "Harry, Harry, retrieve Veronica. She is in the main house."

"Yes, sir."

Their yard man carefully puts down his shovel and walks toward the house.

A beautiful Spanish woman enters and has a seat with us, but she doesn't speak. She smiles and sits quietly. She is wearing a lovely sun dress that cinches in at her tiny waist. Her black hair, perfectly curled, falls below the braided, wide-brim sun hat. Her bright, green eyes are piercing. She waves politely, and then he continues. "I will definitely be referring you to my friends." It's hard to believe this man has friends. "These cookies are absolutely amazing." He looks at his wife. "Aren't they, Veronica?" He emphasizes the first part of her name. I just sit quietly, smile, and listen. Veronica only nods.

"Well, that wasn't so bad." I shake my head.

"I still can't stand the man, myself." Caroline goes on. Rob and I just sit quietly as Caroline vents all the way to the office.

"Y'all girls be safe." We smile. He kisses Caroline and then waves to me. Then pulls off to go to his job site. We grab the quote and head to Mr. Tom's. It only takes two of Caroline's cookies before Mr. Tom caves and approves the quote.

The sun starts to come out, and it ends up being a beautiful day, totally opposite from the horrific storm that started it. For some reason, everything looks happier, brighter, and even cleaner. I pull into my driveway behind Tori's car.

I walk up and let myself in. "Roxy, I need to know!" Tori's usual very put together appearance seems frazzled.

"Tori, calm down and just listen to me."

I walk in behind them and my lips smile, but my eyes scream with concern, "Is everything okay?"

Tori turns to me and starts shouting. "Did she tell you?" Then she looks at Roxy. "Did you tell her?" Roxy sulks and shrugs. "I was at Mama's yesterday, and I overheard *that boy,* the one that is living over at our Mama's house with Roxy"- Tori lets out a disgusted sigh and holds up a hand-"I won't get started on that right now, but that boy is trying to talk Roxy into keeping the baby. If she is going to decide to keep it, I will support her. I will, but I just can't go on an emotional roller coaster. I just can't."

I empathize with Tori because I know she wants the baby. Just like me, when she falls, she falls hard. It's all or nothing with her. However, I also empathize with Roxy because there is no way I could have given up Annika, and I know that hearing the heartbeat could've changed Roxy's heart. I look at Roxy with big eyes and cross my arms, I whisper, "Is it true?"

"Yeah, I mean no. I mean I don't know." Her shoulders rise and then fall. "If she'd just let me talk." She stares down Tori.

I lean back and push open the door to my bedroom. *Annika's not here.* "Where's Annika?"

"I texted you, Mama went ahead and came and got her, so she could go to lunch with Braiden and Bri. Then Mama took them all back to her house."

I nod. *I didn't get a text.*

"Like, I've been trying to say, if she'd just listen." Roxy points to Tori. "I'm not keeping the baby. Chance did try to talk me into it, and he said he'd help. But, I know we are both young, and I'm not even sure if what we have will last. I love the baby so much. I do, and when I heard the heartbeat, I fell in love. I did, but I can't keep him."

Tori and I exchange a glance. I speak up, "Him?"

Roxy shrugs. "I haven't had that ultrasound yet, but it feels like a boy. Anyway, it is true that Chance tried to talk me into it, but it's not true that I have had second thoughts. Tori, I told you this baby is yours, and I meant it with my whole heart."

Tori falls onto the couch. "I'm sorry. I've just been so emotional. Then I heard that, and then I even started thinking about Jace. What if he tries to come back?"

Roxy smiles and sits down next to Tori, pulling her purse on top of herself. She digs in and pulls out a piece of paper. "After Chance saw how nervous I got about Jace not finding out about the baby, he told me that Jace met an older woman and started traveling. He told me he was sure he would be more than happy to sign his rights over because he wouldn't want to mess things up with his new chick. Apparently, she's loaded. It actually took me awhile to find him because he's in Mexico, but look at this." Roxy hands the paper over to Tori. "Bastard signed his rights over. The baby is yours, Tori." Roxy smiles and puts her arms around Tori, and Tori falls into them.

"Becky!" They both look at me puzzled. "Jace...he is with Becky. We met at Mr. Rovert's today to see Rob's finished work, and he said that his daughter was in Mexico." They both look at each other with disgusted expressions.

"She's old!" Roxy scrunches her nose.

Then Tori hits her with a pillow. "Hey, not *that* old."

Chapter 26: And Just Like That She's Three

I longingly look at the calendar and finally cross out the day, March 28th. I think about the day Annika was born, when they laid her on top of me, her first cry, her clenched fists, beautiful and perfect in my eyes. Although she looked the same as most newborns, her cry set her apart from the others. I could always tell when it was her the nurses were pushing down the hall, *a mother's love.*

"Mama, did you get the cupcakes? Mama, Mama!"

She sets her phone down. "Calm down, Natalie, I got them."

"Roxy, did you get the balloons?"

The bubble she's blowing pops. "I texted you earlier. Chance is going to grab them on his way over, remember?"

I look at my phone. I don't have any messages. "You texted?"

"Um, yeah," she says, irritated.

"Look, I didn't get anything." I shove my phone in her face, and she looks it over. "This happened the other day, too. I think my phone is messing up." I hold it close, not sure exactly what I'm inspecting or trying to find, so I jump when it lets out a loud ring. "Thank God, it's Tori!" I know she'll have everything under control.

"Hello, what??? Oh no!" I look at my mom with tears in my eyes.

"What's wrong, Nat?"

"Tori had a leak and part of her backyard flooded. We're expecting too many people to fit in her house. I wanted today to be perfect." It's not like me to get upset over things, but I wanted the best for Annika.

Roxy smacks her gum. "Natalie, it'll still be perfect. Hey! I know! What about Mr. Tom's place?"

I shake my head. "Rob started, so it's already a construction site."

"Well, let's just have it here."

I look at Roxy. "At my house?"

"Yeah, why not? You've got a big yard and a nice-size kitchen."

I nod. "Okay, okay, I think that'll work."

My mom chimes in, "Of course it'll work. Here, help me grab this table and move it like this. There we go, and now I'll move the living room furniture to Annika's room. Rox, put that down, you don't need to be carrying anything."

"I'm pregnant, not helpless."

"I said put it down!"

"Fine!"

"Nat, call Tori and tell her to bring the party here."

I look around. My mom can come in like a tornado and get things up, going, and finished, faster than I can even get off the couch. Every..Single..Time. Her energy and strength amazes me again.

Tori shoves the front door open, letting herself in. Mallory follows behind her with some chairs. They both kiss me on my cheek. Tori starts giving orders and morphs my living room into a boutique-styled birthday party room in less than an hour, absolutely picture perfect from every angle. She stands back and admires her work.

"It's perfect, Tori, thank you." I give her a huge side hug.

She smiles and pats my arm. "This might be my best yet."

Mallory raises her hand. "Hey Nat, do you have a guestlist?"

"No, not a formal one."

"That's fine. Just tell us who all you invited. We'll separate the list, so we know how many goody bags we need to get started."

"Muneca, Raul, and Karisa; you, Ben, and Benjamin; Tor, Brandon, Braiden and Bri; Mama, Rox, Chance; Mr.

Collins; Caroline and Rob; Scott, and I invited Scott's parents, but I'm not sure they'll be able to make it."

"Mr. Tom."

Eyes land on my mom. "What?"

She looks at us and then looks away, keeping her hands busy with nothing. "I said, Mr. Tom."

We all share a glance. "Mr. Tom is coming?"

She nods, walks to the kitchen, and starts washing the dishes. Mallory, Tori, Rox, and I just stand and look at each other, puzzled. My mom's voice floats over to me, "Natalie, it's time to get Annika dressed. Don't you think?"

I shake my head, freeing myself from the puzzled trance. "Yeah, okay."

"Scott's here," my mom calls from the kitchen. "Since he's early maybe he can help out. We still need someone to get the piñata ready and finish setting the tables and chairs up outside."

I nod, but I'm not thrilled about asking him to do anything. I haven't seen him since he got off, and I don't want to put pressure on him.

Turns out I don't have to. "Hey beautiful, I just woke up. I've missed you, and I thought that if I got here early I could help out." He pulls me behind a tree and kisses me sweetly, holding me around my waist.

"Thank you. We just have to unload the rest of the tables and chairs from Brandon's truck. Later, could you help with the piñata?" He nods.

Everyone arrives around the same time, except for Muneca. Scott is holding Annika at the window, pointing to Karisa's truck as it pulls in. Then we notice a black luxury car following behind. "Hey, Annika, there's Pop and Rhonna," he says excitedly.

"Natalie, when you told me you wanted to go to my mom's out of the blue that day, I thought it was pretty crazy, but then after what ended up happening with my Pop, well, it made a lot more sense. It's funny, too, because not only that, but my mom really warmed up to you." I smile, and he pulls me close. "I knew she couldn't resist falling in love with you and Annika," he says as he kisses my cheek, "and she did."

Annika runs to Karisa and grabs onto her waist. Muneca kisses my cheek. Raul shakes my hand and then Scott's. Scott kisses his mom on her cheek as she enters right behind. His dad pulls him in for a strong, one-handed hug because on his other arm he's carrying a tricycle.

Annika runs from Karisa to them. "Pop, Rhonna!"

"Hey there, doll, this is for you!"

Annika's eyes grow big. "I love it! Thank you!!" She smiles from ear to ear.

"Hey, Pop, why don't you join us outside?" Scott doesn't give his dad a choice and keeps talking, nodding his head in my mom's direction, "Mom, you remember Ms. Haven, don't you?"

My mom pulls her hands out of the sink, dries them, and puts one on Scott's chest. "Oh now Scott, please, I've told you, it's Vanna." My mom waves to Rhonda. "How do you take your tea, dear?"

"Unsweet with lemon please." My mom sets a glass in front of her. "And you remember Caroline, don't you?"

Scott walks out with Pop, Raul, Karisa, and Annika to meet Brandon. Rob, Mr. Tom, and Mr. Collins stand in the background admiring the trucks from afar.

"You don't think Mama is talking to Mr. Tom? Do you?" Tori asks. I shrug.

Roxy informs, "I haven't seen him over at the house."

"Yeah, me neither."

We all stop and realize at the same time that Chance has stayed with us girls.

Roxy turns to Mallory and says, "So, what did you think about your aunt and Delilah anyway?"

"Roxy!" Tori's voice overlaps mine.

"What!?" "No, it's fine. Really, I mean I kind of wondered because she never dated anyone, but then again I just didn't think she was into anyone. I'm totally fine with it, and I've already hung out with them on two occasions. Delilah is really cool actually. She's traveled all over the world."

"What about your mom?"

"Roxy!"

Mallory calmly looks at me and Tori. "Guys, really, it's okay. Well, believe it or not, she is the one that invited them over that first time I was around them. She's trying, but it's not coming naturally. She'll warm up though."

We all nod in agreement.

"Wait, so your aunt is a *lesbian*?" Chance catches on.

Mallory slightly turns her head and her eyes glance sideways. She puckers her lips and slowly nods her head.

"Right on!" Roxy pushes him.

"Everyone, it's time to sing Happy Birthday," Tori calls from the front door. Everyone files in. Annika goes to my mom first and my heart sinks, but then she holds out her arms for me. I grab her and hug her at the same time. Scott turns off the lights, and the candles twinkle in the darkness. "Happy Birthday to you, Happy Birthday to you…"

"Okay, Annika, on the count of three make a wish and blow out your candles." I kiss her on top of her head. "One,

Two, Three!" The sound of applause fills the air. I look around the room and take everyone in. Everyone here means so much to me and has supportingly gone on this journey of young motherhood with me. Annika and I wouldn't be where we are today if it wasn't for everyone in this room. I am so grateful for every single one of them.

Annika passes out her cupcakes. "Oh my goodness, this cupcake is absolutely divine," Rhonda says.

"It's like a piece of heaven," Pop finishes.

I look over at Caroline, who's trying to be modest. "Caroline made them."

Rhonda goes on, "Oh my goodness, dear, I think this is the best cupcake I've ever had."

Pop finishes, "Me too, and I've been around a long time, so that's really saying something." Everyone starts to laugh.

Annika pulls Karisa to the kids' table with Benjamin, Bri, and Braiden. I watch as Annika and Braiden lick the icing off theirs, Bri delicately takes small bites that would make her mama proud, and Karisa takes off all the icing and just eats the cake. Then they start talking and laughing. I wonder what they could even be talking about it.

All the adults stay inside to eat their cupcakes. Good conversation fills the air. Caroline's comfort holds onto to everyone, and you can even taste the love in her cupcakes. Roxy's irrational outbursts make everyone laugh; my mom leads most of the discussions; Rhonda and Pop fit right in; Muneca captivates everyone; Mr. Tom sits quietly and takes everything in; Scott sits beside me politely; Mallory and Ben hang on to each other throughout the entire evening. Brandon stands behind Tori, and you can see by the way he looks at her how proud he is. It's absolutely perfect and feels just so real. Nothing is fake. Nothing is exaggerated. It just simply **is**.

We wave to everyone as they leave. Scott had to leave with his parents, so he could help them get settled at his place.

Tori had to get the kids home. Lord forbid they miss their bedtime. Then it's just Annika and me.

"I love you Mommy, always and forever. Thank you for my birthday."

I kiss her and pull her into my lap. "I love you, Annika, more than anything, and I will forever and always."

"I know Mommy."

As hard as I try to fight it, a tear escapes and rolls down my cheek. *Afton.*

"Mommy, don't cry, Daddy's with the angels now." I look at her, astonished. She's told me that before. "He is Mommy, and he is always watching over."

I hold her tightly until she tries to break away. *His promise.*

"Did you have a good party, sweet girl?" She nods her head. "What was your favorite?" She pulls a doily out from under her. "Where did you find that?"

"Nanny," she giggles.

"Where did you get it? Did you find it?" She pulls me over to an old chest I use for decoration.

"It was in here, from Nanny," she proudly says, as she twists side to side. There's an eerie feeling. At the same time, I'm comforted, and Annika's smile eases my chills. I nod. Annika crawls in my lap, and it isn't long before she is out. It was a long day, and she played hard with all her favorite people. Her little arm is still pulled up around my neck. The other clenching to the beautiful dolly. I almost hear my Nanny's voice, "Where there's a will, there's a way."

All of the sudden my chest tightens, and my house seems to go black. I hold Annika as tight as I can. Physical awareness leaves me, and I'm spun into another time. "Natalie, this is taking too long." *Anna.* "I want this to be over!" she is crying, "Please!"

Someone starts shaking me. I open my eyes and see Annika asleep on the couch across from me. I'm on the floor.

"NATALIE!" Roxy shakes me harder.

"What?"

"Natalie, what happened? What's going on?!?"

I look at her. I haven't shared all this about Anna with anyone other than Muneca and only to ask my mom about the lighthouse.

"Natalie, you're scaring the fuck out of me. What's going on?"

"What was I doing?"

"I don't know. You looked zoned out and were just muttering and kind of shaking, rocking back and forth. What is it?!?"

I look at her again. "It's Anna."

Fear strikes her eyes. Her shoulders pull forward, and her head goes back. "Dead Anna??!!?"

Chapter 27: Mary Anne

Pushed up against the wall, we both sit in silence. Roxy leans over and drapes her arms over me. I break down, and Roxy holds on tight.

"So you saw Anna on your own?" She whispers the words. I nod. "Is that something new?"

I shake my head and shrug. "I'm not like Annika, if that's what you mean."

She doesn't ask for clarification. Instead, she nods and holds on tighter. She releases and stares into my eyes. "So what was happening?"

I take a deep breath. It's my choice to tell or not tell. I close my eyes and open them slowly. "Anna has been coming to me. She showed me where she died. She died in the lighthouse. She showed me how she got there and what happened once inside." I take a deep breath. A whisper escapes my lips, "She was raped, and then he killed her."

Silence once again fills the air. Roxy licks her lips and swallows hard, "Who?"

I stare into her eyes now. "That's what she's trying to tell me. That's what she needs me to figure out."

Someone knocks on the door, and we both jump. "Chance, it's Chance. He was waiting in the car. We forgot our keys." She shouts at the door, "Come in!" She walks over to the counter and picks them up, giving them a jingle. She tosses the keys to Chance. "Hey, babe, I'll be out in a minute." He looks at me, and my frazzled state reflects in his eyes staring back at me. Roxy walks over as he turns around to go back to the car, and she slaps his butt. He turns around giving a half smile, and she bites her lip. *Gross*

She walks back over to me. "Are you going to be okay by yourself?"

"I'll be fine. I'm used to it."

"You sure?"

"Yeah."

She turns to leave but stops at the door. "What about Mary Anne?"

Almost as if it's a reflex, and even though I know the answer, I ask, "Anna's mom?"

She nods. "That might help."

I nod. "Thanks, Roxy."

"Love you, always and forever."

"I love you too, Rox, forever and always."

***

It has taken me a month to build up the courage to call Mary Anne. She moved out of this town right after Anna's death; she had to drive in for the funeral. The phone starts to ring. Roxy sits beside me nodding her head in a rhythm, telling me to let it ring, not to hang up, and she has a hand resting on my leg for support.

A lady answers. I lose my breath. Roxy squeezes my leg, and I slightly jump. Then I hiccup out, "Mary Anne, hello, this is Natalie, Natalie Haven." Sobs meet me on my end of the line. I listen to them. I listen to the pain in the gasps. I listen to the pain in the sobs. I listen.

"Well?!?"

"She said I could make a drive to her place tomorrow."

"Well, do you want me to go with you?"

I shake my head. "I think it's something I need to do on my own, Rox."

Roxy nods. "I'm proud of you for calling."

"Yeah, I'm pretty proud too." I smile.

"So you're going to drive all the way by yourself?"

"No, I don't think so, Mary Anne lives about 3 1/2 hours out, and it's on the way to Charles and Rhonda's house. Maybe Scott can drop me off and take Annika for a visit."

"You two sure have cozied up here lately. You haven't broken your sleepover rule, have ya?" She looks at me deviously.

I roll my eyes. "No, I have not. I have to think about Annika."

"Yeah, you're right, but I can't believe you haven't had his fine ass stay yet."

I hit her with the accent pillow I had been clenching. "Hey!"

"Mommy, I love you." I look into Annika's blue eyes that look at me, seeing all her hopes and dreams, and they all seem to surround me. She's still small enough that I am her hero in a sense.

"I love you too, sweet girl, a bushel and a peck and a hug around the neck."

"Hey, that's Nanny!"

I smile and nod. "You're right. That is Nanny."

I finish snapping her car seat and climb in the front seat with Scott. "Ready?" He turns to me and smiles, revealing his dimples and that jawline that makes me hot. I nod and smile.

"Mommy, Scott, are we there yet?" It's the fifth time she's asked, but Scott doesn't lose his patience.

"Nope, no we aren't almost there, but there is an ice cream place at the next stop. You don't want ice cream do you?"

"YES, PLEASE! Ice cream! Ice cream! Ice cream! Yummy for my tummy."

Scott pulls in, and we get out. He already knows her order by memory and mine too. Annika and I sit waiting in a booth across from each other by the window. She called sitting by Scott.

I look at her in amazement. I think about how perfect she is, how cute she looks in the tiny, light blue and white romper, complete with frills around the thighs, a gift from Tori, of course, how sweet her voice sounds as she calls out, "Bird" each time one hops around, picking at all the french fries in the parking lot like it's an all you can eat buffet.

All of the sudden, before I can stop her, she turns around in her seat and taps the boy behind her. "Your pawpaw loves you, and he misses you so much, but you don't have to worry because he's always with you."

The little boy, who looks about eight, looks back at Annika and his jaw drops. His mother sits up tall, and the mother bear comes through in her voice, "What did you say?"

Annika repeats herself louder and prouder, "His pawpaw loves him and misses him so much, but he doesn't have to worry because he's always here." It's happening so fast. Even though I thought I would always have the power to catch Annika, I don't have time to react. I wasn't fast enough, and it's as if I just let her fall.

The mother's jaw drops, matching her son's. She looks at me. "Ma'am, I don't know what…"

Her stern voice is interrupted by Annika, and I'm frozen. All I can do is watch it happen. "The windowsill, you know that ol' windowsill in the kitchen? You know which one I mean. Well, it's broke, and if ya just lift it up, well, you'll find it right there."

The mother covers her mouth and tears stream down her face. I'm left analyzing Annika's tone and her speech, not hers at all.

I quickly grab Annika and bring her to my side. "I'm so, so sorry. I don't know what..."

The woman puts a hand up, stopping me. "That was him. That was my dad. How did she do that?"

"I really don't know." I shrug. Annika tugs on me and whispers in my ear. "She wants me to give you my phone number, would that be okay?"

The woman nods. "Okay."

I scribble down my number on a napkin, too shook up to realize she could've taken it right into her cell phone. I hand it over to her. "

"My goodness." She looks at me. "She is a gift from God, that child." She smiles.

A year ago I would have died if I had pictured myself in this situation, but one thing I've realized about Annika is that she knows when it's okay, and she knows when to fight it. I've also learned to listen, so when she asked me to give this stranger my number, I listened.

Scott comes up holding all three ice creams.

"Oh, sorry."

"I've got it just fine. There we go." Annika starts talking right away about nothing, and Scott answers her back and keeps her conversation company. I'm lost in my daydreams.

The woman across from us grabs her purse and pulls her son under her arm. As they walk out side by side, she pats me on my shoulder and gives me a kind smile and nod. I smile back.

"What was that about?" Scott asks, more interested in the big bite he's trying to get into his mouth.

"Their Pawpaw misses them," Annika lets out.

Scott looks at me. "Ah, that's what all this is about. It happened again?" I nod. "Yep, I should've guessed by the way Annika was all hyped up, and you were dazed out."

"It's happening more, Scott, and it happens so fast I can't stop it."

He squeezes Annika's cheek and looks at her, talking to me, "She's a smart girl, Natalie." He turns his gaze back to me. "She knows when to share and when to hide. Don't ya, sweet girl?" Annika lets out a giggle.

"Are you sure you don't want me to walk you up?"

"I've got to do this on my own."

"Okay, we'll be back to get you in about three hours."

"Okay."

"I love you, Natalie." He kisses my cheek.

"I love you too."

"I love you, Mommy, forever and always."

"I love you too, sweet girl, always and forever."

As I walk up to the door, I think about how I never reached out to her before the call. I always meant to send cards. My mama and Tori send cards twice a year, once on Anna's birthday and once for *the day*. But, I couldn't bring myself to do it. It's like I would be admitting she's really gone, and I had tried to live like she had just moved away, moved away with her mom. *It was selfish. I should have sent cards.*

The door creaks open and a petite woman with curly, red hair, green eyes, and freckles meets me. "Natalie!" She pulls me in for a hug and some tears escape from her eyes.

I turn back and wave to Scott, so he knows it's okay for him to leave. "I'm so sorry I haven't reached out to you before."

She keeps a tight grip on my shoulders but pulls me back so our eyes meet. "Nonsense, we all grieve in different ways, Natalie. I know you were one of us hit the hardest." Tears meet my eyes. "Now, now, there, there, we won't get anywhere if we just sit around cry." She invites me in. I try my hardest to smile.

I'm socially awkward, and I had turned my body into a sweatshop, literally, thinking about how our meeting would go today. All I did morning, noon, and night was come up with different scenarios with one common aspect; no matter what happened, I had always put myself in a difficult position, but this wasn't like that at all. Instead, the hours flew by as we reminisced. They flew by as she pulled out old photos and shared with me the cards my family had sent her over the years. Our drinks were emptied and filled while the walls had echoed with both laughter and cries. Her tiny, cozy living room comforted us, and her sweet pie was like a dream catcher, catching all the bad, only letting in the good. Scott would be pulling up anytime. Almost like when you can sense whether or not a TV is on in a room without any sound or picture escaping from it, I sense Scott pulling up. I look out the window and confirm my belief.

"Mary Anne, it's time for me to go. My ride's here."

She smiles and starts to stand up. "It was so nice for you to come by. I really enjoyed it. Please don't be a stranger. You can come anytime. You're always welcome, and this was just so nice. It really was and much needed."

I hug her tight. "I'll be back. Next time, I'll bring Annika."

Excitement fills her eyes, and she grabs my hand. "Oh yes, please do." Her smile fades as she begins to ponder something. "Hey Natalie, I didn't keep much of Anna's things. Sometimes I regret it, but most days I don't. I just couldn't handle having all her stuff here with me but not having her. It was bad for my heart, but I did keep something." She stops and pulls out a small book from under her coffee table. She grabs my hands and opens them up, placing the tiny book in them. "I want you to have it, Natalie." I look at it and then look at her. I can tell there's no talking her out of it. "The detectives gave it back after it turned up nothing."

I kiss her cheek. "Thank you."

She waves big as we pull out of the driveway, and I keep waving back to her, even after we've pulled back onto the road.

"Did you find what you were looking for?" Scott's voice interrupts my thoughts.

I look in my hands at the tiny book I'm still clenching. I open it to the first page, *"Dear Diary,"*

I smile. "Yeah, I think I did."

Chapter 28: Dear Diary

Dear Diary, I miss my dad. I'm not sure why he left us, why he left me. It hurts so bad. I highlighted that part. *Dear Diary, I wonder if my dad thinks of me.* I highlighted that part. *Dear Diary, Today Natalie and I dressed up in her sister's clothes and put on makeup. Her mom is so cool. She let us drive her car out in the field. I almost crashed in a field.* I laugh as I remember that day.

Tori grabs the book out of my hands.

"Hey!"

"Natalie, really, for like the past two weeks since Scott's been back at work, all you've done is read and then reread that book. It's not healthy." She looks at me lovingly.

"She's right, Nat. I wasn't going to say anything, but you've really got to stop. When's the last time you showered?"

I frown at my mama. "I told you guys. I told you! Someone killed her!" I snap at them, "I have to figure out who it was." I finish sounding more like I'm losing hope than defensively. They all three look at me sympathetically.

Roxy speaks up, "Nat, Nat, look at me. If the answer was in there, and that's saying the detectives missed something, but if the answer was in there, don't you think you would've found it by now?"

I shrug and then start to cry. "Why would someone do this?"

Tori's motherly instinct takes over, so she switches gears, trying to help the situation, to help me. "Well, what do you have so far?"

I look at her through tears, and hope and hunger shine back through. "Well, at first, she talks a lot about her dad leaving. Then there's some stories about us in here." I flip through some of the pages. "All of us, see? And then towards the end she stops talking about her dad altogether, but instead starts talking about someone she called Papa. At first it seems he just gave her rides home from the store, so she wouldn't have to walk home carrying all her bags. Then he started well, look, *'Dear Diary, Today Papa took me out on the water, first time I've been in a boat. He told me that I reminded him of someone he used to know, but she was in heaven now. He told me that she had left him like my daddy left, so it was meant for us to find each other. Dear Diary, Papa brought me some candy today (always red, red like a rose he says). He told me he was proud of me for all the responsibilities I have. Dear Diary, Papa acted strange today, he told me that he was starting to love me too much. When he put my life jacket on, he touched my face with his hand and told me how I looked so much like someone he used to know, but then he stopped. When I caught the fish, I CAUGHT A FISH, he jumped up and said, "That's my girl." Dear Diary, I don't really want to go with Papa anymore, but I miss him too. Dear Diary, I don't think I'm going to go anymore...'* And that's it. Someone saw how much she missed having her dad in her life, and they used that against her. She loved this man. She trusted him, at least at first. He pulled her in, and once she fell, once he had her where he wanted her..." The tears start to burn my eyes once again.

"Shhhhh, shhhhhh, baby. It's okay. You've worked really hard, Natalie."

Roxy interrupts my mom, "Yeah, but like every guy that lives here has a boat, so it doesn't really give us much to go off of."

My mom frowns at Roxy. "Sh!" Then my mama looks at me convincingly. "We'll figure it out. We'll get there."

Annika comes back in from outside, and Bri and Braiden follow. "It's hot, Mommy. I'm thirsty?"

"Three cold drinks, coming up!" Tori smiles and slides off the counter. She pulls all three personalized cuppys down from the cabinet. "One for Braiden, one for Annika, and one for Bri."

They all gulp down the drink before she has time to sit down. "More please, Aunt Tori."

"Okay then, who needs more?" They all raise their cups. She gives them back their cups and a handful of popcorn each. Annika holds out a piece for me, and she giggles as I make pig noises and gobble it from her hand.

My text notification goes off, "Karisa wants to know if Annika can call when y'all get in?"

"Sure."

"I'm glad you texted back. I tried earlier and didn't hear anything. Your phone still messing up?"

I frown at my stupid phone. "Yeah, I'm sorry. We'll call when we get home."

"It is getting hot out. Are you still sure you want to walk home, Natalie?"

"Yeah, once the sun goes down a little it'll be cool enough."

"So, I hope you haven't let Scott get too distant. I haven't seen him in a while."

I look at my mama like, *really?* I decide to answer but only because that means I get to ask a question in return. "No, we talk everyday, and on some days we get to have lunch together. Annika hasn't got to see him in a while though." My turn, I look at my mom. "And what about Mr. Tom?" I say smiling like a fox watching it's dinner.

My mama blushes, not something you see everyday. Then she waves her hand in front of her face. "There's nothing there, so I invited him to Annika's party, big deal." All three of us laugh. My mama shakes her head. "You girls are being silly." She walks into the living room, but we all catch the sparkle in her eye.

"If they are boning, I don't know how because she is at home when she's supposed to be, and he hasn't been to the house."

Tori pops Roxy on the head with a cup towel. "Ew Gross! How are you and Chance?" Tori looks at Roxy, but I know every time she asks, she's really asking how's the baby and if it's still her's.

"We're good. Sometimes he is sooooo boorriiinnnngggg, but maybe that's good for me." She shrugs. "Hey, I'm having my last ultrasound in three weeks. I want all of you to come."

"Of course," Tori says happily. "I wouldn't miss it for the world."

I kiss her on the top of her head. "I'll be there. Just let me know the time."

Mama calls from the living room. "Are y'all going to find out what it is?"

Roxy looks at Tori. "Well you know, *Ms. Plan Everything* wants to of course, but I'd rather be surprised. I can't believe it, and I don't know how I got her to, but Tori's agreed to wait and be surprised."

I look at Tori, and she shrugs. As she eyes down Roxy, she says, "I do hate surprises." Her voice turns from sour to sweet, "But, I'll love this little surprise, boy or girl." She rubs Roxy's growing belly. "You really are cute pregnant. It's not fair. I always looked like a bloated whale."

"She is cute. Isn't she?" Mama calls to us again.

Tori whispers, "Y'all know she is listening to everything we are saying?" She says a little louder, "You know, I think I saw Mr. Tom's car at Mama's the other day."

"You most certainly did not. That man is a quiet, thin creature and not my type at all." We all three share a look. "He wears tennis shoes with slacks," she says in her defense.

"Alright Annika, you ready?"

"I want to stay with Aunt Tori, please, Mommy?"

"I've never slept without you. I don't think I can."

"Oh come on, Nat," Tori says pleadingly.

Roxy looks at me. "Chance and I can stay at your place." She looks at Annika. "I mean we can come keep you company for awhile."

"Please, Mommy!"

"Please, Aunt Nat Nat! Pretty please with sugar on top, please please with berries on top and chocol..."

"Okay, she can stay."

"Yay!" They all three run to me, nearly knocking me over as we all share one hug. "Bri, you owe me a big sundae though."

"Okay, tomorrow!" She wears a smile ear to ear.

"Tomorrow." I smile back.

"Did you want me and Chance to head over later?"

"Yeah, I'm not used to being all alone."

"No prob Bob." Roxy slugs me, "We'll be over after I pick him up from band practice."

I rub my arm. "Thanks." I pull her close and kiss her forehead, forever my baby sister. Baby sisters are like one of your own kids in certain ways. I know the way I feel about Rox is the same way Tor feels about us both. *Sisterly love.*

"Natalie, you call when you get home."

"Alright, Mama."

"And Rox, when you get to Nat's make sure you check in too."

"Yeah, yeah, yeah."

I step out into the air. It's cooled off enough to walk home, but it's still warm enough to soften butter. I feel the humidity heavy in the air, and my hair starts to frizz.

Roxy rolls down the window. "You sure you don't wanna ride?"

I shake my head. "Walking makes me feel good, accomplished, alive."

She rolls her eyes. "Whatever."

My thoughts fly. I think of Caroline and her baking, Mr. Roverts and his unpleasant stature, Rob and his generosity, Muneca and Karisa and how much I could use some of their limonada right now, Scott and his jawbone and those dimples, Annika, my sweet baby, my mama, is she hiding Mr. Tom somewhere? "Ow!" I pick myself up off the sidewalk.

29: Listen

"Hey Natalie, is that you? Are you okay?"

My knee stings and throbs at the same time. I pull my hand away, and the blood starts to run down. The deep pain brings tears to my eyes. I look up at the beautiful yard and perfect flowers. *Wow! I've already come a long way.* "Mr. Collins?"

"Yes, here let me take a look. You got yourself pretty good there, didn't you? We need to stop the bleeding, and that knee's probably going to get a pretty good bruise too."

I look down at my beat-up knee. He's right. "I've got some bandages back in the house."

Mr. Collins, I think to myself, *always so helpful and kind, animal lover, friend to all.* "Thank you so much, Mr. Collins."

He motions for me to sit down at the table. "You know I always thought I'd have grandchildren to heal." He holds up his first aid kit. "But, I guess life had a different story laid out for me." His voice is as soft as ever, and I can hear the anguish in his voice. I feel the spark of hope slamming into reality. "It's okay, Natalie, not your fault."

He smiles as he passes over the kit. I start with ointment and finish up with a bandage. "Looks much better, Natalie."

"Thank you, Mr. Collins."

"Glad I could help." He smiles kindly. I get up from the table. "You need a ride home?"

I look at him and then at my knee. That's probably the most probable thing to do. But before I can answer, something from behind me gets my attention. It's as if his living room is calling to me. "Actually, do you have anything to drink? I'm pretty thirsty."

"Well, I just made some tea. Didn't I, girlie? That's a good girl, Foxy."

I listen and I follow my instinct to the living room, making my way to his couch. There's a small box underneath the coffee table. Something is calling to me. Maybe Mr. Collin's had the answer here all along and didn't even know it. Maybe this can help solve Anna's death. I slowly pick up the box. As my hands glide across the top, part of me feels guilt for touching what's not mine, but part of me hungers for it, something fierce. I carefully start to lift the lid. I get an overwhelming feeling of pleasure, at the same an overwhelming feeling of intense pain. Passing through the garage and into his house flashes in my thoughts, the boat I let my hand glide across as we entered through his garage door. Something slices through me, and I see the words scratch themselves on the side of the boat that has red paint peeling off of it like a manicure that has seen better days. *Red like a rose.*

I think back to when we brought him chocolates. Annika was normal. She even wanted to help him feel better. I think back to the Valentine's party. Muneca said it couldn't be anybody there. It runs into me like a train. Mr. Collins was sick. He wasn't there. I start to feel lightheaded. The time he gave Annika the iris, how he mentioned weeds. I think back to Annika's birthday. Mr. Collins looked on from afar. I remember everyone singing happy birthday, all the faces flash in front of my eyes. In slow motion, I'm replaying the smiles, the applause, the love, the song filling the air. Mr. Collins wasn't there. Oh my God. He left early to come home to Foxy. Goosebumps rise from my legs and engulf my body. My eyes start to sting more than my knee. I try to set the box down quickly. I can sense him about to come around the corner with a coaster and my iced tea.

"OPEN IT!!! PLEASE OPEN IT!!" a voice echoes, *Anna's voice.*

I swing open the lid just in time for him to catch me. "What are you doing?" The words fly into me. Although I'm startled, another feeling plows into my stomach, followed by an uneasy heat that travels through my body, stopping my heart for a second, only to restart it in overdrive. More than anything, I become angry.

"It's her hair. Anna's hair?" I hold up the red lock. "H-h-h-how could you? She was a little girl. She was my best friend. She was a daughter?" I can feel my eyes turn cold. Hatred, a feeling that's new to me, takes over. "You killed her!" My mind tries to wrap around this. *Mr. Collins ??? How could it have been kind Mr. Collins? Am I wrong? No, I'm not.*

I listen.

RUN!

I hold onto the lock of hair like my life depends on it. I pull my cell phone out, trying to get my mama's number to come up. *Nothing. Stupid, stupid phone. I should have fixed it by now.*

"Now, Natalie, I would never." But his voice is different. It's uneasy, and it's all wrong. "Listen, Natalie, Anna reminded me of my late wife. She looked like her, acted like her, and even sounded like her. I tried to take Anna in under my wing." I can't move. I can't scream. It's like I'm living a nightmare. He walks a little closer to me. "Now, I tried to be her Papa."

Oh my God, that word, Papa.

"But she just started loving me too good. She wanted something I couldn't give her."

RUN!

I can't. I can't move, I say back to the voice in my mind.

"But, you see I gave into her." I look at him with disgust. "I gave into her, and it was all wrong. She wasn't my Elizabeth. She was an imposter."

I feel like I might pass out, or puke, or both. I try to stand firm, but I can't listen anymore.

Then his words slice into me like a jagged knife, knocking the breath from my chest. "I realized Anna's not a flower. She's a weed, and we couldn't have weeds. She was in the wrong spot. It was all wrong. She had to be removed. Don't you see, Natalie, she wasn't Elizabeth. She wasn't my Elizabeth."

I succumb to my own fight of remaining calm, and I start shouting at him, pounding his chest. "You gave into her?! What in the hell? *You* gave into her? She didn't want that kind of love from you. She didn't want you at all. She wanted a father." My shouts turn to screams. "She was a little girl! She was a little girl! SHE WAS A LITTLE GIRL!" Tears stream from my face, the same as the day Afton passed.

I don't stop screaming until he grabs me up by my shoulders and squeezes tight. "You shouldn't have opened that box, Natalie. Poor Annika, poor Annika, what will she do without..." He squeezes tight with one arm and starts to grab an accent pillow off his couch.

Fear, anger, a tragic sadness, a deep pain, desperation all hit into me at once. He's squeezing so hard. I feel the pillow go to my face. I see him see a heavy door stop, just a couple feet away. All I see is Annika, all I feel is Annika, but I push it out of my mind. God, she might be the one person that can save me, but I would never want her to have to play this through her mind. I squeeze my eyes closed tight trying hard to push her out of my thoughts when really she is all I want to fall into. I hit the ground hard. My head throbs and then everything goes black.

My eyes blink, everything is blurry. The smell of blood fills the air. My head is throbbing. It feels as though a weight is pushing me through the carpet into the ground. I try to shake the dizziness and fail. I try to move, but something is on top of me. I pick my head up as far as I can. It's him. He's on top of me, and he's not moving. I pull out my phone, but as I bring up recent calls, it begins to ring. "Mmama?" I try to talk, but my mouth is dry, and my throat is sore.

"Natalie!! Natalie, Oh thank God! *She answered*," she calls back to someone behind her. "Natalie, where are you?"

"Miiisster Coll...Mr. Colllll...call co....call co..."

"Tori, call the cops, I think something has happened to Mr. Collins, hurry. Natalie, are you okay? Nat, I just had the most awful feeling, and you haven't been answering. Then Rox got to your house, and you weren't home."

"Mama, I need you."

Chapter 30: Mama's Here

"Ms. Haven, Ms. Haven, can you hear me? Ms. Haven!" My shoulders feel a tug as someone lifts me up. "Ms. Haven, can you tell me what day it is?"

"Sunday."

"Yes ma'am, good job."

I find myself sitting on the edge in the back of an ambulance. "Natalie!" My mama is pushing through the tiny crowd that has gathered.

I gasp, "Mama!" I fall into my mom's arms harder than I ever have before.

"Mama's here now. Oh, thank God! Thank you, God!"

"Where's Annika?"

"Tori has her. They're waiting in the car."

"I want Annika."

My mom looks to the EMT, waiting for advice. He looks at me, "Ma'am, you had a pretty nasty fall, and we haven't ruled out a concussion."

His voice fades out as I see a shadowy figure starting to approach. *Scott, it's Scott.*

"Hello, Dr. Richards."

"Thank you, Mark. I'll take over from here."

"Yes, sir."

He has Annika in his arms. He hands her over to me, making sure he still has a good hold. Tori slowly walks up and covers her mouth.

"Mommy!" Annika nuzzles into me.

Tori comes over and rubs my arm softly with her hand, her eyes full of tears. "How are you feeling?"

"Like I got hit by a truck."

Police sirens cut through the night, piercing our ears and blinding our eyes. Finally the sound turns off, but the lights keep going. I see Chance's car pull up. Roxy gets out of the driver's side and glides over to me.

"You Bitch! You fucking bitch! You did it, didn't you? You really fucking did it!" Tori's mouth falls to the ground. My mama scoots over, making room for Roxy. Her voice grows softer, "Can I hug you?" I nod.

"Careful, Rox," Mama warns.

"I'm so proud of you, Nat. I love you so much, forever and always."

"I love you, too, always and forever." A tear slips from her eye.

An officer strides over until he has met me face to face. "Ma'am, I'm officer Rey," he pauses and looks over at Roxy. "Ms. Haven, it seems we meet again. I'm going to have to ask you a couple of questions."

"Well, you're just going to have to wait a damn minute, sir. She just came to, for crying out loud." Our heads jerk over to Tori. A small giggle slips from my lips and meets the air. My mom tries to hide her smile.

"That's my girl, Tor." Roxy slaps her butt. Tori scoots out of Roxy's reach.

"Excuse me, but the faster we get the details, the more accurate they are. Do you feel well enough to talk this out?"

I nod. Everyone gets quiet, and they all listen. But all that comes from my mouth is, "Mr. Collins?"

My mom looks down. "Natalie, hun"-my mama's eyes meet mine- "He died."

Chapter 31: My Choice

Have you ever known something, something that could make or break a person? Have you ever known a deep, dark secret, or maybe you have committed a deep, dark secret?

Mr. Collins is dead, but he knew I knew. If I tell, it'll ruin him. He was nice, always a kind man. Annika didn't even feel a threat around him. I didn't either come to think of it. Afton never steered clear of him. As long as I knew him, he seemed like a good person, and you know, maybe he was under there. But, you know what? Anna was a good girl; she was, and her mama's a great person, one of the best I know. I owe it to Mary Anne. I owe it to Anna.

"Can you retell me the events of this evening?"

"I was walking home from my sister's, and I tripped on the sidewalk."

The officer looks back, and a colleague raises his hand, covered in a glove. "We've got blood, sir."

"Okay, then what?"

"Well, Mr. Collins saw me and invited me in for a bandage. I was waiting in his living room for a glass of iced tea when…"

Don't tell.

"Well, I saw a box."

Natalie, listen. Don't tell.

"Then Mr. Collins handed me the tea, but he tripped or something."

"Heart attack." My hand goes to my mouth. "There's nothing you could've done, ma'am, go on."

"Well, I guess *that* happened, and then he fell on me. I don't really remember anything else."

I think for a minute, *Anna might not want me to tell.* She loved Mr. Collins. Even when she tried to break away, she couldn't. She had loved him and though he completely twisted up what that meant, she was confused and was still trying to protect him. All she wanted was a father.

Muneca once said, "When she comes to you she is still a thirteen-year-old girl."

She's begging her best friend to help cover for him. It's my choice. Afton told me to listen and figure out which is which.

I notice Roxy looking at me, her eyes bulging out of her head screaming at me, *"What are you DO-ING!?"* If I don't tell, she will.

"Actually, Officer Rey, I just remembered something."

"Good, that's good. Sometimes that happens with head trauma. Go on now, everything you can remember."

***

"I'm going to need that diary," Officer Rey says as he takes the hair I still have wrapped in my hand away from me. Part of me feels as though he is taking Anna away from me.

"I always got a weird feeling from that old perv." We look at Roxy, and she shrugs. "He was weird."

"Ma'am, is that diary at your house?"

My eyes go back to the officer. "No, no, I left it at my sister's."

Scott steps in. "Sir, Ms. Haven needs to get to the hospital, so we can run through some procedures."

"Right, right, of course. Well, can one of you take me to the diary?"

Tori steps in, "Sure, of course, it's at my house. You can follow me."

Tori looks back to me, "As soon as I'm done, I'll be at the hospital. I love you, Natalie, always and forever."

"Forever and always."

Before Tori can even get up to the hospital, I am cleared to go home. "Do you want to come stay at my place?" Scott says, as he passes the discharge papers over to one of his colleagues.

"I think I want to stay at Tori's, so I can be with Annika."

"Natalie, Annika's already asleep. I just got off the phone with Tor." My mom flashes her phone screen in my face, as if to prove herself.

Scott looks at me pleadingly, and I look back. I nod. "Okay." Roxy lets out a satisfied gasp that causes me to wince.

We all walk out into the dark parking lot. Scott whispers something that causes my mother to let out a sound that she tries to block by pressing her hand tightly over her mouth. She nods her head. There's a water fountain that lights up as it flows in the middle of the parking lot. The sound of the water moving is soothing. Scott pulls me over, and my mama and Roxy follow.

"Natalie, I love you and Annika. You both complete my life. I have never met anyone that captivates me and holds my attention as you do." He starts to bend down, and Roxy screams. It sounds muffled to me because all I can hear is my heart pounding. "I wasn't planning on doing this." He smiles, and those dimples... "One day, just not today, but will you marry me?"

I think about what I look like: a bandage wrapped around my head, the little make-up I had on, rubbed off, mascara-streaked cheeks, busted lip, and then I look at him. This handsome, young eligible bachelor. I think about what this means, him committing to me *and* Annika. *Should I do this to him?*

As if he can sense my thoughts, he releases. "You and Annika make me happy. Natalie, all I need is you."

"Okay."

"Yes?"

My eyes are puffy, and there's no tears left to cry. "Yes." I nod.

He stands me up, but just as he is about to hug me, Roxy plows into him. "I knew it! I just knew it!" She takes my hug. "Welcome to the family Hot Scott!" She kisses his cheek. Then my mama pats his shoulder, and he kisses her cheek. Finally, they both move out of the way, and he pulls me in. It feels like home.

Chapter 32: Thank you

"Natalie!" Muneca's voice blares through my phone loud enough so that I have to hold it away from my ear.

Scott looks at me and his love shines through his eyes. He really is happy.

"Yes?"

"You got him! You got him, right?"

"Yes."

"Oh my God! Karisa wanted Annika to call, and I knew something, there had to be something, why she want her to call, but I didn't want to alarm you. Then you never called. I started getting worry." Muneca's words fly so quickly I find myself wondering if it's English or Spanish she is speaking.

"Are you okay? Tell me everything!" I start from the beginning and tell her the whole story. I wait for her response. She is quiet for a long while. "Oh my God, Natalie, I am so happy you are okay. I couldn't even imagine if... No, you are okay. Dios mío, you are okay. That's all that matters. Listen, I have to tell you something."

"Okay."

"Your Anna is free! She is! She is free, and she was able to go home. You did it! She came to Karisa and told her, 'I am free now. I can go home. Thank you for helping me. Please tell Natalie I love her, and I will always be in her heart.'"

A tear escapes and runs down my cheek. Scott gently wipes it away. "Natalie..."

"Yeah."

"She wants you to tell her mama. I know you didn't want to bring anything up about the day she died when you went to visit her, and I think you did a great job refraining, but Natalie, her mom needs to know."

I nod my head even though she can't see me. "Natalie, I let you go now. I know you are exhausting, but you and Annika come over tomorrow. Karisa can help with your headache."

"Okay, that sounds good."

"Wait? You mean Muneca can do what Annika does?" Scott asks wide-eyed.

I shake my head. "No, it's Karisa."

"Karisa? Is there anyone else you need to tell me about?"

I laugh and shake my head. "Nope, that's it, and Karisa's gift is actually what brought us together. I met them recently because Karisa reached out to Annika. That's how we met. I got a phone call, and it was Muneca. It's when I was still in denial." He nods his head. "Karisa is a healer and a viewer. She wants to heal my head."

"Mmhm," he says without looking at me.

I fall asleep in Scott's arms. His apartment is nice and modern, although quite empty. His bed is comfortable and the sheets, heavenly. He is already awake when I start to stir. It looks like he just got back in from a run. "Good morning, beautiful, I didn't want to wake you. I still don't know how you didn't have a concussion." As the words slip from his lips, the vision of my Nanny coming up beside me and placing a pillow under my head comes to mind. There was no pillow when I woke up, and there was definitely blood, but maybe...

"Are you ready to go get Annika?" I nod.

Scott knocks on the door and then opens it. There is a Congratulations streamer across Tori's kitchen. Bri starts making a huge ice cream sundae. "I promised you." She smiles.

"Ice cream for breakfast?" I ask, shocked. I look over at Tori.

"Mama said you get whatever you want today." Bri looks back at Tori. Brandon steps out from behind the counter revealing his kiss-the-cook apron. Meanwhile, Roxy and Chance walk in from outside.

Braiden and Annika squeeze past their legs. Annika runs to me as hard as she can. "I love you, Mommy, forever and always."

I hold her as tight as I can without squeezing her. "I love you too, sweet girl, always and forever."

Annika pushes herself down off my waist and goes to Scott. He picks her up. "I've missed my girl. Love you, Annika."

"I love you, too, Daddy." We all stop and stare.

As we walk up to Muneca's front door, I can hear Karisa scream with excitement. Muneca opens, and she is in her usual tshirt, jeans, and apron. She wipes her hands off on the apron. She flashes a Muneca smile. "Scott, Raul is in the back working on something. If you'd like, you can accompany him."

He nods. "Sure, yeah, that sounds great." Scott has really taken all this in, but he is still skeptical around it all.

Karisa leads me to her room, and Annika follows. The lights are turned down low, and there's soft music in the background. She undoes my bandage and places some kind of mixture on the wound. It feels cool but quickly turns warm, She chants something, words that seem ancient. They are not from a language I recognize, neither English or Spanish. Then she wraps a new bandage on my head. Finally, she gets something that smells of peppermint and rubs it into my forehead and then on my cheek bones.

"All better?" she asks and looks at me with her beautiful brown eyes.

I pull her close for a tight hug. "All better." I smile and look at Muneca. "It really does feel a ton better. My whole body does actually."

Muneca pulls Karisa up around her waist. "Yep, this is my special girl." They rub noses, and then Karisa gets down and pulls Annika to her bedroom.

"I think you should go to Mary Anne's today, that's her name right?"

I frown. "Yeah but…"

She smiles at me as she leans over to pick something up. "But what?" she says feistily.

"Well, I don't know if Scott wants to make that drive."

"Natalie, don't you see the way he looks at you? That man would do anything you ask him to."

"Okay," I say, "but you and Karisa have to come with us."

She places her hand on her hip. "Okay, it's a nice Sunday for a drive."

I choke on my thoughts everytime I try to think of a way to tell Mary Anne what happened. It means telling about Annika and Karisa. It means talking about the day none of us ever wanted to relive. Muneca grabs my shoulder from the backseat. "It's okay. Natalie, it's going to be okay."

We finally pull up. Part of me is ready to get it over with, and the other part is ready to flee the scene.

"Well, there you are, Natalie, and this must be sweet little Annika." She reaches out for Annika's hand. Annika smiles.

Scott holds out a hand. "Hello, I'm Scott."

"Hello, Scott, nice to meet you. And you must be Muneca and Karisa?" Muneca smiles and nods. "Well, you all don't just stand around, come in, come in. I'm so happy you could all stop by."

"Natalie tells me you all have some good news for me?"

I grab both her hands. "I found him Mary Anne." I look at Annika, Muneca, and Karisa. "*We* found him."

"Well, I'll be!"

Muneca steps in, "Before we get started, my daughter wants to tell you something.

Karisa says, "It's okay, Mama. You raised me the best you could, and I love you everyday. I know life was hard for you, but I would choose you over and over again."

Scott looks uncomfortable, maybe even a little scared. It's as if he has caught the monster under his bed with his own eyes.

Mary Anne gasps and hugs herself tight. "That was my Anna, wasn't it?"

"It was her." Muneca nods. "And now, Natalie is going to tell you the story."

Mary Anne squeezes my hands back and nods. "This is going to be hard to listen to; it's going to be hard for me to replay, but at the end we are all going to be freed. We are." She nods.

***

Silence, we sit in silence for about ten minutes. "Oh my God! Bless your heart, Natalie." She gently rubs a hand over my bandage, and her eyes follow with intense concern.

"Now, the detectives are still running all their tests and putting all their pieces together."

"It was him. It was Natalie. Everybody in this room knows it. He got what was coming to him, but he almost took it to his grave." She pauses. "You know, I feel sorry for him. There must have been something in his life that was just horrible." She shudders. "Now all that really matters, all that matters is, my girl Anna is free, and she is home." She pulls her hands together and tears stream down her face, but this time they're happy tears. "I thank every single one of you. I do, from the bottom of my heart, thank you."

Chapter 33: There's Nothing In the World Like It

Muneca looks at me and smiles; her eyes are too kind to say I told you so, but I answer her back anyway, *You were right*.

***

"Grab the bag, Natalie, HURRY!"

"Tori, which one? There's like ten!" I yell, bewildered.

"FUCKKK!" flies to Tori's bedroom from the living room.

"Roxy your language and the kids!" Tori yells out of the room aggravated.

"*I said*, **Mother Fuckerrrrrr!**"

"Roxy, please."

Tori looks back to me. "Natalie, really, grab the bag so we can go."

"Tori, there's like ten."

"There's three, Nat, one for a boy, one for a girl, and one for Roxy."

"Okay, so I grab all of them?!?"

"Natalie, let's go!"

"Okay, okay." I stumble out of the room with the weight of the three bags pulling me down.

Roxy pushes herself up off the couch and stands up, quickly looking down. "What the FUCK!?!?"

"Oh, that's your water. That's your water. Rox, just come stand right over here. There you go, off the carpet and right on the tile, just like that." Tori smiles successfully. Roxy lets out a mean glare.

"Alright, girls, y'all take my car. I've put a towel down for Rox in the front, and I'll follow behind with Brandon and the kids."

Mama is spinning circles around us as usual. She kisses Roxy. "You're going to do just fine, baby."

I help Roxy out of the car and into a wheelchair while Tori parks the car. A car spins into the parking lot like a bat out of hell. "Chance. It's Chance." I smile and nod, but I don't wait for him to catch up.

"Roxy Haven, 38 weeks today, her contractions have been at 3 mintues apart for about the last 45 minutes. Her water broke as we were leaving to come here."

"Your relation?"

"I'm her big sister. She's the baby," I say, and I get tears in my eyes. *My baby sister.*

Just as we enter her room, Tori makes her way to us. Right after, Brandon comes through holding Annika tightly, followed by Mama carrying Braiden. Bri walks herself in and proudly shows me her big-sister shirt.

Roxy's nurse is by her side now, guarding her like a watchdog. "Is this your family?"

Roxy nods and squints hard. "That's my oldest sister and her husband, my brother-in-law." The nurse smiles. "This is my mama."

"Hello," the nurse waves.

"This is my other sister, Natalie." A smile returns mine.

Roxy squints hard again. "FUUUUUUCK!" The nurse looks at us and then at the monitor. She grabs Roxy's hand. "That was a big one, dear. You're doing a great job. I saw in your chart you're wanting to do this naturally."

"Hell NO!"

"Roxy, are you sure?" Tori asks soothingly as she pulls out Roxy's stash of sage and some concoctions out of the one bag Roxy brought. A bag that doesn't even compare in size to the ones that Tori brought. Tori looks disgustingly at all the things she pulls out, but she still holds them up so Roxy can see.

"No, no, I can't. I can't do this."

Chance rushes into the room, and his look of bewilderment by far surpasses everyone's in the room.

"You must be Dad," the nurse says.

Brandon raises his hand. "Actually, I'm Dad." The nurse looks bewildered.

Roxy explains, "This is my boyfriend, Chance. I'm giving my baby up to my sister and broth.... FUCKKK!"

"Would you like the epidural, hun? If you want it, it's time."

Roxy nods.

"Alright, we are going to ask that everyone step out while the procedure is done."

My mama kisses Roxy on her way out. Tori hurries up and slips a big-brother shirt on Braiden and a big-cousin shirt on Annika.

The nurse steps out to let us know it's clear to come back in. She looks at Bri. "So Roxy is your aunt?"

"She is my aunt too," Annika joins in.

"Well, I really like your shirts." She smiles.

Roxy is a lot calmer when we come in. "Sorry guys, Aunt Rox Rox said some pretty ugly words."

Annika goes and rubs her hand on Roxy's face. "It's okay, Aunt Rox Rox, it hurts real bad."

Roxy smiles, but guilt fills her eyes. "Hey, Annika, do you think the baby is a boy or a girl?" Roxy looks at me. "I can't believe no one asked her that yet, come to think of it."

Annika looks at Tori. "Aunt Tori did ask."

I laugh, and so does my mama. Tori hides behind her hands. "It was worth a try." She lets out.

Roxy throws a tiny piece of ice at her. "Well?!? What did she tell you?"

Annika speaks up, "I told her I don't know. I don't know if it is a boy or a girl, but I hope it's a girl." She grins. "I think you know what it is though, Aunt Rox."

Roxy smiles. "A boy."

"Roxy, what are you doing?" My mama goes to the bedside. "I don't know. It feels like I have to go to the bathroom."

Tor's eyes get big. "Natalie, go get the nurse!"

I run out into the hallway. Scott is at the nurse's station. "Hey, how is she doing?"

"I think she is ready to push."

"I'll grab the nurse."

"Alright, Roxy, this is it. The baby is right there. You can only have two people in here. Do you want the mom and dad?" She glances over at Tori and Brandon. Roxy doesn't answer. "Or maybe mom-to-be and boyfriend?" She looks at Chance, who already looks like he's on the verge of passing out. Roxy looks for a minute. "You think about it. I'm paging the doctor."

"Nurse Andrea?"

"Yes?"

"Can I please have three, my mama and my sisters?"

She looks over at us slyly. "If one of you stands over in the back corner, I won't say anything if you don't." She smiles.

My mom stands on one side, and Tori stands on the other. I stand by Roxy's head. "You've got this, Sister. You can do it." I try to make my words into a mantra and hum them out peacefully. She follows my lead.

"Push, Rox, push you've got this baby!" My mama says through the tears in her eyes.

"Oh my God, Roxy, the baby is right there. I can see it's head!" Tori shouts.

"You've got this, Sister. You can do it. The baby's right there. You've got this Sister; you can do it; the baby's right there," I say as I rub her head all in rhythm, all in a hum.

"WaaaaaaaaaWAAAAAAAAAAAAwaaaaaaaaaaaaaaaaaaa aa!"

They place the tiny bundle onto my sister's chest. "It's A BOY!" the doctor calls out as she hands my mom the tool to cut the umbilical cord.

Roxy's head leans back and tears stream down her face. "He's beautiful, so perfect, so tiny."

Tears fill my eyes. This is the most beautiful thing I've ever seen in my life. I remember when they placed Annika on my chest, that feeling accompanied with your baby's first cry is the absolute best feeling in this whole world. There's nothing in the world like it. It's a whole new emotion entirely. I know that's what Roxy is feeling now.

I look at him and touch his little arm. "Oh, Roxy, he looks just like you. He is beautiful."

My mama looks at his feet. "Ten fingers, ten toes, oh my goodness look at his little feet," she says as the tears still fall.

Tori stands back, terrified and confused. She is scared to love but more scared not to. I feel Tori. I can feel her emotions. I go to her and push her up to the bed

Roxy looks at the baby and then to Tori. She carefully hands the precious baby boy over to her. "Tori, he's yours."

Tori starts crying uncontrollably, so hard that my mama has to take the baby. Tori falls over Roxy. "I'll never be able to repay you. I don't even know what to say. He's perfect, Roxy. I love him so much!"

"Me too! And I'll never be able to repay you for giving my son a happy, healthy, stable environment, one that I could never give him."

Tori goes straight over to the bags and finds the girl bag. "Natalie, will you take this out to Scott and ask him to donate to a newborn girl in need." I smile and nod. Then she goes for the boy bag and pulls out a lovely blue blanket. There's something embroidered on the bottom. Rox.

"You're naming him, Rox?"

Tori smiles. "Rox Nathaniel, after you both."

"You mean you're overriding your perfectness and messing up the BR names? Damn!"

"Roxy!! Language!"

Some things never change, and I think those things are the things that make us most who we are.

Chapter 34: An Angel On Earth

"I'm sorry. We don't have any more sprinkled donuts. We still have iced," the lady says with a smile, but her eyes are apologetic.

I turn to the backseat. "Bri they're out of sprinkles. Want a plain pink one instead?"

Her face falls. "Okay, I guess."

"Annika, what color do you want, blue, white, or pink?"

"Blue for boys, like Rox." She smiles.

I look back to the lady in the window and smile. "Alright, can I please get one pink, two blue, and a dozen sausage and cheese kolaches?"

The girls race to Tori's front door. Bri, letting Annika win, busts inside right after her.

"Hey, Natalie, did you remember the orange juice?" I hold it up with a smile on my face.

"Alright, let's get this party started!" Roxy says. Tori sits across from us on the other side of her breakfast bar. She is still in her pajamas at 11:00 a.m. Her hair is in a messy bun, not the cute kind she usually dons either. Her eyes, surrounded by dark circles, are puffed up and tired. Despite all this, her eyes still shine with pure happiness. She hasn't put

Rox down since he was born. I'm sure of it. When he isn't right in her arms, she carts him around in a baby sling morning, noon, and night.

The door opens and none of us have to turn around to see who it is. Mallory walks in, sliding her designer purse off her shoulder and onto the bar. She walks over and kisses each of us on the cheek. "Sorry, I'm late." She holds up a tray of coffees. "There was a long line."

"Thank God!" Tori reaches for one. I grab one, and Mallory hands Mama one. Tori slaps Roxy's hand as she goes to grab one. "Rox, you can't have that. It'll get in your breastmilk and go to the baby. I told you, *No caffeine!*"

Roxy slaps her hand back at Tori's and grabs the cup. "I ordered decaf." She squints and stares back at Tori.

"You realize there's still caffeine."

Roxy looks at Tori and takes a big drink. "Yum."

I'm still blowing on mine, but my mama's already pulled her's to her lips multiple times. "Thanks Mallory, it's really hitting the spot."

Tori adds, "Yes, thanks, Mall. Natalie just got back with the kolaches too." She points to the box as to offer Mallory hers.

"Yes, Mallory, you can tell just by looking at Tori how needed this was," my mama says as she takes another drink. Tori gives my mom the eye. "It's true, dear."

"Well, what do you expect? Mama, he doesn't sleep! I had Bri and Braiden both on a schedule a week out of the hospital but this one! I can't break him. I think he's breaking me." She points to her hair.

"It's the rule of three," Mama says and smiles an all knowing smile.

Roxy speaks up, "The rule of what?"

"The rule of three."

"Alright, indulge us, Vanna." Mallory sits down.

"Well, when there's just two, it's pretty easy. Life is like a balanced seesaw. There's one kid per parent, but once you get to three, well, the tables turn. You can throw the balance out the window, and the parents are now outnumbered. I bet Tori is going to have some new ideas about schedules"-she looks at Tori and smirks- "and appearances here pretty soon."

"Mom!"

"It's true, dear. You look like hell."

Roxy hugs Tori. "I could take him for a night, so you could sleep." Tori pauses, and we all know that none of us are getting this baby overnight. We can read it in her eyes. "No, nope, you're right. That wouldn't work. I need my beauty sleep anyway." Roxy laughs. "I guess you're on your own."

I look around at all of us. We've probably planned a hundred parties, if not more, around this bar over many, many years, and now it's time to plan for a wedding, my wedding.

"Okay, so I made this chart." Mallory goes over and grabs a huge chart off the couch. I've got Tori and Roxy as your maid of honors, Muneca as a bridesmaid. Me, of course, I'm the director." She flashes a smile and bats her eyes. "The Caroline Cookie Bakery is lined up for the cake. I still can't believe she left her secretary work to open the bakery." She pauses and smiles. "I'm so happy for her." I think about Caroline and a smile appears across my face, the same as Mallory's. "Okay, for the guy's side, we have Scott, of course, Brandon as the best man, his cousin Bill as a groomsman, and Chance." She pauses. "Did y'all confirm Chance?"

"We might have to cut him out of the pictures later," Tori thinks aloud.

Roxy glares at her.

"What? You know it's the truth. While I admit he would look nice in the photos, I know you too well. You'd take scissors to a photo that was framed and hanging on the wall. You know you would."

"Yeah, you're actually right." Roxy gives in. "What about Raul?"

"Natalie, why don't you ask Scott if there's someone else he wants to have?" Mama adds.

My phone goes off. I look down at the screen. "Hey, I'm going to take this real quick. It's an unlisted number." I get up and walk to Bri's bedroom.

After I hang up, I replay the lady's words, "Your baby girl is a gift from God. She truly is. My son had been so upset after his Pawpaw passed, and there was nothing I could do to comfort him. I don't know what breaks a mama's heart worse than not being able to comfort your baby, but your daughter gave him what he needed. Yes, she sure did, words from my dad himself. Not only that, but she gave him even so much more. My daddy didn't believe in banks, so I couldn't find the deed to his house anywhere. They were gonna take it away from us, all I have left of my dad. I had searched everywhere. By the good Lord's grace, you'll never believe where I found it, darling, it was in that old broken window sill. It surely was, along with plenty of monetary support. Your baby, I tell you, she's special. **She is a gift.** I'll never be able to thank her, and you, enough. I still just can't even fathom any of this, but I'll tell you one thing, I believe it."

I walk back into the living room, and I feel at peace. I even feel happy, just happy. It's not accompanied by that nagging feeling. Then I notice Tori's face, it looks as though she's seen a ghost. Everyone is silent. Mallory's face matches Tori's. My mama looks like someone hit the pause button right in the middle of a crying scene and forgot to press play. Roxy is the only one that looks normal, in fact she looks even better than normal. I can see the image of her as a small child dancing in her own eyes.

I get that fight or flight feeling and panic strikes me. I uneasily ask, "What?" I try to smile, hoping for the best, but not really wanting the answer because I am fearful it's not an answer I want. My mama covers her mouth and points over to Annika. Annika is talking to someone, someone that's not there. She's playing with them even. It's obvious she was sharing this experience with everyone while I was out of the room and things were probably even said.

I was scared for this moment; I've been scared of this moment for a long time. I've prayed many times that this would not happen and watched nervously to make sure it didn't. Mostly because I had played out Tori's reaction to this very situation over and over in my mind. The day when my sheltered, very sheltered, niece and nephew witness Annika being Annika.

My eyes shoot to Tori. Tori looks at me with tears in her eyes. "It's *Nanny*, Natalie."

Tears hit my eyes. "Yeah, I know."

"You mean she does this. This is normal?"

I shrug. "Our normal." Tori looks at Bri and Braiden, and I don't wait for a reaction. "She can't help it. Tori, it's not her fault. She's just trying to help. She usually knows when it's okay to open up and when she should hide it."

Tori acts as if she doesn't hear me. She hands Rox to Mallory and makes her way straight to the kids as if a heavy magnet is pulling her. I find myself scared for how she is going to react. Is she going to grab her kids and lock them in a room to play? Is she going to pull Annika by her hand outside to play alone? Is she just going to stand there hugging her kids, covering their ears?

She walks over to Annika and picks her up. Tears roll down my face as I watch. "You sweet, sweet baby, you precious child. All the things you've gone through; all the things you've seen; all the comfort and kindness you bring." She holds onto her tight and rocks her back and forth. She pulls her hair back out of her face and kisses her on her forehead in between each thought. "You're beautiful. Everything about you is just absolutely beautiful. You are an angel on earth. You are. You are an angel on earth. Aunt Tori loves you so much, so very much, forever and always."

Annika understands a lot for her age. She always has, but I can tell she doesn't understand why this is such a big deal. Maybe it is because this really is our normal.

My mama's sobs get my attention. I walk over to her and look in her eyes. "What's wrong Mama?"

She tries to look back into my eyes, but then looks away. "I miss my mama so much. Sometimes when it hits me that she isn't here anymore, it takes my breath away." I look at this woman. The strongest, most independent woman I know, and I feel her pain. I feel her anguish, and I cry with her.

Tori comes over still carrying Annika. Annika touches her Nana's head. "Nana, Nanny doesn't want you to cry. She says you're her brave little girl, her best girl, and where there's a will, there's a way. She will always do anything in her power to still be here with us. She loves us, Nana, and she's always here. Don't cry." My mama grabs Annika from Tori and holds on tight. "She loves Bri and Braiden, Aunt Tori, Aunt Rox Rox, Brandon, Scott, Mommy, Rox, and she loves you, Nana, so much."

"You know, Natalie, I didn't call what Annika had *a gift* at first because I didn't really see it as a gift. I know you didn't either. I know sometimes it is tough, tougher than I can imagine, but it seems to always end with a happily ever after. It is like a rainbow after the storm. Natalie, I think it is a gift. She certainly is. This baby is a gift."

My body relaxes. "Me too." I smile. "I think so too."

Annika has a gift, and this is her story.

Chapter 35: We Do

(8 months later)

"Oh my God, Natalie, oh my God! You look absolutely gorgeous." Tori has tears.

I turn around and look in the mirror, but it's Annika's reflection that catches my eye. "Are you ready, sweet girl?"

She nods. "You look so pretty, Mommy."

I rub her nose with mine. "So do you."

"Thanks, Mommy."

"Natalie, you really do look beautiful. Wow!"

"Thank you, Muneca. Roxy did my make-up, and Tori did my hair."

"Damn, Nat! You look fuuu...freaking HOT! I love that dress!" Roxy sets the flower girl flowers down.

"Thanks Rox."

My mama walks over to me and holds my face in her hands, "Natalie, you are stunning, absolutely stunning. You're going to take breaths away for sure. I love you, my sweet girl. You are my sweet girl. You know that, right? Tori is my rock, Roxy is my fire, but you're my sweet girl." She wipes my cheek. "Don't start crying, you'll ruin your face." She lowers her voice and changes the tone. "If you get anything on this dress, I won't be able to take it back." She kisses my cheek.

Mallory comes flying through the double doors, busting them open like the building is on fire.

"What's wrong?"

"Natalie, I am so sorry, but I just realized there's an extra seat at the bride's immediate family table. I don't know how I missed this. I looked over these plans a hundred times. I thought I knew them better than the back of my own hand. I've got your mama, your sisters, Brandon, and Chance. I should have noticed earlier. What do you want me to do?"

She and Tori are so much alike. Tori has already met her, and they're frantically looking over the guest list, trying to figure out who they can put there. Meanwhile, I'm still trying to figure out what's so bad about having an extra chair at the table.

Something escapes from under my mama's breath, "That's for mmm tmmmm."

"Mama, did you say something?" I look at her confused.

"I said, that's for"-she pushes her lips together and a muffle comes out-"Mr. Tom."

"What, Mama, Mr. Tom? It's for *Mr. Tom*?"

"Papa Tom!" Annika says loud and proud.

I give one big nod. "Okay Mallory, you heard the girl. That's for Papa Tom." I smile and point to Annika. I give Mallory a reassuring smile. "Looks like Mama has sabotaged your seating arrangement. See, you are doing a great job!" Tori is still processing the *Papa Tom* thing, and I can tell Roxy is mad at herself for not thinking of a smart comment to add before the moment passes.

"Look! Oh my goodness, LOOK!" I point to Rox. "Look he's crawling!" All of our mama hearts beam with pride. "Look at him, he's going right for the kids."

"I told y'all he was smart," my mama says proudly.

"Of course, he's smart. He gets it from me, duh! Hey, does this mean I can start smoking again? I mean, he's old enough to crawl, so old enough for formula?"

Roxy is ignored. Tori's eyes fill with tears yet again. "Oh No! No! Where's my phone?!? **BRANDON!!!!! BRANDON!!!!**"

Brandon runs in from the other room, "What? What, honey? What's wrong?"

"Where's the phone? Where's your phone? Make sure you hit record. Did you hit it? Are you getting it? Are you getting this?" He puts a hand on her shoulder and the other one in front of her, so she can double check the camera. "Oh, look, Brandon. He's crawling!"

I look over at Roxy. Although she is still crossing her arms in protest, probably even daydreaming of her weed, or pot, or whatever it is, her eyes lovingly watch Rox scoot across the floor. I feel her heart overflow. She's proud.

Against Tori's wishes, I skipped the fluffy, poofy, princess dresses, and went for simple fairytale. "I really love the dresses Natalie. Everyone looks beautiful."

"Thank you, Tori, I was hoping for your approval."

"Well, I know I look freaking hot! So there's that." Roxy gives herself a check in the mirror, turning back and forth as she admires her figure.

"Hey, Roxy, you didn't say the F word." Tori pulls Roxy over to her and kisses her on the cheek. "You're learning."

"I did it for the kids, not so you could go all mushy on me." Roxy rolls her eyes, but then hugs Tori back and smiles.

Rhonda and Charles get seated; Muneca walks down with Brad, one of Scott's childhood friends. Roxy walks down with Bill; and Tori walks out with Brandon. Bri and Annika walk out, not throwing but holding a single sunflower.

My mama leans over and whispers, "Mama loved sunflowers."

I smile. "I know. That's why I did it. They're for Nanny."

Then Braiden walks out, pulling Rox in a wagon behind him. I hear "AWs" as the kids walk down the long aisle.

"It's our turn Natalie." My mama grabs my arm. I smile and nod. Annika comes to my mind. I'm not sure why I feel a little sadness tug, maybe because it's not just Nat and Annika anymore. Now there's Scott, too. Then I look at her, standing there next to Bri, so big, almost four now. She is happy. I can feel it with every ounce of me. She is truly happy, and that makes me happy. I think she's proud too.

Mallory is holding my shoulder tightly and starts to whisper in my ear. "Okay, Natalie, you know I love you like a sister. Okay, okay, okay, this is it. The song is about to change. Ready? Three, two, one, go!"

I walk down the aisle and pass Raul and Karisa. I see Caroline waving big, and it almost looks like Rob has tears in his eyes. He's really the only dad I've ever known. I see Macy and Delilah, and they both look lovely. I see an empty seat, and it makes me think about Mr. Collins, just for a split second and then the thought passes. I see Missy and Edward. Right next to them is Ben and Benjamin. In the very front row, I see Mary Anne waiting for my mama to join her. As I walk up to the arch, I see Muneca, who really has become one of my dearest friends, then Roxy, my Roxy and her eyes only reflect joy. I see Tori, my Tori, and her tears are already falling hard. I see Bri, Braiden, and little Rox. It's overwhelming how much love I have for every single one of them. I see Scott and all his handsomeness. He could easily make it into a bridal magazine. He smiles. *Those dimples.* I see Brandon, who really is like my big brother, and then I see Annika.

My precious Annika, my life, my world. She tugs on my dress, and I bend down to her before meeting Scott in the middle.

"Mommy?"

"Yes, baby?"

She whispers, "Nanny *is* here! Where there's a will, there's a way." She repeats the quote proudly. "She loves the sunflowers. Mommy, she really does love them."

I kiss her forehead. "I love you, Annika, forever and always."

"I love you too, Mommy, always and forever."

I close my eyes. *I love you Nanny, thank you.*

"She loves you too." Her whisper gets a little louder, so I can hear it as I begin to stand back up.

"Natalie, you look stunning, and I get prouder of you everyday. I love you, sweet girl, forever and always."

"Always and forever, Mama." She has tears in her eyes, but she doesn't cry. My mama's a warrior that woman, just like Rox.

"Do you Natalie, take this man..."

"We do." I look to Annika, and we nod.

Chapter 36: Home

My daughter Annika has a gift. It took me a long time to realize it, to accept it, and mostly to trust it. But she does. She has a gift. At times, it's tough. It's so very tough. I still worry. I worry about what's going to happen at the playground when she starts school, what could happen if someone doesn't open up as we pass them in the grocery store and Annika overshares. I still worry about what she might see, might hear. My worry never stops. My worry is different from the mother sitting next to me at swim lessons or the mother in the booth across from me. I know she worries too. The worry begins as soon as that positive comes across on the pregnancy test. It begins right there, and it seems to never leave, for any of us. I know my mama still worries about me, and my Nanny still worries about her.

Sometimes the gift pulls us into the darkness. It's sad, lonely, even scary at times, but those times pass, leaving us with even more peace than before and more happiness than we can imagine. It's the beautiful, sunny day that follows a morning storm. It is a gift. She is a gift, just like Tori said, "...an angel on earth."

I replay the lady from the ice cream shop's words over and over. I never even got her name, but she said something like, "It's more than she can fathom, but she believes it." That's Scott. Anytime Annika starts, he still gets a little uneasy. He can't fathom it. He can write it down in his notebook over and over, but he can't explain it. He can't find the solutions to it. He can't diagnose it. It makes no sense to him. He can't fathom it, but he believes it.

I love Annika more than life itself. I would do anything for her. I know my mama feels the same about me and my sisters. I think back to when Rox was born. We were all around Roxy. I replay everything in slow motion. I remember as if it were yesterday, the love that filled that room, the bond that we all have, my mother and my sisters, it's something fierce. I think about Macy and Missy's relationship. I think about us girls and our relationship with Mallory. I think about me and Muneca. I think about Missy shortly breaking her bond with Macy, only for Mallory, her daughter. I think about Mary Anne and her love for my sweet Anna. I think about Roxy and her face when the doctor placed Rox on her chest. I think about the lady at the ice cream shop and how she wanted to protect and comfort her son so bad it hurt. I think about Mallory when she was falling apart, but trying her hardest to be strong for Benjamin. I remember my Nanny when she was still alive and how she was the only one that could pick my mama up when she fell. I remember Muneca and the heavy weight that could change her whole personality when Karisa went through certain things. I remember. I remember me, and I remember Annika.

It's a friend's love, and it's powerful. It's a sister's love, and it's powerful. It's a woman's love. I believe a woman's love is the most powerful thing on this earth, and even more powerful, is a mother's love. A mother's love is the absolute most powerful thing in this whole, wide world,and where there's a will, there's a way.

"Mommy, Mommy look! Mommmmyyyy! LOOK! LOOK HURRY!" I look up, and my eyes fall onto her. She is an angel. She pushes her hair out of her face and gets ready to go back up the ladder to the slide. Scott walks out of the house. It still smells of fresh wood and paint, one of my favorite smells. As I breathe it in, the smell of rain meets me, too.

"DADDY! DADDY, WATCH! LOOK AT ME!"

"I see you, Annika, you're doing a great job!"

"All by myself!" She points at herself.

"All by yourself!" He smiles and sits next to me.

"Smells like rain." I smile.

He frowns and pulls something up on his phone. "No, nope." He shows me his phone. "Not today, clear skies until next week."

I look back over to Annika, and she is talking to someone. She's pretending to drink from a teacup and then passing the teacup over, holding it for someone else to taste.

I point over to her. "I think Nanny's here." I smile. He smiles back, and then tiny drops of water start to sprinkle from the sky. Scott looks at me. I smile and shrug. The sprinkle gets a little harder, and it starts to rain.

"I should have known. Yep, that's all I can say. I should have known." Scott nods as he talks.

The backdoor slides open. "Natalie, what is she doing? NATALIE, I just bought that from the boutique on main. Natalie!!!!"

Bri and Braiden push right past Tori and join Annika in the rain. Roxy holds up a glass. I'm pretty sure it has more than just lemonade in it. She dances out towards the kids holding the glass up in the air.

"Tori, hun, it really is just rain," my mama says as she sits her cup down. Mr. Tom pulls her chair out for her. "Really, Tom, I can get my chair myself." She lets out a sigh, but let's him push her up to the table anyway.

Brandon has a seat and brings his finger to his lips pointing at a sleeping Rox, "Please don't wake him up. I just got him down." We have to read his lips.

Somethings never change, and those are the things that make us feel most at home.

My eyes find Annika, and I am captivated as she dances in the rain. M*y little girl, your little girl, our little girl dances in the rain*, not just now, but every single moment for her entire life.

"Mommy, Mommy!!!" Annika says out of breath as she runs up to me, soaking wet.

"What, baby?"

"I love you, Mommy, forever and always."

"I love you too, always and forever." I watch as she runs back out into the rain, laughing, her rosy cheeks, her big blue eyes, long eyelashes, her sweet little laugh. I soak this in, forever and always.

Made in the USA
Middletown, DE
03 February 2022